The Death of all Things Seen

MICHAEL COLLINS was born in Limerick. He holds a Masters of Study in Creative Writing from Oxford University and a Ph.D. in English from the University of Illinois. Collins was the 2010 Captain of the Irish National Team 100K. He earned a bronze medal at the 2010 World Masters Championships. Other victories include The North Pole Marathon, The Last Marathon and The Everest Marathon. Running and writing are his twin passions.

Also by Michael Collins

The Meat Eaters

The Life and Times of a Teaboy

The Feminists Go Swimming

Emerald Underground

The Keepers of Truth

The Resurrectionists

Lost Souls

The Secret Life of E. Robert Pendleton

Midnight in a Perfect Life

The
Death of
all Things
Seen

Michael Collins

HEAD
ZEUS

A catalogue record for this book is available from the British Library.

ISBN (HB): 9781784974947
ISBN (XTPB): 9781784974954
ISBN (E): 9781784974978

Typeset by Adrian McLaughlin

Printed and bound in Germany
by GGP Media GmbH, Pössneck

Head of Zeus Ltd
Clerkenwell House
45-47 Clerkenwell Green
London ECIR OHT

WWW.HEADOFZEUS.COM

To my wife and children

Thanks to Maggie McKernan, David Godwin, Dominique Bourgois and Kim McArthur for faith and guidance.

To Amal Chatterjee, Joe Lemrow, Will Tomory and Karl Ameriks as early readers. To Heidi and Nora for editorial insights, advice and countless hours of reading.

And to my parents for the early years of sacrifice and love and showing me how to live life and take chances.

The world breaks everyone,
and afterward, some are strong
at the broken places.

—ERNEST HEMINGWAY

PROLOGUE

IT HAD BEEN over a decade since Helen Price had driven along the Gold Coast in the push of an early afternoon commute. This time, however, she was driving against the flow of traffic, heading to the city and not out toward the suburbs. The direction sat as a point of significance, figuring in the literal transformation of her life these past few years, the run against the grain of any true forward momentum, a life pushing backward in time toward old memories, to islands of remembrance of who she was and who she had once been.

How had it come to pass, this vast sweeping change, this passage of time, so she found herself at a point where life appeared, neither here nor there, but belonged to the past? Maybe this was the melancholy essence of growing old, of *being* old.

There was only an hour to go before her doctor's appointment. Yet, Helen couldn't help weigh the significance of

a receptionist's polite insistence that she switch her appointment from Monday to Friday, and to Dr Marchant's downtown office where allegedly a last minute cancelation had
opened up in the late afternoon, the concatenation of facts
hemming her into a reality that there could be no further
happiness, *no further life.*

She considered staying on Lake Shore Drive, then,
deciding against it, she changed lanes, exiting into merging
traffic along Michigan Avenue. She felt an almost immediate sense of déjà vu in having taken this route so many
times before.

It was not, however, quite as it had been. Nothing
was anymore. If she could alter the perspective ever so
slightly, if she could beg such small mercies on this day of
remembrance, reclaim the past for a moment, she would
swap her compact Toyota Corolla for one of those bygone
fin-tail floating Detroit fortresses.

What she had in mind was the 1963 Buick 4600 Invicta
with the tomato red leather interior she and her husband
Walter had purchased the first year of their marriage – the
Invicta, the first and last car she ever drove straight off a
showroom floor.

She'd adjust, too, the garish fluorescence of the Michigan
Avenue storefronts, temper them with the Technicolor
warmth of *Breakfast at Tiffany's*, filtering everything
through a Hollywood cheesecloth that had defined an
America of pillbox hats and high heels. How one appeared
to the world mattered once.

And, if she could effect those changes on this melancholy

day, she would go back further through the blur of history, undo so many events, finding a point of re-entry into life when she had the thread of continuity. She would begin by re-aligning historical details, remote and yet personal to her, events as she now remembered them – reinstate the Shah of Iran, unhood and march the hostages back to American shores, send Khomeini back into exile. Reinstall Nixon, unplug the Watergate devices, silence Deep Throat, undo Nixon's visit to Red China. Fill the empty gas pumps of the 1973 Oil Embargo, keep the bigness of US cars and the monopoly of Bethlehem Steel, resanctify the unions, resurrect Jimmy Hoffa. She would also lead a retreat out of Vietnam, dislodge the bullets from the brains of MLK, Bobby and John F. Kennedy. She'd repeal, too, the benevolence of the Marshall Plan, spinning back time to some twilight pre-adolescence of first cognition, stop time somewhere after the dropping of the bombs on Hiroshima and Nagasaki, begin it again in the Cold War brinksmanship with the defined enemy of the Communist Soviet Union.

She was aware she had not included undoing the recent horrors of 9/11, not started at that new point of national hysteria. It was not her history, not really. She felt the emotional slippage. The inconsequential piling of new histories that no longer impinged on her immediate life with any sense of real urgency, just as untold tens of millions before must have surely arrived at certain points in their own lives where events, even as monumental as Pearl Harbor, just floated, unmoored of any real significance – psychological life lived, not in a forward trajectory, but built up around points of personal perspective – each generation, no, each individual at the end, an island unto itself.

Helen Price was conscious of how upset her son Norman would be with her in expressing this melancholy sense of loss. Undoubtedly, he would have stridently argued against her present vision of history, pointing out her incongruous lament for a succession of generations who had slaughtered themselves across a half-century of two world wars, plunged themselves into the shadow of nuclear annihilation, not to mention the protracted economic miasma of the preceding age of Robber Barons, The Stock Market Crash, and The Great Depression.

She could almost hear Norman's voice in her head, his rarified, injurious assessment of other people's lives that had already coalesced in his indignant, hurtful one-man shows, from *Confessions of a Latchkey Kid*, to his follow-up, *Angry Man*, a scathing indictment of Walter that had become a minor Chicago theatrical phenomenon.

How would Norman now title her life – *Sad Woman, Dying Woman, Lonely Woman*? She tried to imagine the exchange, her story unfolding as a natural corollary to Walter's life, a companion piece to *Angry Man*, another black box theater production, her offstage voice playing against Norman's voice, carried over the stilled dark. This, the perceivable endgame, a pitiless assessment of two people who had gone broke educating what turned out to be a recalcitrant gay man who had decided to damn the history of civilization for perceived homophobic injustices.

She felt her heart race even as she reached for the word *homophobic*. The estrangement was Norman's doing, and yet, in coming again to her own life, she would have to cede to some of his points, to a revisionist history now taught in schools that gave him his confidence, his optimism, his distaste and distrust of the past.

And yet it wasn't exactly how history had unfolded, not really, not how she remembered it. She found herself shaking her head ever so slowly, seeing further back before Norman, memories of her early courtship, the drive-in ice-cream parlors and drive-in movies; the solidarity of small-town homecomings, the flotilla of convertibles escorting Kings and Queens to the floodlit fields of night game inter-county rivals, everyone seeking simply to reclaim the familiar, to set aside recent horrors, to fall in love with poodle-skirted girls in push-up bras, cashmere sweaters and mother-of-pearl earrings. It played just so in her mind, in spools of old reel turning slowly against the foreground of a more recent, but disconnected, debased present.

Time was running out for Helen Price.

She had started to think of herself again in the third person, remembering how she self-consciously had identified herself as *Helen Price* when first married, writing out her signature over and over again with a trembling adult resolve, and now to come upon that name again, *Helen Price*, her name, and all that it once represented, and to think of it on a headstone.

She felt her eyes blur. She remembered how the end had ignominiously started in the nadir of an itinerant Thanksgiving at a suburban Red Lobster less than a year ago, a compromise in the absence of a family, an experience so unsettling it had set her and Walter on the high seas a month later for a lavish Christmas Caribbean cruise ultimately overshadowed by a low grade salmonella outbreak linked to a dubious barrier reef buffet of crustaceous delights. It was the persistence of stomach pains in the months after the cruise that had augured all was not well with her. Cancer was in her uterus and then in her lungs.

How often had she thought, what if she had never gone on the cruise? The entire fiasco opened up again, the Medevac rescue efforts off the coast of St Croix, a quotient of elderly summarily helicoptered to an island hospital for precautionary reasons, her included, and against her better judgment. A month later she had discovered that travel insurance had not covered the six-minute airlift, the Medevac outfit billing an astronomical $11,000 to their credit card.

Helen turned after crossing the Chicago River, edging along Upper West Wacker. She knew she should have turned earlier onto Superior, toward the vast medical complex of Northwestern Hospital and the Oncology office of Dr Marchant.

Instead, she followed the contour of the river's bend. She wasn't going to Dr Marchant's office. She gave herself to this truth, lost in the elongated fall of shadows. She passed across gelled bars of afternoon light intersecting the East/West streets in a roll call of presidential names – Washington, Madison, Monroe and Adams – before turning east again toward the lake on Jackson, crossing Franklin until she finally passed the intersection of La Salle. This was where she had worked until 1992, the ground zero of her existence.

She craned forward. Above her, two hooded figures stood atop the Mercantile Exchange, an Egyptian grasping a sheaf of wheat and a Native American holding an ear of corn. Time seemed to have stopped here. The commodities exchange and the Federal Reserve Bank belonged to another age, to a time when the nation's wealth had been tied to the Gold Standard, to a cache of gold set against the float of currency.

'There you go again!' she heard Norman say in her head. And yet it meant something to her. It defined the way she had experienced life for so many years, the ticker tape of futures tied to the breadbasket of grain, cereals, and soybeans grown out on the great plains of Oklahoma and Nebraska, to the dairy farms in the glacial moraines of Wisconsin and Minnesota, the railway yards of livestock movement, the trundling shunt of railway gauges coupling and decoupling, trains snaking out toward the East, South, and West.

Maybe it was just nostalgia, the same story generationally played out time and again, but no, it was different! The slippage all the more stark now in this new age of informational management and digital superhighways, in the Wi-Fi bandwidth of things unseen, in the derivatives markets tied directly to Walter's retirement account, based on what exactly? Calculated wagers securitized against something.

Helen felt a shudder run through her. Was there ever such a sense of loss as the one she now experienced? In times past, be it plague, famine, war, or simply the wrath of God, there was some sense of an ending and reasonableness to it. She thought of Lot, walking away from all that had come before, but toward a future. That was the difference, the prospect of hope, of a new beginning.

Helen was willing to admit to her own failings. It was just her perception, her way of seeing the world. She felt the need to defend herself again. No, nothing made sense anymore. Not really. She felt her lips forming the name Theodore Feldman, reeling in time again, finding a way back to the most distant and yet respected man she had ever known. Mr Theodore Feldman, distinguished, decorated veteran of World War II. He called the Japanese 'Gooks', his one betrayal of his personal history in the Pacific carnage. Where had men like that gone, men of means, manners, and material substance? She knew where. Life detached from a fading, tangible, older world of physical materiality; life lost to a digital age.

She recalled fondly the arterial vacuum suction tubes running through her office building. This was how commerce had worked once upon a time, in the hive of corporate activity, with its division of labor between the sexes and ages. Memos materializing as items of substance, memos first taken down word for word in a cryptic shorthand secretarial script, then passed on and typed up by pools of girls.

It still existed within her mind, the gurgle of the water cooler serviced by that lifelong Culligan Man in his dickey bow and crisp white short sleeved shirt with the hitched polio limp passed off as a war injury. She observed all this sitting in an outer office of bubbled privacy glass, opening the morning mail with a dagger of a letter opener, screening all calls for Mr Feldman until he buzzed and called her in, whereafter she spent the greater part of her day transcribing, pen and pad in hand.

She remembered, too, how Mr Feldman strode back and forth punctuating his ideas with a series of affectations that perhaps even he was unaware of inhabiting, stopping mid-stride in a slanting sunlight, then shifting into the colder grey of more rational deliberation, moving to and fro in a mental cursive of looping patterns through the office, finding his way toward some coherent thought.

She could almost smell his aftershave and how, through all of it, she had remained an undeniable physical presence into which she had allowed Mr Feldman to pour his professional expertise. At times, Mr Feldman looking askance in her direction, at the way she shifted ever so slightly, whereupon he subtly readjusted a phrase, because of her influence, her presence – who knew, really?

She thought if she were to explain the business memo process, if there was something she could pass on to this new generation, it would undoubtedly include reference to this spatial sense of awareness, this fluid movement in time, this assemblage of thoughts found here and there in the touchstone of physical things and spaces. Yes, that was it, her sense of physical presence in time.

And there were other memories. That time Mr Feldman took to using a gold-plated putter that came with one of those automatic cups that spat the ball out again and again, a corporate Christmas gift when such tokens were expected, Mr Feldman sighting up his points of managerial reprimand for the salesmen in the field, a series of balls hit in slow, methodical succession, the ball's silent roll across the billiard green of the carpet.

She remembered, too, the speeches Mr Feldman spent days constructing for the board of trustees. The attenuated way he had of coming to subtle points regarding the general running of the company. Mr Feldman looking off toward Lake Michigan for a word or phrase to capture a thought just so. The old-world, soft-shoe way he had of speaking around and not particularly to an issue, circumscribing points of business suggestive enough to land upon the overall challenges, but lest anybody forgot, for this was a nation of optimists, the opportunities that still existed – remarks that always inspired the corporate board members to nod approvingly amidst desserts and cognac, leading to furtive considerations concerning drinks elsewhere – Mr Feldman politely retreating and placing a jocular call to the office with uncharacteristic warmth in the hum of accomplishment to ensure the office, as he put it, 'hadn't burned down!' A remark that always made Helen flush.

On these occasions Helen had always found comfort, hearing the raspy scratch of Mr Feldman's five o'clock growth on the end of the receiver, and so, too, the clink of china plates being gathered from the impressive spread of tables, the general hubbub of corporate entitlement which made her feel all was well, that everything which mattered in the world was in the capable hands of irreproachable men of sound character and good moral judgment. She would never, ever have thought Mr Theodore Feldman would have bowed out, stepping from his corporate office window atop the Chicago skyline on the Black Monday of 1987, but he did.

That was when her life had most surely ended, or so said Norman in the years afterward, implying improprieties of a most sordid sort, pressing against her loyalty and fond remembrance of Mr Feldman with his general cynicism of all things past, the accusations surfacing at being left in the nurse's office because she simply could not leave work. 'It was as simple as that, Norman!'

She heard herself shout it inside her head.

Helen felt the dull ache of her insides. Shouldn't she turn now and head toward Dr Marchant, face the coming realities? And yet she didn't, circling again her former life, passing the burnished brass revolving door of her old office building, casting back to a time before Mr Feldman's suicide, re-aligning life again, finding her way to earlier memories.

She tried to find that essential old happiness, to inhabit an early freedom as a newly liberated woman of the late sixties. She had such fond memories, rising in the morning in a hustle to get Norman to the school bus on time, leaving the utilitarian suburb of a modest house in a car financed on affordable down payments for the throng on the commuter train platform. She remembered it all with absolute clarity, parking her car amidst the gleam of other new cars, proceeding in the push of life, venturing toward the stenciled ceiling and frescos beyond the revolving door of her office building.

Even now, she could see in her mind's eye the gold-leafed topaz and onyx tiffany mosaic in the building's lobby, the entire pageant of Midwestern history captured in a series of stylized mosaics, the collective first landings rendered in a two-dimensional flatness suggesting an uncomplicated arrangement of bringing a Christian God to the natives – a sharing of gifts between frocked French missionaries, Bibles in hand, with olive-skinned natives in ceremonial headdress offering a peace pipe at some appointed canoe portage.

No matter the real history. She could almost hear Norman in her head shouting, and she wanted to scream back at him, for who *now* didn't know the true history!

'Yes, Norman, the ravages of smallpox and measles, the internment of natives and the Trail of Tears... I *know*... I *know*... you are so *damned* right...'

And yet in the mosaics' audacious simplicity, set before the people as artifact, it had served as a stylized myth

12

of life as a system of exchanges, of deals, where the only underlying principle was the decorum and manner of how one negotiated.

It was in these early first landings, these ceremonial exchanges, that the glory of a new world was founded – from a humble barter of animal pelts to the glorious reach of skyscrapers in a span of mere centuries.

No *single* history could account for such progress. It was all too vastly complicated, and yet so manifestly real and literal, the inner chamber of the lobby a crypt holding the sacred transactional truth of Adam Smith's *Wealth of Nations*. It had all come together so beautifully once-upon-a-time, the perfect inning, the improbable no-hitter of American dominance, and all of it coinciding with her youth.

Helen turned east on Jackson toward the lake in the evening traffic, intent now on what needed to be done. Snow had threatened all afternoon. It fell now in drifting flakes of a snow globe. This was the contained reality of her life, or how it had once been. It had passed.

In retirement, for the better part of a decade, she had huddled in a housecoat in her basement inhabiting a remote history of distant lives and times, re-enactments on the Discovery Channel – entire eras and civilizations compressed into hour shows – the Crusades and the Dark Ages, the spectre of plague and famine, the rise and fall of the Roman Empire, and on through the plundering conquests of the Norse, Vikings, and Vandals, all of it a tumbling distraction of dates and events. This had been the sarcophagus of her hours, days, weeks, and years.

She thought of Cancer as blithely unaware of her absence; Cancer, taking in a mid-morning Western before getting up to torment her in the toilet in late-morning agony, the cloud of blood in the bowl after she went. She imagined Cancer, slovenly, up-to-date. A reaper in a college hoodie and sweatpants, shuffling out of the den; Cancer standing in the grey light leading up to the first floor; Cancer whining for her, in the way Norman had over the years. It sent a shudder through her.

It was tempting just to close her eyes, to end it here. She circled the block of her former life. It was all there, arrested and contained, so like she remembered it. She wanted to pull over, park her miserable Toyota import, go stand again in the mosaic lobby and feel the overpowering reassurance of her own existence.

She passed the gleam of her office building once more. Why had she come down here? When she got the news of her illness, her first thought had landed on Mr Feldman, that she might yet meet him again on the other side of life.

What did such thoughts say about her? Had Norman been right in his accusations? Such questions, and in the lateness of life! No! She *wouldn't* answer them! She would not.

She sniffled. She wanted to go deeper, find that place within herself where it all still existed, the time before her illness, before that godforsaken 9/11, before the accumulation of joys and regrets that had somehow, quietly, rubbed out her significance.

It was decided. The choice had always been hers. She felt a control she had not felt in a long time. Yes, that most surely was it, why she had come here one last time: to reclaim the feelings of those years of comfort in what had been back then, the incalculability of life in an emerging modern world of options, where she had continued to work after marriage, and *even* after Norman's birth, the surrogate infrastructure of daycare overseen by attentive professionals in child psychology, all vastly more equipped to nurture growth than any mother sequestered with a child and a TV in the doldrums of the mid-afternoon soaps.

How forward-looking it had all seemed. How liberating! The delegation of tasks per one's merits, one's interests, the uncompromising vision that everyone could have everything one needed, or at least the opportunity to seek it. And now it was gone.

Helen felt her eyes tear, intent on what needed to be done. On the seat beside her lay a letter from the State Attorney's Office, a subpoena requiring her testimony in a case she had thought long closed, now reopened, alleging Walter's criminal obstruction of justice in perjuring himself by providing an alibi for two officers accused of executing two gangland dealers who had been set to testify against members of Chicago's South Side vice unit.

She was sobbing, her thoughts settled on Norman, on his *Angry Man* show, on the quiet indictment of a fiction that might yet be appraised as fact, as evidence. What would he say about her and about Walter, about their lives? Helen ran the back of her hand under her nose, tasting her own tears, drifting in the blurred flow of traffic against the falling snow. The subpoena was already a week old. It had been served to her door, which she had obstinately refused to open despite the persistence of the serving officer. She had not yet formally acknowledged its receipt, not even against the stiff formality of the follow up messages left on her answering machine.

She thought again of the hours running up to Walter's departure earlier that morning and what a court would demand of her again, a reinvestigation into monies she had allegedly laundered for Walter in the grim years of a greater city corruption. It was come upon them again, the entanglement of her secrets with Walter's, what had not yet, and might now, be discovered. She had survived it once, just barely. She couldn't do it a second time.

She looked through a blur of tears, seeing again her own effigy seated by the small telephone table picked out so far back at the beginning of her marriage, listening to and then erasing each call from an attorney, then hearing the call from Dr Marchant's office, the polite insistence of the voice asking her to come down on a Friday and in the late afternoon for a consultation. How was such a coincidence possible, such an alignment of Fates, this convergent sense of an ending?

No, Helen Price was not a religious woman, yet something was being asked of her, some grave and purposeful decision.

She reached for her pills beside the subpoena. In opening the bottle, she tipped her head back, feeling the reflexive gag of self-preservation. She managed swallowing them, their effect almost immediate in the sudden euphoria of knowing how it would now end.

In the long corridor of her funneling exit, in the falling snow, she headed south on Columbia. Driving parallel to a desolate Grant Park, she was startled by the wail of a police siren, a sound hard to pinpoint against the tumbling end-over-end effect of the pills.

In her rearview mirror, she caught sight of something she could no longer face and, closing her eyes, felt the disembodied sponginess of the accelerator pedal beneath her foot. Beyond the broad six-lane stretch of Lake Shore Drive, she imagined the cradling grey of Lake Michigan like a vast subconscious stirring.

PART I

*The darkest places in hell are reserved for those who
maintain their neutrality in times of moral crisis.*

—DANTE ALIGHIERI

1.

NOBODY JUMPED TO their death in the Global Financial Crisis of 2008 as they had in the Crash of 1929, and though the losses were equal, there was no run on banks or the chaotic dissolution of so many lives.

The crisis was more a *correction*, the lightweights on the morning shows, educating the ignorant about the volatility of the bond, securities and derivatives markets, while down on Times Square, outside the glass enclosure of the *TODAY* show, the faithful held up signs that said, 'We Luv U Al!' or 'We Luv the Big Apple!'

In their so doing, it confirmed an undeniable truth for Norman Price: that whatever the outcome of the crisis, life would go on. There would be no revolution.

In truth, for anybody who gave a shit, it was difficult deciding *what had happened* and *who was at fault*. Sometimes too much freedom, too much democracy, too much choice, too much talk could – and did – achieve nothing.

For Norman Price, in the midst of his own crisis, the financial crisis was a distraction signifying there were no longer any essential truths, no longer a beginning, middle, or end to events; a realization that eclipsed, among other things, the passing of his parents. It spared him mourning them, or otherwise trying to understand the events surrounding their deaths. Their motivations were as convoluted as any accounts related to the financial crisis.

Initial eyewitness accounts suggested that Helen Price, in hearing a siren, had hit the accelerator instead of the brake. It was a reasonable explanation. Helen Price was old and ill. She had been on her way to a doctor's appointment. There were, however, other circumstances that told a different story. The officer driving the unmarked police car had been Walter Price. He had witnessed the incident, and yet he had neither assisted at the scene, nor called 911. He had simply driven away.

There was much made by the police of *what was known* and *when it was known*, given how in the early hours of the morning, Walter Price had been granted unrestricted access to a comatose Helen Price at Cook County Hospital, where he had ended her life before taking his own with a single bullet to the head.

Allegations of racketeering, extortion and money laundering surfaced. Just days before, Helen Price had been served a subpoena in a reconvened grand jury stemming from an investigation into systemic extortion by the South Side police. It was an old story of city corruption, the twists in the story, Walter and Helen's age, and the fact that Helen had been suffocated. It signaled how brutally unforgiving the system had been, and so, too, underscored the culpability of the police who had allowed Walter unsupervised access to Helen.

Norman stood apart from it now. Walter and Helen's respective wills served as eventual directives. He hadn't participated in their funerals. Helen was cremated. Walter detailed a similar wish. Norman had uncovered it in a grim correspondence of legal documents that eventually found their way into his life. He inherited his parents' collective possessions, the house, and associated bonds and stocks.

Norman looked up. Beyond his window, snow fell. It was not yet seven in the morning. He had been writing for almost two hours, or trying to. He lived for this feeling of accomplishment, sifting through the silt of an awakening subconscious, unlocking life in a word or line. He believed mystery and understanding lay at liminal thresholds of awareness in the way ascetics prayed and believed there could be communion with a greater power.

What mattered now was that he was at his desk again.

In the interim since his parents' passing, life had changed. Not least his jettisoning of his philandering partner, Kenneth, who had been carrying on a long-term relationship with an investment financier, Daniel Einhorn, whom Norman had introduced to Kenneth during discussions concerning Einhorn potentially financing an off-Broadway run of one of Norman's plays that was eventually never financed.

There had been, in the not-too-distant past, heady days of a potential breakthrough and rising fortunes, when the climate of investment largesse had funneled down into the Arts with gallery openings and a burgeoning interest in theater. That was over now.

Much had changed. If the decision to dump Kenneth dovetailed with his parents' death, which it had, it was coincidence, or so he believed. You moved through stages of existence. What you endured at one point, what sustained you, suddenly couldn't. It was how he might have described his father's life, his mother's, his, too, and the life of the city.

Today, Norman was aware of a Chinese language CD playing in an indecipherable babble in his daughter, Grace's room. He had adopted her three years previous from China, claiming her against the eventualities, that whatever happened in his life, she might be there to establish a normalcy and continuance in his own life. He had retained custody of her after the breakup with Kenneth.

He felt that continuance, but so, too, the burden of her influence in hearing the Chinese CD. Yes, he could have tried to learn Chinese, but he had decided against it. The linguistic distance ensured his influence would be as unobtrusive as possible. What Grace brought of herself would remain intact. Principled ideas of autonomy, justice, and sovereign independence were important to Norman Price.

Norman stared at the sliver of a hallway mirror, Grace, reflected in the image of another mirror, lost in a sort of repeating Escher effect. She was earnestly arranging her Barbies in a bleak tribunal outside a Victorian dollhouse guarded by a porcelain pair of salt-and-pepper shaker Scotty dogs. If Norman had one pressing regret, it was how Grace had changed since the adoption. He consciously connected a coldness settling over her to a latent survival instinct that she must have perfected in response to the way institutions, such as the one she had been rescued from, functioned, on the absolute uniformity and anonymity of those it housed.

Or perhaps he was overthinking it. Maybe it was his sense of guilt, his aloneness and disconnectedness from life when he was writing. Or maybe all Chinese were like this, the billion faces so absolutely the same, or apparently so from Norman's perspective, if he could submit to such an idea without racist intent – it was hard deciding.

In truth, losing Kenneth was a burden lifted, a feeling that eclipsed most everything else going on around him, a self-imposed austerity measure like how it felt to cut up your credit cards, as attested to by the honest folk who talked on the conservative radio stations about assumed personal responsibility as a quasi-religious atonement for wrongful purchases, and how there was nothing wrong with America or capitalism. It was the people who needed to atone and make amends.

There was a new beginning. He felt it everywhere, in the sweep of change, in the simple pronouncement of 'Yes we can!'

As evidence, he had ventured out into the cold dark of a Chicago night in early November, holding Grace's hand as the throng pressed down on Grant Park, to experience the rousing sense of history being made, John McCain, distinguished and decorated former prisoner-of-war, unable to overcome the rainbow coalition of minorities unsettled by the lies which had led to war in Afghanistan and Iraq and the collapse of the economy.

Norman consigned his parents' deaths with McCain's defeat, with the passing of an era, with a generation that had served and died for the American cause. It was not that Norman didn't care, or that the nation wasn't thankful or respectful. It was just that certain types, certain histories, mattered less in the emerging narrative. In defeat, McCain, like Norman's parents in dying, quietly surrendered the past to the present.

Norman saved his file for the day. At times it was enough for a writer to show up. Turning, he watched in the hallway mirror his live-in nanny's blue-grey Weimaraner, Randolph, stir and go toward the bathroom. This was part of what he was calling *The New Existence*. Norman listened to the faint lapping sound of the dog's tongue drinking from the toilet bowl.

Joanne Hoffmann, Grace's nanny and Randolph's owner, was also up and performing a series of contorted Yoga holds in his living room, her flannel pajama bottoms riding low on the spread of her pelvis. Beside her was a tent-like structure – sheets draped over a table in the living room – a conceit that still persisted from when Joanne had first moved in. In observing it, there was the resurrection of a routine, a filling in of life in the vacuum of what had come before. He was not fully reconciled with what it all meant, but it was part of *The New Existence.*

Norman had hired Joanne on New Year's Day, Joanne, his neighbor, fallen on hard times. Her long-term partner had dumped her. Norman had learned the disconsolate details on New Year's Eve in the apartment hallway as Joanne was coming out to walk her dog.

She'd mentioned her separation with an oblique apology related to the fights that had raged in the final weeks before her break-up. Fights Norman 'must undoubtedly have overheard'. He hadn't, but he had felt obliged to pretend he had, to respect the implosion of what he learned had been a long-term relationship.

He learned it all in one long sentence, how management had been disinclined to extend her lease, her credit shot. She wasn't working. She confided she was considering returning home for good, but there was a family complication. She stopped abruptly. She had a dresser and an antique table, family heirlooms, on Craigslist, priced to sell. She asked if Norman might be interested. She could show him after Randolph was let out.

At midnight they rang in the New Year together, Joanne, in the minutes before, removing cellophane from a tray of cheeses, crackers and dips Norman had bought in the eleventh hour of the dying year. He dusted off two champagne flutes, opened a bottle of champagne, so it was done just in time, the clink of glasses after the ball dropped at Times Square, each counting down the seconds, each standing at a distance, watching the television, whereafter, Joanne produced a joint from the turned-up cuff of her cardigan. She grew her weed on a windowsill in a makeshift window box greenhouse.

Back in the living room, Norman talked about Grace's adoption, the trip to China, ending with the eventual undoing of his relationship with Kenneth and Grace's delay in speaking. Joanne, in turn, talked about her ex-partner. They toasted with an understanding of their own shortfalls and an emphasis on their partner's failings. It was good to talk.

It helped that Norman had tangentially known Peter Coffey, a pedantic, long-standing post-doc, who, as Joanne explained, after a dissolute eternity as adjunct faculty, had finally gained a tenure track position at a small community college in Oklahoma. At the time of his departure, he was already dating a former student. He took the girlfriend with him, not her. Joanne described Coffey as a second-rate poet, and, truth be told, a poet with a small penis, but then wasn't that what was behind most bad poetry?

Under the influence of liberally poured wine and pot, Norman learned that Joanne could become truculent. She had a way of scrunching her nose when she got mad, absentmindedly rimming her wine glass in a circular motion, her eyes glossing with a deepening hurt.

Norman turned to his computer again. He pulled up the website for the realty agency he had contracted to offload his parents' house. He had not gone out to the house. He simply wanted it gone. He stared at the low-res feed of his childhood home on the realty's Virtual Walk-Thru. A grainy fisheye sweep of a wavering feed stalled in the hallway. To go any further required an email address. It said so in a pop-up window. Then another pop-up offered financing options – three- and five-year arms, balloons, variable and fixed rates, a flashing banner indicating *Bad Credit Isn't a Problem*, a legacy banner, pre-financial meltdown. There were, of course, no such loans anymore.

Another flashing pop-up offered a trial membership in FreeCreditScore.com, the pop-ups reminiscent of garish billboard signs he had seen on a trip taken in his early adolescence with his parents along Route 66. At the time, the roadside motels were already diminished in the way Hitchcock had prophetically anticipated, so that, much later, Norman, in looking back on it, would understand that *Psycho*'s deceptive genius was not the shock of Janet Leigh's shower scene murder, but something further reaching, more innominate – the death of the American love affair with the car and the open road, and, with it, a certain aimless, transient freedom that had allowed snake oil salesmen to pitch their wares town-to-town in the shadowy in-between of promise and despair.

There were, among the greats, many ways to tell a story. Truth had to be played like a good poker hand, concealed until the end, though what he feared most was that freedom and understanding had been eclipsed, so there was only sensationalism and no substance anymore. Maybe that was just the lament of the pedantic, the contrarian, the literalist, the fate of the Chicken Littles of the world.

In staring at the jittery images, in inhabiting what had been his former life, Norman was reminded of the opening scenes of *Titanic*, the modern submersible sending back a grey feed of pictures from beneath the Atlantic to the aged heroine. That was the genius of Art, its power to encapsulate, in the case of *Titanic*, to apprehend the great folly of human hubris that had so defined the age – the push across the Atlantic at breakneck speed for the record, icebergs-be-damned, along with all on board – the film's essential allure, everyone on board living the last days of their lives and not realizing it, while everybody watching did.

On this morning, Norman felt the inherent stirring of a re-energizing intellect. He was wandering into a creative and searching space, the unmoored flotsam of events washing up in the scud of the subconscious. He was building, from what remained, some kind of raft, something that would sustain and carry him forward, liberate and connect him again to his craft. He liked the double meaning of the word *craft*, how the right words could be carried in a riptide of understanding, a process that required not so much strength as patience to assess and reconfigure life, so one could stare back toward the coastline of the inhabited world, then make for shore once more.

Norman stared at the images of his former life. Neither Helen nor Walter existed anymore. They had been incinerated.

Tightness gripped his chest, a register of emotion he was not aware he still possessed.

He pulled up the Internet memorial site to affirm Helen had ever existed. Not a single person had signed her virtual memorial book. A question mark placeholder showed where a picture should have been uploaded and never was. An American flag wavered like a flag plangently planted on the moon, suggesting that the afterlife was somehow the province of an American holding.

And yet, it somehow fit with a certain understanding that Helen had of the American experience – its striving greatness and sense of possibility pursued and then abandoned in the lunar grey of a destination reached and then forgotten – so he understood, the journey had been the point, and not the landing, not the conquest. It was the story of the moon and so much of everything else in life.

Norman was suddenly glad now for the Internet, for the impersonal expediency of how all matters of life and death could now be so negotiated in a disconnectedness of connectedness. All a real funeral would have revealed was that there had been nobody in his mother's life for a very long time.

Helen had opted for an insignificant departure, a literal dropping off the earth into the depths of the great lake, seeking the fathoms of her own grave, taking with her the argosy of her dreams, the air pocket of her retirement, ending in the literal rising of a water line in the cab of her car. It fit her temperament, the attempted, self-contained death, the tight circle of her own thoughts and ideas, her immense capacity to withhold opinions, to stay in the orbit of her own existence.

For a moment, his thoughts settled once more with the *Titanic*, on the sullen passing of life in the cold reaches of the North Atlantic far from shore. He hadn't watched *Titanic* in a long time.

In the falling snow, he thought, why not seal off the outside world for a lost day of tragic remembrance? Why not submit to this quiet reprieve, rerun history in the wavering stills, the opening sequence draped in the raiment of the dirge of Uilleann pipes against the siren's lament of Celine Dion?

He was, he felt, the Rose Dewitt of a lesser tragedy, but a tragedy nonetheless. Maybe he could dive as the submersible did, dredge back a history long sunken. Yes, maybe that is what he would do.

2.

To NATE FELDMAN, Helen Price was always just *The Other Woman*, so he didn't immediately recall her name when he first read it in a letter sent to him by a law firm out of Chicago.

Nate snaked along a logging road against a pale luminescence of banked snow and out along a rut of iced road. His bladder ached from the grind of the snow-chained tires. He was at the age when the signs of mortality announced themselves. He edged toward the glow of Iroquois Falls, the world encased in a domed dark that in late January held past nine thirty.

A storm was forecast. Nate had the radio tuned to the Canadian weather service. The barometric pressure was dropping fast, but he had errands to run and just this window of opportunity. He didn't meet a single car on the road. His eyes focused on the funneling cone of his headlights, old growth pines running sentinel along either side of the road. There were times when he felt like the last human alive, as if only he had survived a great cataclysm, which, in a way, he had.

The town was all but deserted, though there were lights on at various establishments. He shuffled through the mail in the cold vestibule of the post office. What struck him first was the airmail blue of the envelope. He felt an overwhelming sense of déjà vu, so he had to lean for support against the burnished patina brass of the PO boxes.

He fingered the waxy weightlessness of the envelope, recalling a time when weight mattered, when the envelope itself was the medium on which one wrote, and when it was done, the letter written, the folding origami, making it an envelope again, the tongue running along the sweet bordering glue.

He felt the stab of memory. His father had sent him letters to this same PO box with the affectation of *par avion*, letters asking after his health, but more pointedly after Nate's wife and newborn child, though their names were never mentioned under the presumption that all letters were opened by the United States government.

Back in the pickup, Nate let the vents pour a dry heat over his hands. He ran his thumb along the crinkled give of the envelope. It was upon him, all that he had left behind.

He recalled the first summer of his escape, the encroach of wildfire, the sky a sanguine blood orange, the thunderous stampede of wildlife in a pitiless retreat toward rivers in a natural divide of a fire line, and then the soot and ash, the torrents of rain that darkened the midsummer as though it had all been delivered unto him alone.

He had endured those first months with a moral indecisiveness so it was hard to find the measure of who he was. He braced against the knifing advance of autumnal days he knew would come, and did. Inside his cabin, he had penned letters against the throw of shifting firelight, grappling not with the immediacy of what was happening, but seeking a grander assessment of life, writing with the instinctive understanding that what he set down would be read again and again, not for the hard and fast facts, but as an epistolary of a life lived.

A shudder ran through him. Guilt dogged him. He struggled for the right metaphor. How best to describe it, this past? An old scar in the boggy tenderness of flesh never made quite right; his history an escape that would outlast the conflict in Vietnam, the pull-out from Saigon, the receding proxy of Cold War conflicts fought in far off jungles.

Maybe that was why he had felt such swelling euphoria on first seeing the Twin Towers come down – *not* for the loss of life. He was philosophically against death, but he aligned with the literal act of aggression. War had come to American shores, so it wouldn't be a case anymore of shipping young men overseas, for the fight would be fought on American soil. It turned out not to have been the case.

Nate didn't open the letter right away. He was past the insistent pressure of youth. He would wait, though he felt a thumping in his chest as he went about his business. He exited the pickup under the bowl of a streetlight.

The wind took the door. The hinges creaked and strained. He pushed the door shut with both hands. A dusting of snow blew around his face. Storm was in the air.

In the warm store, he picked up his supplies: coffee, evaporated milk, an assortment of meats, three bags of flour, rice, beans, a kilo of sugar, an allotment of canned goods. He had emailed his order ahead. The goods were sitting in a crate with his name stapled to the slatted wood. It could have been the nineteenth century.

He checked the contents against his list. The proprietor, Pierre Arouet, came out but neither of them spoke. The store bell trembled on a coil spring. There were highlights of the previous night's game between the Oilers and Canadiens on a big screen TV in the background. Roars filled the silence. This was how wars were settled, in the contained rink of Canadian ice, the rapacious frack of the gas boom western province pitted against the militant Québécois Francophiles, and yet Canada held.

He used a bathroom off to the side of the general store. He went in dribs and drabs. Blood in his urine clouded the bowl. He should see a doctor, but knew he wouldn't.

Above him, a spider held a corner in the web of its own spun universe.

On the way out of town, Nate looked again at the letter. He set it beside him like a passenger come a long way. He would address the matter at home.

Ahead, snow fell in a soft, swirling veil that took on

the opaque blue-grey of a bruise, the northern facing hills cast in deep cavernous shadow, the western sides a pale, butter yellow that had long since sent animals toward the instinctive drowse of hibernation.

He felt the same, drugged effect in the shunt of blood toward the vital organs. His hands and feet were always cold in a way they had not been years before. Maybe it was his age? He was undecided. He yawned into the back of his hand.

What he liked to watch on the television in his aloneness, in the deep freeze of winter, in the satellite beam of new choices, was reruns of *Hawaii Five-0* – the azure sea and palm fronds, the scooping dig of island natives in the break of waves in their long canoes, and, of course, the immaculately dressed Jack Lord, the signature turn of his head at the show's beginning. Jack Lord, a colonial viceroy, a man Nate connected with the calm, judicious equanimity of his own father.

How strange, the insistent drag of history, a show that could find him here alone and could breathe life into events connected to shots of his father in his time out on Midway Island in advance of the attack on Japan.

Nate opened the letter at the kitchen table. Helen Price had been known as *The Other Woman*, and before that as *The Coat-check Girl*, a title his mother had settled on in the early days.

There was a brief description of some film reels, recordings that had belonged to his father and that had come into the possession of Helen Price who had subsequently bequeathed them to Nate. In view of the reels' age and fragility, the law office was seeking advice on how they should be sent.

Nate looked up into the gauze of falling snow, the world gone flat and two-dimensional. The letter was still in his hand. He looked down at it. His eyes adjusted to the glob of floating light and found their focus.

There was no indication of the content of the reels, or of how many there were, though what was significant, what could not be discounted, was that the reels had been kept all these years, and bequeathed, not through the execution of his father's will, but through his father's mistress, Helen Price.

Nate searched for a sweater in a cedar chest he had built with his own hands. The piney tang of it dropped to the depth of his soul. Wood shavings curled amidst the folded wool sweaters, socks, and hats, all hand-knit. He had become fastidious in his solitude, in the quiet arrangement of everything. He stood in the room, as if everything had been awaiting his presence before it took on the approximation of existence.

He was a clockmaker, moving the hands of his own existence. Or he was a drowned man in a well, staring up through clear water. It was life seen through the wrong end of a telescope, small and isolated, and just beyond comprehension. He hugged himself, his throat tightening as he stared at sunlight streaming in an angled light on an empty mattress. A shiver ran through him. He leaned toward the frame of the window, wincing against the snow's incandescent shock.

On the Internet in his study, he searched for Helen Price. He found a brief mention of her accident, then a series of articles related to her death at the hands of her husband in an apparent murder-suicide. Walter Price had been involved in a systemic, long and protracted extortion scandal. At the end of Helen Price's obituary, there was mention of a surviving son, Norman Price, an established playwright in Chicago's theater.

Nate went out toward the kitchen. He was still absently holding the letter. When he noticed, he balled it in his fist. He was not obliged to answer. He was angry and sad in the same instance. He had been discovered and sought out.

He looked at the date at the top of the letter, the postmark two weeks old already. He could ignore it, or simply write and refuse delivery. He could instruct that the film reels be destroyed. It was his prerogative. He muttered a catalogue of excuses of why he should not respond. The tapes meant little to him.

It mattered little what his father might now say. His correspondence with him had declined when the threat of the Vietnam War had receded and ended. A congressional act was passed that had eventually dropped federal indictments against those who had dodged the draft so Nate had been free to leave his place of hiding, to return to America, but he hadn't. He felt he had somehow lost the right to call himself an American. It hadn't mattered when survival was everything. But it mattered later, when it was over. His father had simply stopped writing to him, and Nate, in quiet deference, had quietly and dutifully receded.

3.

IT WAS MID-FEBRUARY already, in the first year of *The New Existence*. Joanne's makeshift tent was still there in the living room. Norman had silently anointed her 'The Refugee of Suburbia'.

Norman had offered to foot the bill for a futon to end Joanne's encampment. She had declined the offer. She preferred her improvised tent, what she called 'the monastic aesthetic of the hardwood floor', when the issue was that her heirloom table had not sold on Craigslist, when it was, in her words, 'a real steal'.

She was suffering from unreal expectations, or that was how Norman saw it. He wasn't an economist, but he liked working with logic problems, and under the terms of *The New Existence* he had begun to take an active interest in the table. He saw it as part of an experiment to show how life was actually lived – the rise and dash of expectations, rational or irrational, because expectation figured in how markets worked. It had become one of his projects.

In the case of Joanne's table, he wanted to work out the difference between how she saw the table and how he saw it, as a pile of shit!

He had devised a formula. The heirloom table signified as (x) with its value based on two factors: the table's *perceived valuation (pv)*, what x was allegedly worth, and the *purchase price (pp)*, what someone actually paid for x.

Denoted mathematically, in most cases $pv \neq pp$. He had the table drawn on a white board with intersecting lines connected to various formulas. The table (x) could work out as $pv \neq \underline{pp}$, $pv < pp$, $pv > pp$. No transaction he denoted as $pv \otimes pp$.

It was the sort of passive aggressive formulation of life that Norman thrived on.

Joanne took it good-naturedly. She *believed* in the table as $pv \odot pp$.

In the background, throughout the day, Norman kept a small TV playing on CSPAN in the faint belief that this was how democracy worked, and that this too was part of *The New Existence* – reform, self-analysis, accountability, and transparency – the great show of collective reconciliation.

In truth, he thought it was crap, but the hearings captivated Joanne who liked the crispness of congressional and senatorial members and their staff, the polite decorum of the process. She seemed to have plenty of time to wax on life and politics, on her sense of how the world would reform under Obama, who raised great hope in her.

Joanne was interested in the power of talk, in the power of reconciliation. She communicated all this with sincere conviction as she ran her tongue along a joint.

Norman watched her move between the playroom and the TV room. She had a way of running her hand through her hair. She was quoting figures – the extent of the losses was astounding. Norman obligingly pretended to write it down.

Joanne was, she told him in all sincerity, absolutely for law and order. She was interested in the process of transparency. She wondered if the Lehman Brothers would eventually testify, then made a face when Norman said nothing.

She knew the Lehman Brothers were dead! Was Norman even listening to her?

She wanted his opinion on whether a certain senator wore boxers or not. She liked sincerity in a man more than anything else. As she talked, she crossed her arms. She was talking and simultaneously looking between the TV, Norman and Grace playing in her room, while in the kitchen, Randolph pushed his food bowl across the floor with his nose.

It went this way, Norman guarded in his criticism in a way he might not have been with Kenneth. In intertwining with her distracting influence, in allowing her into *The New Existence*, he believed Joanne was drawing him closer to a feeling of empathy and understanding, leading to a flattening of life's ambitions and hopes, connecting him with the velvet hammer of assumed and perhaps welcomed responsibility.

What he wanted at a deep level was to flush irony from his vocabulary, to tear down that essential wall that kept him from actually living life. He was looking elsewhere for inspiration without being fully cognizant of doing so, where the stated goal was not actually the stated goal, and that, in the margin of anxiety, perhaps genius would find root and surface.

There was, of course, the practical care and keeping of Grace that Joanne could provide. It wasn't all about his own mania, his own interest. Grace survived as the singular event that could not be undone. What he tried to convince himself, in the distancing of Kenneth's absence, in the silence of days, then weeks, and now months, was that Grace represented the watershed of a personal commitment toward ideas of hope and humanity, toward ideals that outlasted the flame of passion or intimacy. She was exerting a needed influence on his life, changing him for the better, normalizing him.

What Joanne Hoffmann was teaching him, what he was seeing when he stared into her image in the hallway mirror, was the power of the accumulation of small actions, an atomized life.

He noted Joanne's attentiveness when she dressed Grace, matching socks and color-coordinating outfits. He would come upon them in the kitchen, Joanne cutting food into bite-sized bits, steamed broccoli, cauliflower, sprouts, and spinach to be eaten before there was even a mention of dessert. Joanne inflexible in her resolve, her arms folded in stand-offs that could last a half-hour. At times Joanne sent

Grace to her room to think about 'making good choices' (*gc*), when Norman would have simply given in, not out of love, but expediency.

He wanted to put Joanne on the spot about her own apparent bad choices (*bc*), but managed to quell the cynical reflex. He was beginning to see how, through the act of talking and an associated pantomime of actions, a child might eventually navigate the world.

He wrote it all down in its exact details, revising and adding to his new formulary for life's grand equation. Was this, in fact, how you raised a child? He thought of Romulus and Remus. Raised by wolves, they had founded the city of Rome. He considered the question under the working title – *What if Joanne Hoffmann had raised Romulus and Remus?*

And he could catalog a series of other distractions. Joanne said that Grace would need to be kitted out with a new coat and boots for the walks she, Joanne, and Randolph took along the lake, so Norman was obliged to turn from his own preoccupations to notice the bare outline of defoliated trees, to see that winter had already settled upon them.

Since the purchase, there was the added equation – Joanne and Grace's pre-walk routine. Grace demanding that she be allowed to change out of her Princess Jasmine underwear into Princess Aurora underwear, or Belle underwear, the demand made with such petulance that the formula was skewed by a tantrum (*t*), as Grace thrashed her legs on the floor like something out of *The Exorcist*. A tantrum (*t*), could rise exponentially, denoted by $(t)^x$.

The tantrums and the socio-political reality beneath them – the polyester underwear purchased at Walmart – shot to hell his stand against globalization and child labor exploitation. It was, he reflected in his most sanguine moment, part of the new poverty. This was economic life under *The New Existence*, in which princess underwear could be bought for the price of a Big Mac.

He had his working formulae, seeking what he called the elusive dark matter of the human condition. He felt himself on the far reaches of a profound understanding, where there might be no single solution, where each case might be the exception, a concept that had at its center a dark nihilism.

This was life in *The New Existence*, and it didn't end with the morning routine.

Norman began to face the 24/7 reality of childcare. After the reprieve of the morning walk there was another change of clothes, a smock for finger painting, the mounting pile of laundry, all part of the monotonous sinkhole of commitment a child's life entailed if you decided against daycare, or didn't simply hand a child over to *Sesame Street* and *SpongeBob SquarePants*.

In this he better understood his mother's choices. Hers had been the new era of delegated responsibility, where a life no longer had to end with marriage, and the rearing of children didn't have to be a soul-killing proposition.

But, of course, it was never that easy. He was, as he had described in the opening of *Confessions of a Latchkey Kid*, 'Formula Fed!' with its double-entendre in that spirited age of dehydrated foods and pills, where nobody wanted to suffer the recourse of slaving over a stove.

How it had changed, that sixties lightness of existence, a calculated minimalism that might be ascribed to a processor, to the functionality and purpose of something, and not the thing itself, not its beauty. He was thinking of Warhol's Campbell's Soup cans.

Something had changed in the interim. Why were chefs now so popular, why was the kitchen part of a new eroticism, and why were there so many goddamn cookbooks on the market?

He now bore witness to it. The mid-morning snack, the organic lunch with the sugar allowance noted, the small juice box and the wholegrain animal crackers, the calorie-counted dinner, and, at the evening's end, his concentration broken in the midst of reviewing the day's work by the quack of a rubber duck, the splash of the ritual bath, so that he was forced to get up and close the door.

For the longest time, life had thrown up nothing but a quiet stasis of days. He had forsaken the tempestuous shouting and making up of a sexual relationship for *The New Existence*. There were agreed terms of civility and order to maintain with Joanne Hoffmann.

At one point, Joanne called Norman into the hallway. He compliantly appeared. She was in the process of putting a sticker on the top of each of Grace's winter boots. Each kitten had its paws raised. Joanne explained how when the kittens' paws aligned correctly, they completed a heart. Then Joanne made Norman do it.

Joanne swept her hair off her face and lit a joint, observing as Norman dutifully brought the kittens together. In so doing, Norman gained an insightful awareness into how, even in the teaching of the simplest of tasks, the act of communication required one to take into account the other's temperament and self-awareness, so Grace learned not so much her right from her left, but a strategy to complete the task.

As in all things, a balance needed to be struck.

4.

A MERICA HAD ITS great stories of rags to riches, and so, too, did Canada, though celebrated in a different way. Canada didn't lay claim to greatness. It didn't set men on pedestals.

If Nate Feldman were to tell it, Canada had been a providential lifeline. He had made a small fortune in organics from the late twentieth-century obsession with all things natural and had gotten in on the ground floor of the Green movement long before it was fashionable.

He did it out of necessity, eking out a subsistence existence in the early years after his escape. He tapped a line of trees around his small cabin, drawing a viscous maple syrup, and later, in the disaster of the early onset of one winter and a briar of grape vines freezing, he'd fallen on the idea of making an ice wine that went with a salmon he'd caught and smoked.

These items – the maple syrup, the ice wine and the smoked salmon – became synonymous with a rugged Canadian mystique. He added honey and unleavened bread later to his gift baskets. The world, or at least a part of it, was seeking a point of reconnection.

It accounted for a small fortune, but a fortune founded on a dark secret. He remembered, at one time, a teacher asking, what of the fortune of a man who makes it on an initial sum of stolen money – was the investment and return thus tainted? How could one make reparation? Could an immoral act be made right?

In the quiet of his kitchen, he felt a reflexive ache of deepening loss, how his life had unfolded in those first years, the serendipity of events, the alignment of chance, the run of good luck that might otherwise have seen his ruin. He had been watched over. He truly believed this.

He gathered wood around the side of the house, then set a blaze going in the fieldstone firepit. This was home now in the enveloping warmth of a dry heat. He felt its deep pull in the throw of amber light contrasted against the outside brilliance. He had cords of wood piled high to see him through winter, a cache gained during the summer months.

He had come to live in anticipation of future events, to set his perspective in the reach of the next season. He considered this a great personal realignment with the natural order of the universe. He thus accounted for his days in a labor of advancing effort.

He was seeking excuses to not acknowledge the letter. He might retire now and sleep as the animals did. He was due it. All things must rest. He was stalling. He knew it.

*

The letter was a week old and curled at the edges by the dry heat of the fire. He passed it on the way to the kitchen. He found and opened a can of soup, poured the contents into a pot and set it on the stove.

A crown of flame whispered over his thoughts. He stood in an oblong shadow and stared into the monotony of falling snow. Memory floated in a grey static that cleared and played when he focused and closed his eyes. There was always another life playing within him.

Where to begin? In 1971 with his arrival into Canada? *Yes, there!*

Thank God for the Canadian wilderness and the length of an undefended border. How easy it had been to cross the divide under cover of night, venturing into the far north, passing unnoticed through a drift of human settlements, brief flickers of habitation that had grabbed a living from the inhospitable land. It was still there, the legacy of trading posts that held on long enough for towns to take hold and give rise to generations who intermarried and stubbornly survived long past the boom times of gold or silver mining, or whatever it was that first brought them together.

In the weeks before he left for Canada, he'd torn pages from an encyclopedia in the public library, circled the names of towns. Havre-Saint-Roche had caught his interest. It was described as a ramshackle town, once beset by debauchery and gambling, where civilization had never quite taken hold. Its original French-Canadian population had been joined by Russian and Ukrainian immigrants lured to the

Canadian wilderness with the promise of arable land that had proved unable to sustain a livelihood, let alone a family. Though, as indentured figures, most had been compelled to repay their debt and thus forced to push further west. Most had come down with malaria, smallpox, or trench foot. Some survived, others died, while others walked into the wilds and were never seen again.

He had arrived in Havre-Saint-Roche following a night and a day hitching north after crossing the border near the shoals of Sault Ste. Marie. He was affirming certain truths to himself about life, how hope and progress could sputter and die without ceremony. He was seeking examples of a truncated and lost history, seeking tangible evidence of the reality of human insignificance, a point of disconnection.

Havre-Saint-Roche wasn't really a town anymore by 1971 – just a weigh station surviving on a post office and a Department of Forestry and Land Management Bureau.

Nate stayed in the vicinity almost a week, pitching a small canvas tent along the river's edge. He set fishing lines in a pool of still water, jigging them until he caught three speckled trout which he gutted and salted to add to his supplies. He started a small fire in advance of morning's pale light, then wandered amidst the remnants of an elaborate network of rigged lines where teams of horses and men had toiled under the boil of black flies and mosquitoes, felled logs carted through the marsh toward the rush of fast-flowing rivers.

Nothing had survived intact. A dormitory house roof had all but collapsed. He stood in the dappled light, a blue sky shining on a series of identical cots, suggesting the compact sameness of an early settlement. In the wide yawn of a dark stable door, he looked at the crucible of what had once been a firepit that had burned in the service of shoeing horses, making sleds, chains and irons, along with all manner of tools required for extracting old growth timber. In the center, an anvil sat near a tarred accordion bellows like the folded wing of a monstrous bat.

In inhabiting the stillness, in surveying the creep of vegetation, the ruin, it had the feel and fallout of a great calamity, but that was what had drawn him there. He had not been seeking to restart life, but to hold life in abeyance, to sit out the rush of destruction in the conscientious objection that too much life was discarded by generals in the vainglory of conflicts that might have been resolved if young men simply refused to serve, if they laid down their arms on both sides, if they chose to run away.

At times, in the vast stillness, in his aloneness, Canada rang with a certain unassailable truth that all could and would be subsumed and undone by nature. He said the word, *Canada*, like a mantra when the overwhelming insignificance of it all brought on a flutter of trembling anxiety.

In the torn encyclopedia pages he brought with him, he had circled a reference to one particularly ill-conceived mining operation. Financed out of Ottawa, it had sprung up in the dying days of wood, just as steel began to be used to rebuild the metropolises along the lakes, after the great fires of Chicago and Toronto.

He had found the entrance to the mine, the grim, black mouth agape in the agony of collapse, a splinter of blackened beams within. Twenty-two miners were buried alive a half-mile into the side of a hill in a flash flood in the spring of 1929, the calamity meriting just a footnote in the encyclopedia. The event, and the town, had all but been forgotten after the onset of the Great Depression.

All things changed. Nate let the thought settle. After the depression, men no longer went into the wild, and instead lined up at soup kitchens in the great metropolises on both sides of the border. What it signified was the destitution of the body and the mind, a destruction of the spirit of the age.

It was the prophetic ending Nate had needed when he first arrived, that solitary pilgrimage into desolate lands, inhabiting the cleaving sense of how time could and did outrun the ingenuity of the best-laid plans. *Oh, Canada.*

He left Havre-Saint-Roche in the light of early morning for what was his true destination, the town of Grandshire. He extinguished his fire with the stomp of his boot, and made his way along a dirt road following a page with a map torn from the same encyclopedia.

He had read that Grandshire was a town built by an enlightened industrialist, Augustus Grandshire, a prominent socialist with progressive New England sensibilities who had transported his vision of a Utopian collective across the border into the wild Canadian backwoods.

Upon first arriving, Nate surveyed the town. It emerged

from a break into a clearing of land run along a river's edge. It survived in its shabby grandeur. In accordance with its founder's Utopian reach, a pulp mill had been set at a distance from the residential district, so Grandshire achieved, at the time, a rarefied divide – separating the toil of one's daily labor with the reprieve of nature.

In the town center stood the remnants of a chapel. Prayer services had been read from a belfry over a loud speaker, so when the wind blew, people forty miles away had been given to proclaiming that they could hear the word of God carried on the wind through the whispering pines.

It was not then the place it had once been, but it showed how one man's influence could make a difference, how those who might not have fared so well could be saved by being born into a place where attitudes and ways of conduct were well-established. In a way, it reminded Nate of the influence of John F. Kennedy on his own adolescence, how the decade started with a promise of putting a man on the moon. How strange, Kennedy long dead, and Nate out in the Canadian wilds, while at the decade's end, a man *did* walk on the moon, and the world knew all about the *Sea of Tranquility*, while, in South East Asia, war raged unabated.

How could it have been, that anomalous proposition, the claiming of a moon when there was so much yet up for grabs on Earth?

Nate lodged for the first few months in what had once been a plush hotel, complete with a grand tearoom with

velvet-covered couches and a dance hall with draped curtains and a stage.

At the time, everyone understood what brought an
American up there, and yet he was regarded with neither
suspicion nor interest. Vietnam was not Canada's war. The
work at the mill kept the workers busy and attentive.
The whirling bite of a blade could cut a man in two. Nate
was hired and worked a year that shaped him into a man.

He met Ursula Abenakis right after he arrived. She was
a twenty-two-year-old half-blood native who worked at the
hotel. She met his stare with the greenest of eyes, her sallow
skin framed by a black sheen of hair, betraying her lineage.

She wrote his name into a leather bound ledger, the
languid sweep of her writing style suggesting a convent
education. She had, in fact, been brought up in a Catholicism
that never took hold. In the pulse of nature, in daily life,
there was a more powerful God.

She became his fascination, this Ursula Abenakis. He
took his meals at the hotel, tipping with a view to catching
her attention. He watched the way she filled the pepper
and salt shakers, topped up the milk jugs, turned over the
damp brown sugar in the glass bowls, and at the day's end
dutifully changed the fly-strip paper.

He learned, in the coming weeks, sitting by her in the
dying evenings, that her father had been a fur trapper, three-
quarters First Nation and a quarter French-Canadian, as were
most trappers in the region after centuries of interbreeding
along the Saint Lawrence and the fur-trade routes.

Nate was fresh-faced back then, a young man destined

for great things. Or so Ursula told him. It didn't take her long to come out to the cabin he found in the fall, her housewarming gift a rhubarb pie and a pound of ground coffee beans.

At the hotel, she had called him 'My American', smiling with a beatific grace. He had thought her a beauty he could never possess, and he carried the thought of her in the way men carried lost dreams into battle. He loved her for her intelligence and mystery. When she poured him coffee, he felt like weeping. He thought he would never have her.

When she arrived with the rhubarb pie, she wore nylons under her jeans, but no underwear or bra. It was revealed as she removed her top and then her jeans, placing them by her side, and doing so without the slightest sense of urgency or impropriety. She observed a polite restraint in the wake of their lovemaking, which was full of struggle and passion. She never asked directly about his family, or if he might return to America. Vietnam was the reason for his being there, and yet it seemed so remote, it didn't bear mentioning.

For her part, she revealed she was from the Anishinaabeg tribe, a name which literally meant, 'Beings made out of nothing', a conjuring that set Nate into a swooning sense that, yes, all came from nothing, that all things had to be envisioned and decided upon and then made real. He considered their relationship the same way, something made out of nothing.

Of course, Ursula came with a past, something before the current nothingness. She was honest, open and proud. She had been with a First Nation man, Frank Grey Eyes, born into the Wolf Clan, a ponytailed, equine-faced native with wolf eyes and a temper. He wore a black bowler hat and a poncho. His favorite things in the whole world were scratch lottery tickets and booze. This was where mystery and revelation had gone, or so he believed.

They had ventured to Toronto in 1968 so Frank could work construction, but Frank couldn't handle the booze or the loneliness and, though he complained that Toronto was killing him, he stayed and got attached to white women in bars where his kind fell easy prey to women on the way down, white women who held a certain allure of what non-white males felt was a conquest, a victory of sorts. It just exacerbated the decline, because it felt like something other than it was, when it was nothing but the end.

When Frank was sad he used to trace the outline of a circle around himself, shuffling in a circular, tribal, tomahawk-wielding dance, a slow vortex spun against the spin of the cosmos, as though he could create some concept of home. He wore his bowler hat, so it was sobering, sad and moving to witness him dance in the dark of the apartment.

Sometimes he scratched a lottery ticket, the silver filings sifting through the air like a spell. He was looking for small, contained miracles. He was fascinated, too, by fortune cookies. He felt revelation was hiding in the most unlikely places, and that you had to work against the petulance of the spirit world. Toronto seemed like a place that the spirit world might inhabit. It was worth a look.

Frank was good like that in understanding the ways of the spirit world. But it was white women that destroyed him. They didn't understand his energy. They could reach in and tear his heart out. There was no magic against white women. Frank was helpless. They passed right through the circle.

The last time Ursula saw Frank he was in a Drunk Tank. He called her not by Ursula, a Christian name bestowed upon her, but by a native name, which translated meant, 'Something Good Cooking by a Fire'.

Frank was bestowing a grace on her, releasing her. His face and nose were smashed in. He kept drawing an invisible circle around himself so the cops thought he was nuts.

Ursula watched him through a one-way mirror before she left for the last time. She drew a circle around herself. Then she was gone. She took a bus back home in the magic of her aura, and so ended the summative history of what had been almost three years of her life.

Frank was eventually stabbed and died in a Toronto hospital.

She revealed the story, working a fire that Nate couldn't start. There was a trick, the bedding of embers had to be packed with sawdust dipped in a gel paraffin, which, when she lit it, gave off a bright blue light like the star of first creation. Nate was taken by the flint of light caught in her eyes, the light licking the sheen of her cleavage and up under her chin as she turned and faced him.

By seven thirty, after a day and night of snow, Nate eased toward the outskirts of Windsor. Almost thirty-eight years had passed since he had crossed the border at Sault Ste. Marie as a desperate nineteen-year-old.

If felt like a lifetime ago. Ursula was dead almost eight years, her radiant face still the trademark design of the organics enterprise he had sold the year after she succumbed to cancer. He had sketched her face up by Handsome Lake in the first year of their marriage.

He didn't go out of his way to tell those who didn't know the story of the origin of the company logo when it might have increased the sale price of the business. Nor did he reveal his own personal story, his Vietnam history and exile that, equally, might have lowered the price. His voice had leveled, with a broadening of his vowels, so he sounded Canadian without consciously trying. He sounded like a man without a history.

In approaching the border crossing, he could see how the divide between America and Canada had diminished in the push of global sameness, the eastern Canadian cities running along the border filled with the same big box stores – the Walmarts and Lowes and Sears and Targets – the same fast food franchises, the same car manufacturers. These Canadian cities now inhabiting just a slightly altered version of the American experience, a reprise of the American experiment overlaid with a sense of decency and socialist tendencies, though it was all becoming a oneness, so there was no real understanding of a divergent past, or it didn't much matter anymore.

He considered calling his only daughter. They had not talked in a great while. Against his and her mother's wishes, she had married a Pakistani immigrant, Rahim Hafeez, who had gone on to great success with a controlling interest in a call center in Karachi, and whose view of English Imperialism was exceedingly gracious.

Disconcertingly, Rahim had made his daughter dress according to a conservative Muslim code, while he dressed like any one of the terrorists who had hijacked and crashed the planes into the Twin Towers – in button-down shirts, Levi jeans, Nikes, and a Blue Jays baseball cap. It was a fight Nate knew best to put off for another time. Perhaps he would visit, but not just then.

In truth, Nate's mind was elsewhere. He had found Norman Price's email address on a theater website. He might contact him, making polite reference that he was returning to Chicago.

In fact, he knew he would contact him. It was decided in his heart, though it would be a delicate matter, how to broach the subject of Helen Price, but for now there was the advancing line of cars ahead of him, and America awaiting his return.

5.

JOANNE ENTERED NORMAN'S office, asking casually, 'What are you working on?' as she handed him a mug of coffee.

He looked up with a determined seriousness shot through with a good-natured roll of his eyes. 'A grand theory of relativity that will account for everything we have ever felt or experienced.'

'And it's coming along well, I trust?'

Norman took the mug, 'Not really...'

Joanne smiled. 'Well, there's always tomorrow!'

In so saying it, Norman understood the impasse of his life and work was of no great significance. He was arriving at the point of awareness that, if he never found greatness, it wouldn't matter, not to the larger world, or to Joanne. It was small comfort, but true, and then Joanne was leaning on Norman's shoulder, staring at the wavering feed of the realty site.

Norman said preemptively, 'It's a house I inherited.' He qualified the remark, 'My parents' house.' He stopped.

Explaining his parents' recent deaths, which he hadn't done, would have only revealed a deeper hurt that there were secrets yet kept from her. Then he thought better of it, and mentioned Walter and Helen by name.

An airy quality was gone from Joanne's voice. Taking a step back, she said flatly, 'You're putting it on the market or keeping it?'

Norman hesitated. 'There's no liquidity in the markets now. You've listened to the congressional hearings.' It wasn't an answer.

Joanne cleared her throat. 'Were you ever going to bring it up?' Her eyes glossed, her gaze moving from the screen to the white board. She looked at the stick figure of herself, along with the rendering of the Craigslist heirloom table, and at the center of the formula the stick figure of Norman (N) ⚲. Arrows connected Norman to Grace in the bathtub, to Joanne, Grace and Randolph's departure each day for The Walk (w), his stick figure with an exponential joy quotient $(j)^x$ at their receding image.

Joanne said, 'Can I be honest with you?' as if it was hard containing what she felt. Her eyes met Norman's. 'It's about your work.' Her eyes were on the board again, and then on him.

Norman went to reach for Joanne's hand but she pulled away. Her voice rose. 'I went to one of your shows once with Peter. He knew all about you. We ended up seeing *Latchkey Kid,* and what I honestly felt while watching it was that your work lacked humanity.'

Norman tried to breathe quietly.

Joanne kept talking. She would not be dissuaded from discontinuing. Lines showed around her eyes. 'The things you said about your parents... It wasn't that I didn't believe them, but there was no restraint. It was downright pathological.' She turned to the board. 'Sometimes restraint is what's needed.' She had begun and she would finish. This was not anger as much as truth speaking. Norman knew it.

'Of course, Peter defended you. He said you were...' She raised her fingers for the effect of quotation marks. '"Re-appropriating darkness, embracing a rarified pathology of male pessimism characteristic of the American theater of the forties and fifties."'

Norman forced a laugh. 'You're almost making me like Peter.'

Joanne turned on him. 'I bet you would like him. Peter was always generous about the *failure* of others.' She did the quotation marks thing again. 'He said something like "there is exalted genius in facing a darkness too few try to confront anymore".'

Joanne was staring directly at Norman. 'Of course, he was talking about his own work as much as yours. And you know what I said to Peter when he finished with his explanation?'

Norman didn't risk responding.

'I said, "That's all well and good. Norman Price might be a genius, but he's also an asshole."'

Norman flinched.

In the sudden silence, Randolph appeared. He needed to go.

Joanne went out with him, closing the door behind her so Norman heard the receding echo of her footfall on the cold tile.

In Joanne's absence, Norman felt a trembling feeling of guilt. He understood his capacity to drive people out of his life – his parents, Kenneth, any number of men he had dated, and now Joanne. He went and faced Grace's room and thought that whatever about adult life, about the injury one could inflict on another, Grace was different. She represented a permanence and hope. This he had against the world.

He wanted to suddenly reclaim her, to front her at the center of his existence, and yet, in observing her, in compelling himself to love her, he felt instead what he felt most times when he looked at her, an unsettling emptiness and lack of any genuine connection.

Guilt jumped in him like a live wire. In truth, he had come to see his relationship with Grace as akin to the sort of chasm that opened in those awful castaway plays that went nowhere – ideas and plot lines that existed at the liminal horizon of something conjured but never made quite real. The play that never formed, not so much for a lack of will, but because of a failure of the imagination to sustain the mundane, the ordinary, to buoy existence in the float of sorting through the infinite possibility of what a minute, an hour, or a day might hold, then aligning it with a guiding foreknowledge of where it might lead and eventually end.

It struck him how he had so failed in the imaginative reach of conceiving a life with Grace, so there was no ordination of what might be accomplished or what was to come, no foresight of even the landmark moments – her first day of school, her first date, her graduation, or eventual marriage, nothing.

Norman stared at morning light caught in the small, paned windows of Grace's dollhouse. Within, he could see the porcelain figurines – the miniature proprietor, George Crumby, respectable banker, enjoying an eternal breakfast with wife Esther, son Harold, and daughter Polly; a proper Victorian family seated in a second-floor, wallpapered room with a white tablecloth, overhanging chandelier, and portrait of the queen on the wall.

It was so self-contained, so real that it was easy to conjure up a life lived inside the dollhouse, this world fashioned and conceived in a time before two world wars and the collapse of the British Empire, in a time before the slow leech of civility, good manners and proper dress.

Norman had the relevant history, the facts, the apparent mood of crusty manners, the staid voice of George Crumby – authoritatively clipped, sensible, George Crumby speaking over the rasp of a knife in the spread of butter on toast, with a measure of rebuke, reprimand or instruction. He felt he could begin right now with a play of sensibility and manners, and yet, in standing there, it fell on him, the revelation of what was far more difficult to capture – the in-between time of the great mansions and what came after George Crumby and his family – the subtle shift when a time was no longer as it had been. It took a keen insight to understand that what was felt was not the thing itself, but its after-effect. Though, somewhere in the in-between of in-betweens, he felt that an understanding could sometimes register – and just barely – if one had the acuity to feel it. This is where greatness lay.

In looking in at George Crumby, in seeing the small black umbrella stand, Norman was reminded of the depth of Lennon and McCartney's lament for the passing of an older England; their transformation from clean cut pop stars to the strung-out, long-haired gurus of an Eastern mysticism. How had they navigated from the perfunctory vacuity of 'She Loves You Yeah Yeah Yeah', 'It's Been a Hard Day's Night' and 'I Want to Hold Your Hand', to the melancholic dirge of childhood memories of standing in the English rain? And so, too, capturing the inexplicable litany of those most English of moments in 'Penny Lane' where a pretty nurse sold poppies from a tray, to the dirge of 'Eleanor Rigby' in the church where a wedding had been, all of it a slurred past seen through a yellow matter custard dripping from a dead dog's eye.

Norman recalled a naked John and Yoko in the bed-in protests in a world come undone by Vietnam, John and Yoko a contrite Adam and Eve reckoning with the grim reality of what the snake had so offered in the Garden of Eden.

Norman looked away, felt a shudder run through him. He opened his phone, scrolled through some photos. He settled on a shot of Grace. Both her hands were earnestly fixed on the steering wheel of a miniature ice-cream truck.

He scrolled to another image of her. How strange to mark time against physical change in the way a child grows with the passage of weeks and months. He could see with the distance of three years how exotically Oriental she had looked upon arrival, her large doll face, her body so shockingly tiny.

Grace had suffered apparent malnutrition, or that was the determination of a doctor who had cautioned that, most probably, her adult teeth, when they came in, would need dental work. She was missing an enamel coating on her baby teeth. It was advised she not eat processed sugars. Her bones, too, had been deprived of calcium. She was suffering rickets. There were things that happened during her lack of prenatal care that might yet manifest. Norman learned all this stateside.

Norman navigated to an image of the orphanage in the southern region of the Guangxi province, a province, until then, unknown to him and not disclosed before he left America. There had been that much secrecy in the adoption.

The house warden was a small, withered peasant dressed in Maoist style standing outside a dilapidated government building that had served as a place for indoctrination during the Cultural Revolution. Against the dark background, he could see a constellation of lights, the eyes of the children caught in the camera flash.

When Joanne came back inside, she announced, 'I can give a month's notice if you like.'

Norman rallied. 'I just checked. There's no law against practicing literary criticism without a license.'

Joanne didn't take the bait. She said, 'Whatever you think of me, I have a job, and I intend to go on doing it. I just want you to know I have more feeling than you give me credit for.' She pointed in the direction of Norman's office. 'That board is *not* my life!'

Norman acknowledged it. 'It was a mistake. I'm sorry.'

Joanne's eyes were glossy. Clearly, she had other things on her mind. 'Last week, I looked up the college where Peter's working. Somehow, you suspect the life others are leading is better than yours. I thought Peter had found happiness. The college out in Oklahoma where he works, it's like that Columbine High School where those awful killings happened... He would never have dreamt of settling for it in a million years.'

She kept talking, something about Peter having been hired to teach Composition to students, farmers' daughters aspiring to be nurses' aids, medical transcriptionists and bank tellers.

Her voice was suddenly faint with a rising misgiving. She was emerging from a great shock of self-awareness. She looked at Norman. 'Looking Peter up doesn't constitute a betrayal, does it?' She had misgivings about having revealed it by the time she had it said.

Norman paved it over. 'So what were you saying about Peter?' There was within his saying it a pandering sense that all might yet be navigated.

Joanne said as much. 'You want to hear it, really?'

She didn't await his answer.

'When I first met Peter, he talked a lot about New England. There were liberal colleges tucked away in Vermont. He was trying for one of those jobs. I think what he was doing at the time was coming to terms with his lack of real talent. He talked a lot about chickens and white fences. I was the alternative to his life as a famous poet, or Peter thought that greatness might be snuck up upon, that in not seeking it, in our retreat, he might find it there in the quiet of a life simply lived. We hoped for it, both of us, without ever saying it.'

Joanne looked at Norman. Her eyes were set beyond a beseech that Norman should hear this, or that it mattered what he thought. It had to be simply announced.

She raised her voice. 'Fast forward five years. We dressed in a shabby bohemian way, as if we were decided on being that way. We were pretty much broke. And then I got a call about my father being sick. Nobody had bothered to tell me before.'

Joanne's eyes widened again with emotion.

Norman looked down because he felt it was the decent thing.

The heart of the matter lay in a sisterly rivalry between Joanne and her sister Sheryl, a complicated and entangled story that involved Sheryl and her husband Dave, and a marriage a week out of high school, whereafter Sheryl had got busy pumping out four children in quick succession, while Dave had been hired, fired, hired and fired again, so he ended up signing with the National Guard, which apparently had increased in Sheryl an emerging patriotism that got her talking a lot about Communism and American values.

It was a hell of a lot of detail. Norman listened as best he could. He suppressed the urge to yawn. He could see there was reproach in how Joanne described it all, the venial quality of a small life and small details, and yet it mattered greatly to her. That much he was willing to acknowledge. It was complicated, as were most family relationships. Some of it didn't make sense, what Joanne really had against Sheryl.

Then Joanne got to the heart of the matter. Her father had come down sick and nobody had called her. He was sick a long time, suffering from dementia.

Joanne hugged herself against the settling memory of it. 'Sheryl was so cold on the phone when she called. It was right on the eve of Thanksgiving. Then she got to the reason she was calling really. Dad and Mom were selling their house and moving in with Sheryl. There were papers that needed to be signed and witnessed. There had always been an agreement that the house would be split between us, but then suddenly there wasn't. They wouldn't let me speak to Dad. I didn't know what papers they were talking about. When I asked about *what* papers needed signing, Sheryl slammed the phone down.'

Joanne's voice trailed off for a moment. 'Sheryl has always had a way of making me out to be *the bad guy*.' She made quotation marks with her fingers to signify the inconsequentiality and triviality of it. She was suddenly self-conscious. She looked at Norman. 'Why is it the lives of others, or even our own, can mean nothing when we speak about them?'

Norman said softly, 'I don't believe that's the case.' In doing so, he advanced her right to continue.

Joanne nodded in a rallying sense of needing to tell it. 'I wouldn't have gone. I knew Sheryl, but Peter insisted. He hadn't earned more than $12,000 a year adjunct teaching, and I could see he was seeking to find in Sheryl and Dave's life a reason to feel more sure about his choices, when Sheryl and Dave weren't to be messed with like that.'

Norman advanced the story by degrees. 'So you went?'

Joanne nodded. 'We went. Dave answered the door in a camouflage jacket. Sheryl had turned huge. She was in a church lady's floral dress and pink slippers and busy in the kitchen. She didn't say hi or anything. I saw Dad in a chair by the TV. He was already adrift of everything. He didn't recognize me, and then he did recognize me, then didn't again. He was sitting forward, watching a Bills game in a Bills sweater. Mom hardly said a word to me.

'Dave started talking about Gulf War Syndrome. He and Sheryl were patriotic still, but in that rabidly anti-government way conservatives can get. Peter thought he saw an inroad when we had been there a half-hour and Dave hadn't even bothered to take our coats. Peter had worked with veterans. He told Dave how he had used poetry to help with their PTSD, while Dave just wanted to talk about the NRA and protecting the Second Amendment. I could feel a disaster coming. Dave was talking to Dad and to Sheryl like we weren't there. Then Peter said something about a constitutional democracy and the power of the ballot box, while just then Dave saw a doe and a fawn in the yard outside and pointed it out. Something about it struck Peter. I saw it then. It was a Thoreau moment he tried to write a poem about later, and then he denied it was about that Thanksgiving, when the poem, for Christ's sake, was called "A Deer Comes to Thanksgiving".

'Peter asked Dave if he thought the deer had any concept of Thanksgiving. This was how Peter started his classes, asking open-ended, inane questions, while Dave just looked at Sheryl like they were sharing the funniest joke. Dave said, "First off, deer didn't come over on the *Mayflower, Professor*!" That's what they called Peter, *Professor*, like the Professor on *Gilligan's Island*.

'Meanwhile, Dad wanted a round of root beer floats for the kids. Sheryl said it would spoil dinner, but Dad got his way. I went down to the basement for the ice cream just to escape. Dave followed. He came up to me and said, "You know the problem with you? You need to get laid by a real man." I had my head in the freezer. When I turned, I said, "I'd just as soon have you keep your opinions to yourself," and he said, "You want to know something? Your sister is twice the woman you'll ever be. What are you doing with that *fruitcake*?" Then he reached into his pocket and presented me with a card. It turned out Dave was a card-carrying member of *Promise Keepers*. He explained it as a pact between God and men.

'Upstairs, Sheryl's middle daughter, Misty, was giving a command performance for Peter. I'd heard about Misty's exploits, the phrase Junior Olympics bandied around for years, suggesting in reality nothing more than you could pay the entrance fee to a regional tournament. I hated Dave at that moment, and yet, the truth was, Sheryl and Dave deserved credit to a certain extent. I wasn't beyond acknowledging it. Sheryl had sat through all the practices, Sheryl holding to certain family values like this was a Tea Party political battle she'd understood was always coming and had now. I might have said something, but I didn't.

'There was maybe a point of reconciliation. I was willing to concede to my own shortcomings, but weakness never played with Sheryl, so in just standing there, I kept thinking this was it, this was the extent of all our lives. I kept staring at Dave staring at Misty, and knowing that it didn't get better than this for most everybody, and that what I was witnessing was the contained dream of all those tramps who lived with the ever-lasting hope that they might make it onto a Wheaties box. All you needed was one tramp to make it onto a cereal box to keep it all within reach.

'I thought Peter must have been thinking the same. This was all grist for the mill. Dave was standing with a Genesee beer in his hand, watching me out of the corner of his eye. They had a signed autograph of Mary Lou Retton alongside Bela Karolyi. Sheryl made Misty go get it, like it was a testament to her talent. It said something like, "Keep reaching for your dreams!"– something vague and inspirational, but *not* specific to Misty's actual talents, or lack thereof. It was never established if they'd met either Mary Lou or Karolyi.

'At dinner, Peter got talking to Sheryl about an idea for a cookbook, some potential collaborative project they had been discussing while I had been downstairs with Dave, when Dave reached for Sheryl and said, "I have a marriage license that, among other things, entitles me to exclusive rights to Sheryl's cooking, and, anyway, we'd have to ask Sheryl's campaign manager." And that's how it came to light Sheryl was considering running for the State Assembly in Albany.

'I nearly shit myself. Even Dad looked up. He had gravy all over his lips, Dad, who couldn't stand Dave at one point, and now it was all changed. There was already talk of building an extension onto the house for the two boys that was a vague cover for anticipating the long-term care of Dad and Mom. I was a cast-out. It was like I didn't know these people sitting around me. A trial and jury had been convened in my absence, and I was found guilty.'

Joanne looked up, so Norman could see her life was there before her, in the way life can sometimes make itself known.

'When I got back, I looked into the Peace Corps as a way out. But, you know, it's not easy to give yourself up to the prospect of cholera or typhoid or malaria. There are waiting lists of people ready to sign up. Nobody ever says, "I'm going to lose myself in Cleveland!" That same year, I got pregnant a second time. I didn't tell Peter. He was lost in another round of national academic job searches and had come up empty again. I knew he was cheating on me. We were maxed out on credit cards. I saw a receipt from the John Hancock, a revolving restaurant we had gone to early in our relationship. I was aware of him telling the same stories, but to a different girl, like we were all interchangeable characters on this merry-go-round. He asked me, not long after I saw the John Hancock receipt, if I had ever been with another woman, or if it had any appeal, so, for the life of me, I thought he was trying to shore up all his options, that perhaps the burden of life was better shared with more than one person, in the way certain religions make the allowance for the taking of more than one wife. I told him I wasn't interested. It wasn't the answer he was looking for.

'That Christmas, we got a postcard of Misty in a plaster cast, a family Christmas portrait. Dave was holding Misty like Karolyi did that little girl who won gold. Misty had broken her femur. It ended her career, the capstone of what might have been, and never would have, but it set Misty on the path of gracious acceptance of what the Lord ordained, like the Lord had time to look down on Misty, but that's how she thought about it, and that's what counted in the end. They had all these trophies behind her, like the spoils of Tutankhamun's tomb.

'In the end, Sheryl was beaten in a primary for the State Assembly, but she ended up getting Dad to enter into some ungodly tax shelter so he got on Medicare. They got the extension built with government money. Dad put his house into a Revocable Living Trust, so I don't know what I'm entitled to. When I've tried to speak with Sheryl, she tells me, "Ask a lawyer to explain it!" It's a war of attrition, and I've been shut out. I'm just coming to terms with that reality.'

Joanne used the heel of her hand against her nose, blinked and blinked again. 'This is just heartbreak talking, right?'

Norman didn't disagree. He said, 'I think you understand life in a way most will never fully realize. It's part of the process of reassessing and finding peace.'

Joanne seemed appeased, when Norman wasn't sure he wasn't just lying, or lying was the wrong word. He just didn't believe in enlightenment and reform in the way others believed something could be come upon and overcome. The reality was, Joanne had, in fact, talked too long and too candidly, so the essential mystery of her life was settled. Ordinarily, talks like this ended in the payoff of an entanglement of sheets, in a succor and commitment.

In the stalemate of words, Joanne seemed to understand it. She offered an alternative: 'I could make eggs and toast if you're hungry?'

Norman put his hand to his stomach for exaggerated effect and said, 'Starving!', paving the way to recommencing a normal routine.

Joanne, in her genuine honesty, had set her finger on an essential fault within his work, and, in so doing, Norman felt a deepening understanding of how the drift of days should intersect with the fears and joys of others, and how the megalomania of his life had destroyed a crucial sense of perspective and balance.

6.

IN THE WINTRY light of mid-morning, at the entrance to Lake Forest Cemetery, what Nate Feldman noted was not the solemnity of the cemetery, but the large number of rules there were for a place where only the dead resided.

It took time to find his father's grave. The newer part of the cemetery stood on a rolling tongue of hill. The grave markers were recessed into the grass. Flowers and wreaths could not be left. It said so on a sign, an ordinance that facilitated the living – namely, the grounds crew – in the expedient sweep of their commercial grade lawnmowers.

When Nate eventually found the grave, he scuffed the snow away with the toe of his shoe and read the marker:

THEODORE L. FELDMAN
SGT
US NAVY WWII
SEPT 16 1922
OCT 19 1987
BELOVED HUSBAND & FATHER

Anyone walking through the graveyard would know that here lay a man who had served bravely and faced the line of fire when it was most demanded. But in this regard, Nate thought, his father's individuality, his exact service, the nature of his personal history, was erased, so he was as faceless and anonymous as the heaps of corpses who had been bulldozed into mass graves.

His father had found no valor in survival, or, for that matter, in the act of service. He had avoided the fetish of the dead, avoided the rousing sentiment of Veterans Day, when a nation's thoughts were obliged to settle on the collective heroism of all those who had passed, when history and truth were always far more complex.

He said it to Nate in as many words one evening, his father coming out to the perch of the carriage house out back of the main house to call Nate in for supper. A panel on a TV show was debating the constitutionality of the draft. Nate had been engrossed.

In listening to the show, his father was decided that too much life had been lost in what Eisenhower had called the Industrial Military Complex. If the time came, there was the National Guard as a measure of last resort. His father had connections. It was the best of both worlds. Nate might save face, serve and never see action.

In the interim, there was life to be lived.

Nate used the carriage house out back of the main house as his domestic quarters. His father had been liberal and generous and impressed on Nate that he felt that trying to dissuade men from their natural desires, as he put it, was a perversion of the natural order of things, implying a salaciousness in Nate that was never the case. At times, Nate felt he was being absolved for sins he hadn't actually committed.

His father communicated his tolerance not in so many words but in the way he announced his arrival at the carriage house, his noisy footsteps across the flagstone crossway, ostentatiously sniffing the scent of someone who, he imagined, had just gone scrambling through the back egress. In reality, few girls ever visited Nate in the carriage house, and those who did were acquaintances or study partners.

And yet, his father swore he knew all Nate's girlfriends by their perfume. He called them *Duchess* and he called Nate *Swank*. It was just one of his foibles.

When his draft number came up in the fall of 1970, Nate was attending Northwestern but living at home. He decided that he would not seek a college deferment. He told no one, least of all his father. Nate would not be pressured. He kept his father at bay, while in the back of his mind he was advancing on the idea of seeking his place in the world in the act of serving. It was the unpopular choice, no doubt, but it carried with it, for men like him – college men who did not defer – a noble and gratifying significance.

At the time, he was in a platonic situation with a junior in high school whom he was tutoring in Math – Janice Marsh, the kid sister of his best friend. He eventually told his mother of his decision and begged she say nothing to his father.

A week later his mother betrayed him.

His father arrived at the top of the carriage house stairs while Janice was sitting at a table beside Nate. A book was open between them. The fire threw shadows on the exposed red brick. It could have been a scene from a hundred years before.

Nate had grown. His hair was long. He had the beginnings of a goatee beard. He was wearing bell-bottomed pants with a hip-hugger waist and a paisley shirt.

It was one of the few times that Nate had ever seen Helen Price. Below, he saw her leave in the crescent arc of the circular drive in his father's car. His father was that loaded he hadn't been able to drive.

His father insisted on being introduced to the duchess. He was aggressive and lurching in his advance.

Janice Marsh hardly understood what he was saying. She looked for her coat.

Nate's father had a bottle of Scotch in his hand. Nate reached out to steady him. His father swung wildly. He would not be handled, not by his *goddamn son*! It was the most awful Nate had ever seen him.

Janice Marsh let out a squeak like a mouse. With her books clamped to her chest, she was the very picture of what men were fighting so hard to keep safe.

Then Nate's father wanted to shake Nate's hand in a sudden shifting reconciliation in the way a drunk might advance and retreat on an argument. There was no call for language like that. He was sorry. He insisted Janice stay. He wanted her to hear what he had to say.

Nate stood protectively by Janice.

His father blocked the stairway. He set his Scotch on a step beside him and began to show them how you strangled someone. He had strangled more than one gook with his bare hands. That, he said, was what hand-to-hand combat was about, his hands still around the throat of an invisible enemy. The Japs, they had to be flushed island-by-island during the push through the fortified caves of Saipan and the lesser islands along the Marianas archipelago, the weapon of choice – the flamethrower.

He took a long drink, one foot on the step above. He had seen GIs bleeding out on the hillside quagmire of godforsaken islands, heard the murmuring phantasmagoria of the rumored kamikaze attacks that had sent a thousand souls into the listless blue of the Pacific to endure insufferable thirst and the circling menace of sharks.

He said how he'd seen armies of crabs with the faces of Samurai warriors pouring onto the beaches, as though the enemy they'd killed was coming back again and again.

What he said he learned in the atolls was that people fought hardest for the things they didn't believe in because there was no alternative. Kamikaze attacks and ritual hara-kiri, the war in the Pacific was nothing like the known terror of the Nazis with their *Lebensraum*. The Pacific theater of war was a journey into the vegetative tangle of nameless archipelagos of what should have been Paradise Found, with its parrots, palm trees, and eternal sunshine, when what it had ended up being was a proving ground for obliteration.

He explained why they took so few prisoners. The *Japs* wouldn't submit to surrender. They fought to the death, so the bomb had to be dropped on them. There was no other way. They had to be brought to their knees. Each American fighting had that settled in their hearts. They had nothing in common with the Japs. Independent thinking was an alien concept to them. They were bound to their imperial emperor, to collective ceremony and tradition. America with its democracy and convertibles offered them nothing. Their understanding of Uncle Sam was all pin-up girls and Coca Cola.

Nate's leaving party was in the carriage house two weeks later in the détente that nothing could be said between him and his father. Nate was served papers to appear for active service at Fort Pendleton out in California. He avoided his mother for her betrayal.

He stayed at the college in the dorm room of a friend in advance of leaving. His going away party was a divided gathering. Present at the party were those who supported Nate and supported the war versus those who supported Nate but not the war.

What they all shared though was a feeling of awe for this young man who was willing to lay his life on the line.

Nate's father came out toward the end unannounced. This was how the carriage house should have been lit up every weekend. He moved through the throng, amidst the smell of pot and the sweet odor of keg beer, amiable, cordial and convivial. He called the girls *Duchess*. They thought he was charming, or they lied and said so.

Then the speeches started, the eulogies, his father staring over the rim of his glass. His eyes were locked on Nate. It was apparent then, what his father would do, that he would eventually intervene. It was what Nate had subconsciously hoped.

But just then there had been a charade to uphold, and if Nate had not succeeded in high school, if he was never captain of the football or hockey team, if he played lacrosse, and played it badly, here was a moment when girls might later name their son after him, remembering him for the innocence of a boy who had stepped forward, when nobody in school had looked closely at how brave Nate Feldman really was.

Nate looked up. His breath frosted in the coldness. He was standing vigil to a pile of bones six feet beneath the ground. He had been a day and a half in America, and there were things still to be settled, not just with the dead, but with the living.

Back in his car, Nate took out his phone. He could not bear to call Norman Price.

Instead, he wrote a brief email.

I am contacting you on the off-chance you might remember Mr Theodore Feldman as longtime employer of your mother. I should be delighted to make your acquaintance if you have the time.

7.

THEY WERE ANTICIPATING a mid-morning departure for the journey out to Norman's home to view and appraise a property that wasn't moving in the doldrums of the post-financial crisis. Credit had dried up. He described it on the white board as a case of perceived value not equaling purchase price, or $pv\otimes pp$.

It was a small miracle getting ready, what with the issue of Randolph obstinately refusing to go into his cage. Given his size, there was something grotesque about the entire operation.

Joanne moved in the harried clip clop of her heels. In a flounce of blouse, she looked like a buccaneer. She wore a push-up bra. Her cleavage showed. She leaned and waved a newspaper squeak toy encouragingly under Randolph's nose to lure him into his cage. It didn't work.

Exasperated, she dropped the toy and went back to working a pair of earrings into her ears. She hadn't been out in the real world in a long time, well, not in the company of a man. She made a pout with her lips, applying lipstick and blush. She looked suddenly appealing, or more feminine, and all that she had lost was suddenly apparent.

Norman might have said something kind, but decided against drawing attention to the situation. Joanne was up on her toes in her high heels. Along the back of her left thigh where it widened above her knee, there was a run in her tights. He decided not to mention this either, while Grace shouted in her aggressive Chinese, her face right in Randolph's face, in the way Chinese did not yield personal space. She left momentarily and reemerged with a naked Barbie doll.

It did the trick. Grace talked to Randolph, and then to the doll, as though it was necessary and unavoidable, like how a general might speak to his troops on the eve of some futile battle. Randolph entered the cage, the quarry of the Barbie between his slobbering jowls.

On the way out the door, in the turn of the double-lock bolt, Norman was suddenly aware of the disconcerting sound of crunching and snapping plastic.

Norman's driver's license had expired. It had escaped his attention until they were downtown before the Hertz agent. Joanne had a license, but, embarrassingly, all four of her credit cards were maxed out. She set them down, one at a time, like a bad poker hand, before a tanned, buff assistant manager in the corporate yellow of a Hertz polo shirt that made him look gay, even if he wasn't, which he was. Norman was sure of it.

What struck Norman was how the agent barely noticed him. The essential *gaydar* of how he had lived his old life was eclipsed in the presence of Joanne and Grace. He tried again to make eye contact with the assistant manager, the exchange not reciprocated.

On the fourth card, the assistant manager traitorously turned his back and made a phone call, so Norman understood it would have been more awkward explaining Grace's presence in the company of Joanne than if he had been in the presence of Kenneth. He felt his virility, his sense of who and what he was, under threat. He felt a sudden seething reverse discrimination at this outright betrayal by one of his own kind.

Eventually, the manager, an African American woman of considerable bulk, came forward as Joanne began an unduly complicated story of how she had gone through an acrimonious break-up and had been cut off by a vindictive partner. It didn't explain Norman or Grace, or how they figured.

The manager interrupted Joanne. All four declined cards were not in Joanne's name. Furthermore, the authorized cardholder had canceled the cards. The cards were being held for security purposes. It was company policy. For a moment, it seemed the police were on their way.

Norman preemptively offered to pay with his card. He put on a voice of gay affectation again. He couldn't help it. He made his appeal to the assistant manager, who disconcertingly looked to his manager, as if Norman was being confrontational and downright politically incorrect and homophobic. This was suddenly more than about a goddamn car rental. There was again the insurance issue, which couldn't be covered by Norman's card, since Norman wasn't a licensed driver. It was company policy. It took a trip to an ATM to withdraw funds from Norman's account, and then a trip to Joanne's bank to pay down the sole card in her name before they could rent a car.

They went with Alamo Car Rental, a downmarket rental agency along the L track, where the wind swirled in the dark hulk of shadows. A train rumbled overhead on a steel spine of track throughout the transaction. All told, it cost him $2,645 to pay down Joanne's card and secure the rental. They went with the full-sized at a teaser rate of $399 plus tax for the week. They then discovered Joanne couldn't decline the supplemental coverage at $29.99 a day, since she had no car insurance.

There was no actual total cost, just a line item of costs and associated taxes, and they were coerced into purchasing the full tank option, so the car was to be handed back on empty or as close to empty as possible.

It was 1.15 p.m. before they were done and paid when the issue of where to eat reared. Grace was hungry, and she had to go as well.

They ate on Randolph Street, the street name bringing to mind the caged specter of Randolph, back in the apartment, suffering the interminable nature of their absence and the terrifying possibility they might never return, the Barbie long dead, and Randolph never understanding why they left in the first place.

In the clawing, protracted indecision, against the run of time, as Joanne purchased a Happy Meal, in the quiet salvage of something fast sinking, Norman reached for a napkin and wrote, 'Why They Left and Where They Went – Theories of an Abandoned Dog'.

The day brightened into an incandescent blue sky. They left the funneling shadow of the downtown heading for the shimmer of Lake Michigan and the northern suburbs. The air had a sudden windblown crispness. This was a Wednesday in deep winter, the cold freeze of an Arctic high-pressure system that dipped into the south. It was good to be out among the living. Norman felt it suddenly, after the anxiety passed and they were on the road.

Joanne hadn't driven in a long time. In fact she hadn't since her days driving her infamous Pontiac Sunbird that her father had cobbled together for her drives to and from Chicago during college. She talked with an overriding sense of brimming enthusiasm. She was recovered from the debacle at Hertz. It was good to be behind the wheel of a car. She liked movement and the feel of the open road and held the decided understanding that money, despite what people said, could and did buy happiness. She said something to that effect on the run up along Lake Shore Drive, passing the intersection where Helen Price had driven into the lake.

Norman let the coincidence pass without comment. A bleak awareness registered, but only for a moment.

It passed just as quickly. This was the discharge of a life. He had moved on, or felt he had. He was, at least, trying.

He looked up and had to catch his breath. In truth, it was difficult deciding what he thought about the house really. It was one of those post-war ranches tacitly conceived for all eventualities, not least of all for returning amputee war heroes looking for the unencumbered run of a wheelchair through a house with long hallways and well-lit rooms, a GI, still young and finding a wife in the flush of youth willing to accommodate stumps, so a great intimacy might be shared, so there would be children eventually, and the children of children yet, and they would see it as a couple, in this house, before their lives were over.

These homes, they were mausoleums really, passed from one anonymous family to another. He felt the act of home buying should have come with an exorcism, or perhaps something less mordant, a prayer for continued journey, a reading forth of names, if simply to acknowledge and appease the dead.

Norman looked away from the lake. He was trying so very hard to contain a feeling, to move toward a point of normalization, when beyond the cutting cynicism lay a deeper reality of why, if he'd had his way, he would not have gone out to the house. What he remembered of the house, what he thought about it, was something else entirely.

He had captured it in one of his early shows, a converging homosexual awakening that had coincided with the unfolding bogeyman drama of John Wayne Gacy.

What had frightened him at the time was the contained life a person could live, how Gacy had lived and murdered in the precincts of his own home. It taught Norman how life could be concealed, compartmentalized, how a perverted sense of one's desires – or, equally, one's ambitions – could be serviced amidst the lives of others.

In the associated coming of age of his own homosexuality, in stashing his magazines in, of all places, the crawlspace in his home, he had come to align himself with Gacy – sexual release associated with the smell of crawlspaces, mildew and fetid darkness; sex connected with the rasping scrape of a shovel; sin spaded in mounding dirt; the grey slur of concrete poured in the finality of a conquest, desire literally paved over when things were done.

Norman crawled from the memory.

Joanne had a tendency to drive too close to the break wall barrier. Norman watched and said nothing. Joanne was in the process of trying to angle out of her coat. She had the heater on high.

A car behind beeped. Joanne swerved and righted with an over-corrective measure. She beeped at another motorist who beeped back and gave her the finger. She rolled her eyes at Norman when it had been her fault entirely.

Norman was glad of the distraction, Joanne pulling him back into the orbit of normal life. She started the story again about her beloved Sunbird in the general non sequitur of how she negotiated and made connections in life.

The Sunbird had died near a Wendy's out near Skokie on the very night she and Peter had gone to see *Schindler's List*.

She described the theater as packed with what she called 'sniffling Jews' with boxes of Kleenex. She said it without provocation, her statement connecting with her working class Buffalo roots, though Joanne could see in Norman's eyes the remark needed further explanation.

There was a story to the story in most everything Joanne said. So it was the case with *Schindler's List*. It turned out that back in high school she had dated a junior of Armenian heritage, a wrestler. It accounted for her nascent anti-Semitism. She asked Norman if he knew about 'The Forgotten Holocaust', because, apparently, the Jewish holocaust sat as a great and particular national grievance to the Armenian people that their holocaust had been one-upped by the Jews.

Norman knew about the Armenian genocide. He pretended he didn't, leaving Joanne to communicate the scant details of what she knew. This was how history was best come upon, or so Norman believed, Joanne processing the travails of a high school boyfriend's parents that in all likelihood had allowed this boyfriend to get into Joanne's pants in the fumbling reach of new boundaries, in the way life and history were more fully revealed in the act of lived experience than in any history book.

Norman was confident Joanne couldn't pick out Armenia on a map, but he felt a deep authenticity in the run of her words, in how she couldn't shut up. He was more interested not in what she said, but how she said it, how the profane, blasphemous and plain hurtful could be so wrapped up in such a good-natured heart, because Joanne was all that, kind-hearted and strong, and nobody could deny it.

She was, he understood, the sort of ingénue, one of those daughters, who, under more pressing and simpler times, could be coaxed into believing almost anything about anybody and counted on to bear from her hips a race of madmen.

He might have said so and ruined what they had between them, so he kept his mouth shut. Minutes then passed in silence.

Along the dappled light on Sheridan Road, Joanne pointed to the palatial homes of those who had made it in Investments, Securities and the Law. She slowed down, shielding her eyes against the mid-afternoon glare.

'You see all this, Grace? In America you can be anything you want to be.'

Norman said, without turning around, 'Joanne and I, we just didn't want to be.'

Joanne fake-punched his shoulder. 'Don't tell a child that.'

'Okay, let me clarify. We wanted it, but we couldn't get it.'

Joanne shook her head and looked into the rear-view mirror. 'Don't listen to him, sweetie. You think positive and anything is possible.'

Joanne eased back into her seat. She shook her head in mild admonishment and bit the underside of her lip. A half-minute passed. She seemed deep in thought, her lips moving silently. 'Why do you have to go tell her something like that? Her success is not predicated on whether *we* fail or succeed. That's a legitimate fact.'

Her face was suddenly serious. She looked at Norman as she finished, so he was struck by the inclusive *we*, but he said nothing.

'I think being a realist is not the same as being a pessimist. Look at Obama. Son of an immigrant Kenyan, raised by his mother and grandmother.' She shrugged her shoulders. 'I think that speaks volumes for who we are as a people.'

Norman added compliantly, '*The Audacity of Hope.* I read it, and the companion volume by Clinton, *The Audacity to Grope.*'

Joanne's eyes narrowed. 'And you want to be taken seriously as an artist?'

The word *artist* got to Norman in a way few other compliments could. He felt a sense of her view of him. He was an artist.

He conceded, 'Maybe you're right about Obama. It's a significant step toward equality, or the perception of equality.'

Joanne looked at him, trying to determine whether he was serious or not, and deciding he was, she said, 'And that's the first step, the ability to dream.'

Norman nodded. 'Right.' He let it play out in a way that gratified Joanne's view on life and politics. So much of life was compromise and biting your tongue. He said, by way of further advancing her optimism, 'I think you can divide the political parties along a diverging line of ascendancy. Either you come from somewhere or nowhere. Republicans don't come with a history or backstory in the way Democrats do.'

Joanne turned. She was the typical community college student, willing to sit through night class, having come from not one, but two, jobs. No doubt Peter Coffey had taken his chances with a series of self-improvers like her.

Norman prattled on. 'Think about it, FDR and his fight with polio, or Carter, a peanut farmer from the Deep South. What was it Carter said in that *Playboy* interview? "I've committed adultery in my heart many times." He's probably the only man who ever had to pretend to have had impure thoughts. And Clinton, brought up by his grandmother. Everybody knew what the White House meant to him. It was part of his humanity. There are stories of him campaigning, shaking a thousand hands, and afterward eating a bucket of Kentucky Fried Chicken with those unwashed hands. That's democracy.'

Joanne added, 'Peter says Clinton passed more laws against the poor than Republicans.'

Norman marveled at the sense of how a mind could be so formed by the guiding opinion of another, by even someone as unfaithful as Peter Coffey. Peter, the phantom limb felt long after its amputation. It was something worth understanding, how someone's influence could outlast their departure.

Norman added, 'Peter's right. Politics is all about

perception. Clinton's infidelity made him vulnerable in a Faustian way. All through the impeachment hearings, he cut legislative deals to survive. The great problem for Obama, there's no dirt on him. You need an essential flaw. It constitutes how compromise and change happens.'

Joanne looked off toward the lake. Peter Coffey jumped in her heart. Norman was aware he had been too cavalier in referencing peter. He had crossed an invisible border, exposing the tolerable life they were sharing in the shadow of lost loves, so it was suddenly obvious they were doing their very best to be civil and cordial, and it wasn't quite enough.

Joanne recovered a bit. 'You forgot Kennedy in your grand theory.'

Norman rallied, anything to get them through the day.

'Yes, Kennedy had money, but, with him, idealism trumped money. You throw Jackie and Marilyn into the mix and you get the sort of president most any man would want to be. Money is the preoccupation of the Republicans. You have to grow up with money to respect it, to invest it, to make it work in a way that those who don't grow up with it will never fully comprehend.'

Joanne conceded, 'I think you're right.' She said it on an up note, like the awkwardness had passed. She looked in the rear-view mirror at Grace. 'Your father, he knows a lot about politics. He's very, very smart. You should listen to him.'

As she spoke, she put her hand on Norman's thigh and said quietly, 'I'm planning on paying you back every red cent you put on my card. I don't welch on my debts.'

*

They were all suddenly tired. It had been an eventful day, and yet they had survived, or negotiated the day as best they could. They were out here at last.

Norman mentally ran through a list of positives. He was trying very hard to be optimistic.

In the ensuing quiet, Norman's phone buzzed. The realtor had postponed their meeting until 4 p.m.

Norman stared at the text. His inclination was to turn back. There was little point in seeing the house. He might have suggested it, but he knew Joanne had other ideas about the house. He said nothing. Instead, he checked his email in the quiet stalemate.

Amidst the spam, he came upon an email with a .ca suffix. The name Feldman caught his eye. He read the email quietly.

He looked up. Joanne was preoccupied with the radio and searching for a station.

She eventually looked across at him. 'Anything wrong?'

Norman cradled the phone in his lap. 'No, it's all good.'

Joanne was again distracted. She used the tone she used when explaining things to Grace. 'This is where people live if they don't live in the city.'

Norman smiled and added compliantly, 'Like your dollhouse, Grace, and Mr and Mrs Crumby. Everybody has a bedroom and a bathroom of their own.'

Joanne enthused. 'Right… like Mr and Mrs Crumby.'

Grace didn't respond.

Joanne averted her eyes. She knew enough about

psychology to know that important milestones had been missed in Grace's development.

Norman broached an explanation. They had talked little about anything of substance since the revelations of New Year's Eve.

'When we first got Grace, I was dead against the imperialism of English. I read that if you spoke just your language, and let a child maintain their language, the two languages could work alongside each other. I felt she deserved to have her heritage intact. But maybe it was a mistake. How much can one person hold on to?'

With it said, there was a quiet indictment of his life, his past, and Joanne's, too.

Joanne was forgiving in her answer. 'Grace just needs friends, maybe that's all it will take. I see *potential*, real potential.'

In her voice was the charge of a clinical and compassionate concern, the true measure of who she was, stern and loving in the way a child needed direction and the assumed role of a strong parent. It was obvious Joanne loved this child.

Norman looked out of the window. He turned his phone over in his hand. He was aware his mind was processing Nate Feldman.

Joanne angled in the impropriety of wanting to see it, asking, 'What are you hiding?' so Norman held the phone up as a part of full disclosure.

He read the message, broaching its greater context.

Joanne interrupted, 'Is this Mr Feldman even still alive?'

Norman advanced the story by degrees. 'Mr Feldman committed suicide on Black Monday, 1987. He jumped from his office building.'

In Norman's voice there was a tone that betrayed a greater intimacy.

Joanne half-turned with a familiarity that came from simply being in the presence of another's life and asked, 'You knew him?' She was holding the wheel with the determination of a captain steering a ship.

Norman looked ahead at the advancing street. He said with a tone of quiet remembrance, 'I used to go to my mother's office. Mr Feldman did this trick. He'd reach behind my ear and pull out a silver dollar. I was young. I always wanted to know how he did it and my mother used to say he couldn't tell because that's what made him the boss. He could make money out of thin air.'

'Your mother liked Mr Feldman, huh?' Joanne said it as though it was the stuff of ordinary life.

It meant little to her, a story to pass the time on a drive together.

Norman felt it in the act of telling it. He offered as a point of continuance, not for Joanne as much as himself, 'I have a vague memory of my mother telling my father something about Nate.'

The word Canada formed under his breath. He said, as though it was revelation, which it was, 'Nate, he was a draft dodger.'

Joanne didn't know these people. She was presently distracted. She looked in the rear-view mirror at Grace.

There was the ever-present to occupy the totality of one's existence. 'You okay, Grace?'

She turned to Norman with the pressuring sense that perhaps there had been too much talk and not enough attention paid to Grace. She said by way of reconciliation, 'Grace can get a doll for being so good, right?'

Norman said, 'A new doll, why not?' just as Grace leaned forward and threw up in a spew that hit the back of Joanne's head.

8.

NATE WAS A day early for his appointment at the office of Weatherly, Sutherland, and Saunders, Lawyers. He called in the mid-afternoon from a coffee shop out in Winnetka, politely asking if he could be slotted in at the end of the day perhaps. He was in town ahead of plan. He could be at the office in less than an hour.

He was put on hold, then the message came back that he could not be accommodated. Documents needed to be drawn up. Nate heard the receptionist opening and closing a ledger or scheduler. She confirmed his appointment. He thanked her and assured her he would keep to the schedule.

There was no need to head into the city. He used his phone to search for a hotel in the area and found a Comfort Suites room, breakfast included. An immediate upgrade pop-up appeared as he was registering – a California king sized bed for an extra $9.95, including a spa upgrade for the gym. It was too complicated to decline, or navigate back through the site, so he booked it. Margins were met on $9.95 upgrades. The final price was never what you were quoted.

The old carriage house was off to the side, not visible from the road, but Nate saw its distinctive rooster weathervane and felt its presence loom over him. He heard the word *Duchess* in his head.

It still hurt. He felt it and winced. It was all there again in his heart and head. In wartime, gear and supplies had to be meticulously packed and weighed. This was how his father packed for him, military style, deciding what to take and what to leave behind. They had the lie rehearsed.

They were going on a fishing trip, wilderness gear packed into the car, canned provisions, oil-slick parka and wading boots, thermal underwear, a Swiss Army knife, flint, and a cache of dry kindling. His father weighed it all in the carriage house on a scale taken from the kitchen.

In pulling out of the drive, Nate saw his mother in the upper floor window of his old bedroom. A curtain moved. She was then gone from his life.

They talked among themselves eventually miles out of Chicago. His father drank whiskey from an engraved pocket flask set between his knees. At times the car swerved and had to be corrected. Thankfully, they didn't run into anyone as they drove along the funneling timberline.

Business had been going to hell, or so his father had determined, or it was getting so. He saw bad times ahead. There had been mistakes made at all levels of government.

It wasn't even about governments anymore, but multinationals, about prevailing interests that transcended any one border.

His father cast into a great pool of discontent. He was then anticipating the rise of the Japanese imports. He had a head for understanding the ways of the world, or it was his hatred of the *Japs* that keyed him in on them specifically. In looking back, it was hard for Nate to decide what was prophetic and what was rage within his father. It was perhaps both.

Whatever the case, the Vietnam War was a great distraction. His father announced it, banging the dash of the car, the joke of those early Toyota and Honda four-stroke engines – a lawnmower motor in a car – the compacts that nobody in their right mind would think of driving, and didn't, but then did eventually, in what would be the subtle narrowing of dreams and skyrocketing inflation.

It was never about Nate. That was one of the fast truths emerging at the time. There would be no succor. His father was lost. It was the *Japs*, what he had experienced in war.

His father pulled over and pissed into the desolate landscape against the onset of evening. He wavered and steadied, went round the front of the car, shielding his eyes against the cone of light.

Getting in, he reached back and touched his hunting rifle with a strange reassurance that it was still there, so it had frightened Nate what might have happened if they were stopped, or what might happen after he was gone across the border.

The anger was suddenly gone from his father. He was exhausted. He took another drink. They talked again eventually, or his father did. What he described was not the act of desertion, not the act of disgrace, but something far nobler, something connected to the Feldman past.

They were heading up into Feldman territory connected to a band of heroic Norwegians going generations back. They were, in fact, more Ingebretson than Feldman. His father turned and faced Nate in the compelling sense that this was all true, or it should be believed.

Nate could do nothing but acquiesce and listen.

It was a complicated story. The Feldman name had entered the family through a mercurial Norwegian who had given birth to a daughter of immense beauty, but also petulant character, who broke camp eventually and was seduced and bedded by a fur trapper named Feldman, so the mirthless Ingebretson Norwegians, those dumbfounded giants who had come across the Atlantic, had their bloodline infused with a sagacious, nomadic taxidermist from the Urals who knew something about fox fur and ermine and its value to the Imperial Court of czarist Russia. This, according to his father, was how a rarified beauty, a daughter who struck out and found another life, saved the Norwegian side of the family from a great obscurity.

His father had been brought up outside Saint Cloud, Minnesota. The family name was Engelstad, and he was christened Angar, a name he had always associated with a clod driving oxen, so that when he distinguished himself in school and left Saint Cloud eventually, he took the lifeline of the ancestral, Semitic Feldman name. As for Theodore, he chose the name from a haberdashery storefront sign seen fleetingly through the window of a train on his way down through Saint Paul, believing he might find favor in circles of money in the metropolis of Chicago, Philadelphia or New York. He did. He was such an anomaly with his flaxen hair and great strength, and to be counted a Jew, to have that lineage.

He earned a scholarship to Cornell, enrolling in ROTC simply because he had no respectable civilian clothes. He wore his uniform exclusively, compensating in the way certain men can turn disadvantage to advantage. He was described in the Yearbook as a student of great patriotism, featured in his uniform, inspiring and deferential, and he came to understand that you could be a fraud, or not a fraud exactly, but that your true self, what you felt and thought, could be so concealed from others, and from yourself, too.

He had a head for applied mathematics and a penchant for philosophy, and also the steady hand of a carpenter, given the thunderhead Norwegian Engelstad and Ingebretson in him. His height and his looks gave him a physical stature. He was wildly courted and admired. This was an established fact. There was nothing he couldn't do, because you had to do everything in Saint Cloud, Minnesota, and he had done everything well by necessity.

A Vanderbilt had her claws into him at Cornell. She didn't care a whit where he had come from, not then, but he knew it would come against him, and yet, for a time, he described a growing self-awareness, how he could elicit a recklessness in women. They were rough in their lovemaking, and there was always the possibility he would sire a child. There was that much in him, that much explosive charge. This was the frontline of a war that might be won, the war over the heart.

Nate had heard the story. His mother had verified certain facts during the trials and rows of a contentious marriage, relaying what his father could have had, and what he left behind in the first great act of selfless love in leaving behind his Vanderbilt. There was a lamenting sense that he had passed on true love and was never whole again. So it wasn't the war entirely that had changed him, but what he left behind, what could never be recovered, and would most surely have ended, if there had been no war, anyway.

Nate dared not ask about the Vanderbilt. It wasn't a question of facts and understanding, but a story of perceptions and deepening influences. His father described how he had been influenced by his studies in philosophy and engineering at Cornell, where, notoriously, existential devotees of Sartre and Camus regularly committed suicide at any of a number of bridges along the gorges near campus. He revealed how, during his sophomore year, he used to walk out toward the gorges with his Vanderbilt debutante, both sharing the mutual understanding that suicide was a genuine option in a world without a God, and that, each time neither jumped, they were making an existential choice to go on living and felt the better for consciously making a choice.

His father held the whiskey between his knees. He drank liberally, looking out into the unfolding landscape. There was the surging sense of what had passed, the rush of great and undeniable passion, and all of it begun before his father was Nate's age, the indictment laid out before Nate.

At times, his father found it hard to contain it all, the car swerving so it had to be corrected and accounted for, but, thankfully, there was nobody going north or south along the funneling timberline. These were stories pulled from his father's head and his heart, the stream of words, the Feldman nomad and the giant Swedes, or was it the giant Norwegians? Yes, the *goddamn Ingebretsons.* His father corrected himself, lost in the quiet incantation of how life could be otherwise invented and lived, peopled by great and noble nomads who must surely have existed in how the land was first discovered.

Nate listened, his father coming round toward an awareness of his own disaffection, tendering the tremulous and humble opinion that, at a certain point in history, just before the Industrial Revolution, when men still lived without the hitch of industry and machines, when distances meant something, a man could find the measure of his strength and temperament in Nature, in lands yet uninhabited.

He alighted on the story of a great ox of a man, Per Ingebretson, their Norwegian primogenitor, who, of his own volition, neither from religious persecution nor any real ambition, just a wandering sense of wanting to see the greater world, had left home at age sixteen, crossed Iceland and Greenland, before making shore in North America. Per, a towering, uncomplicated figure in the tradition of Paul Bunyan, a man who would find his true calling logging in what would eventually become Minnesota. His passage to America had been secured through a trading company out of Hudson Bay, his first true landfall along a meandering river at a bleak outpost near Pictured Rocks on Lake Superior at a supply shed on the way to nowhere, where he was given the vague mandate to begin work further north and simply keep chopping until someone came and got him. There was enough in a lifetime to keep him busy.

His father told the story driving into the upper mitt of the Michigan peninsula in a thinning tree line of spruce and pine. How he knew the most intimate details of Per Ingebretson was not up for debate. It was just understood he did.

His father shifted, took his hands from the wheel, and, describing the strength of Per, made the halted chop at something that could never be felled in a single blow. He described the stance, the measured series of blows, the angled cuts, impressing at all times the absolute isolation of it all.

In those years of first discovery, he explained, men lived rough, authentic lives and gathered in encampments at season's end in the trade of goods and services. A breed apart from others, they were all alike among their own kind, because of the physicality of the work, their shoulders broad, their arms and legs thick, hands like shovels. But, lamentably, they were a sort others did not willingly suffer drawing alongside, the comparison too striking in their collective favor, so, when camp broke, each giant went its own way.

In the clearing of the far North, his father maintained, there were no stories of drunkenness or disaffection with life. Each could carve, and did, reeds planed to a fine-grained translucent parchment, wood whittled to release the fluted trill of a songbird's call.

They were on a grey scratch of road.

His father drank again from his tumbler of whiskey. He imagined Per, in the metronome swish of a weighted axe, in great advancing strides coming upon a stream, drinking like a horse in a satiating quench, and, at day's end, pitching an impoverished tent, flint struck against the coming dusk, a glow of kindling coaxed with a whisper, the sudden bloom of his shadowy form and his hand cupped like a teller of a great secret.

It was thus told, in the way stories are, for the listener, but for the teller, too. His father filled with an emptiness of his own days pitted against a heroic life that most probably never existed, which made it all the more irreconcilable, more tragic, because he believed it in his heart, and he would not be dissuaded that there was another way, when there never was.

9.

JOANNE DIDN'T KNOW anyone could still get carsick. Maybe it had been the McDonald's. It was a plausible alternative explanation.

They were in the suburb of Winnetka. Joanne rubbed Grace down with baby wipes. Norman was out of the car, too, compliantly holding the box of baby wipes.

Joanne pointed to a shop across the road from a café. Maybe Norman could get a coffee, while 'the girls went shopping'. Joanne turned to Grace. 'Maybe they have dolls?'

Norman acquiesced, left them and went over to the café and ordered a double espresso. In a day waning toward a darkening sky, he saw already, beyond a tree line of oak and cedar, the visible glow of city-light pollution, a soft, bathing light belying an afternoon of falling temperatures and the gridlock of a treacherous afternoon commute.

They might yet be trapped out here. There was the issue of Randolph. Norman didn't want to think about it, the piling of responsibilities that could pull you under and take you from any central and focused interest. There was much beyond his control.

Norman felt it. All that had been so recently lost to him. Not least, the loss of Daniel Einhorn's investment that might have propelled Norman toward greater success. Money accrued in the essential fraud of how so much of the world had been built upon deceit. It sickened Norman, not least that it had ended before he could cash in. There was the sudden and unsettling sense that his life had reached a point where the best years were behind him. It struck out here in the most unlikely of places, not in the confines of his office, but in the run of life and the coldness of an advancing afternoon.

In the quiet indeterminacy, Norman opened and reread Nate Feldman's email. What struck him again was the language, the authoritative but ingratiating, accessible tone. Here was a man who could find a broad and accomplished reach in the measure of a single line or two.

It irked Norman. It must have been this way with Mr Feldman. The executive shorthand of a voice and lines that could communicate a buoying optimism or reprimand, without ever using the exact words of praise or indictment. Mr Feldman moving around the center of an emotion, so he was never any one thing, but the sum of a continuance in the aftermath of great slaughter, and at the end, sequestered in a skyscraper, among a pantheon of demi-gods surveying the antlike procession of what now constituted the emerging world.

Norman looked up in the contained world of the coffee shop. He felt like a man long submerged, breaking the surface of water again. His breath came in fits. He should have stayed at home. This advance on his old life, it meant nothing. What did the Feldmans want from him? He felt himself asking it.

Despite his better judgment, Norman did a search on the name Nate Feldman. There was an article concerning a Nate Feldman and the sale of Grandshire Organics to a Toronto-based multinational for 15.5 million Canadian dollars. The article was dated April 11 2001. In bold lettering, midway through the article, Nathaniel Feldman was listed as founder and CEO.

There was an insert photograph, the evidence incontrovertible. Nate Feldman, the spitting image of his father. His age was listed as forty-eight, the same age Mr Feldman had been when Helen had come under his sway of influence. It did something to Norman, the alignment of these men in his life.

He pulled up Mr Feldman's obituary, the lauded account of his heroics in the Pacific, his subsequent rise within the Insurance industry. He was an avid outdoorsman. His interests included golf, fishing and carpentry. He was born in Saint Cloud, Minnesota.

Norman set his phone aside. He felt an out of body experience. The Feldman men, they had a shared acumen for making money. He felt a fitfulness of breath. He wanted to go home. It was too much to bear. He had been wrong in appeasing Joanne when she had suggested they go see the house. His first instinct had been right.

Goddamn the Feldmans! Goddamn Nate Feldman! He felt the mantra of words repeated. They undercut an understanding he had always believed, how the universe worked in relation to one's efforts and hard work, when now, it was all too patently apparent that the universe didn't align with that at all, and that greatness was bestowed on certain persons. He had read about it, fundamentalist sects attesting that certain men were predestined to salvation and that God, in showing favor, allowed them to stand as pillars of virtue and examples of God's favoring grace. There was nothing unabashed about wealth and success. It accounted for every televangelist in a three-thousand-dollar-suit asking for tithes from the faithful, the sick and indigent alike.

Something inside him dropped. It was envy, yes, that, but also a sense of his own shortcoming, an unsettling and fundamental misunderstanding of the world, and how it could be negotiated by a man like Mr Feldman and seemingly, too, by his son, Nate Feldman, when he, Norman Price, had failed so miserably, he, along with Walter and Helen.

How could he not help but compare the Feldman trajectory, their greatness, the Feldmans' sentient awareness of trends and markets, and the ennobling reach of Mr Feldman, who had come from nothing. It was there in black and white, goddamn it!

A half-hour had passed. Norman felt obliged to order another espresso. He got up and stared into the approaching dark. They should head back home. There were times when nothing seemed worth it.

He was on the verge of a meltdown. He thought of alternatives to going back into the city. They could push on north into Wisconsin, stop at some rest area and search the Internet for some mid-winter, cut-rate deal at a boutique hotel along Lake Geneva. Why not salvage the remainder of the week, make use of the car, spend a quiet reprieve around the languid history of a lake where the robber barons of old had retreated in the midsummer heat? He could call and simply extend the car rental.

He would suggest it to Joanne when she got back. He thought of Randolph, the infuriating reach of this responsibility. They would go and simply get Randolph, or maybe Norman would simply drop off Joanne and Grace, and then return the car himself, but then the car was in Joanne's name!

Norman struggled to regain a sense of perspective. It didn't matter, the particulars, what he did, or didn't do. It was about what Nate Feldman thought Norman was doing. That was the goddamn point. He felt the fury of distraction. He had never worked well under pressure.

He would not meet with Nate Feldman. He took a deep breath to reorient himself. A reasonable lie coalesced. He was vacationing at Lake Geneva. It was all that needed to be stated, no explanation given. It was just a stated fact. He liked the idea very much. A mid-week retreat was just the sort of casual ease Norman wanted to project on goddamn Nate Feldman. Yes, any meeting with Nate Feldman would have to be postposed. *Fuck* Nathaniel Feldman.

If he had showed as requested, it would have favored the Feldmans. He knew it. Nate, rising to meet him, a sherry or brandy proffered, something Feldman-like, the gracious reach and quiet accommodation, and Norman, the obsequious and simpering recipient of such airs and graces, where there would be no question of Norman paying. It was billed to the room, all taken care of, the expediency and decorum of a man versed in gaining the subtle upper hand.

It coursed through Norman, the sense of envy, this Feldman stock, this great breeding, and Nate Feldman, in crossing his legs, in the attitude of relaxed consideration, would begin, and so politely, conveying his sympathies, how sorry he was for the tumult and violent nature of Helen's death. He had read about it. Such a dreadful business, the way it occurred, quietly suggesting that he hoped it had nothing to do with his father.

It would be textbook Feldman, Nate seeking not so much to exonerate his father, but to extend his father's influence, advancing some preternatural hold Mr Feldman had over others, all this serving the Feldman name – the Feldman mythos.

Norman could see it no other way, and what the Hell right did Nate Feldman have to interfere with his life? This was the Feldmans' presumptive pedigree – all they were, and what he, Helen, and Walter weren't.

Fuck the Feldmans! There was a name for a play. He said

it under his breath. It stood as a singular indictment. If Nate had the audacity to impose on his life, then Norman would hang the name Feldman out to dry for the world to see, Nate, that goddamn Draft Dodger, and that insufferable father of his, that mincer of words, that ineffectual fop. The truth of it, the insurance company had gone near bankrupt under his charge, the Chicago office slashed and re-staffed with temps. He was a goddamn drunk, and everyone knew it! No wonder he jumped to his goddamn death!

Norman was indisposed. Yes, that was it! His secretary had just informed him of the conflicting date. He had a pressing deadline on a new play. He hoped Nate would understand. He was muttering words as he began writing out the email, suddenly confronted in the construction of a lie, whether he should give his secretary a name or not, and, in the imagined sense that he had a secretary, he thought of his mother and Mr Feldman and all that had come before. It made him angry that Helen Price was his mother and that he was attached to a past and to a woman like that.

He was still in the midst of writing his excuse, when he looked up and saw Joanne advancing across the street with Grace.

Grace was dressed in a smart black wool blazer, pleated tartan skirt, white ankle socks and patent leather Mary Janes. Joanne slipped Norman a primrose-colored envelope with a raised seal that contained the receipt. She made Grace turn like a figure on a music box.

In quietly observing Grace, Joanne said, 'We are all being slowly poisoned. You know that, right?' She was referring to McDonald's.

Norman knew, or he had heard the story umpteen times, about a chicken nugget that had purportedly lasted six months beneath a car seat and showed no sign of decay. It had gone viral on YouTube. Joanne began to repeat the story.

Norman added in a mildly contentious way, 'It's the sort of event that would have constituted a miracle in biblical times. Maybe we're just tired of miracles.'

His comment was met with a *tisk* of mild admonishment. Undeterred, Joanne said, 'Doesn't she look beautiful?'

There was no denying Grace's exoticness. In her outfit, she looked to Norman like a smarmy character from an upmarket children's book. *Madeline*. He wasn't quite sure if the story was set in Paris or New York, or if Madeline was even French.

It didn't quite matter. What mattered was that the *Madeline* series was there in his mind at all, suggesting a lamentable downward reach of art and story, the economy of words and sparse images, one diminished form propping up the other in the shorthanded way these stories worked; parents trawling to unearth what might engage a four-year-old or, more accurately, what might engage the sensibilities of overbearing mothers who felt they knew what might engage a four-year-old, when it wasn't established what a four-year-old might genuinely be interested in at all. It didn't matter, the entire children's book industry was in the service of parents, not children.

There were times when Norman lamented the service-ability and truism of the TV shows of the fifties and sixties, a confederacy of ordinary left to sit before shows like *Tom and Jerry*, *Tweety Bird and Sylvester the Cat* or *The Road Runner*, when the message was less ambiguous, when life was all about the chase, and where, in just about every scene, you got a frying pan in the face, or you stepped in the spring of a bear trap, or you ended up holding sticks of dynamite that blew up in your face. These characters should have been on currency for the Truths they harbored.

Norman kept looking at Grace, the cardboard cut-out of her features, the flat face and the slanted eyes, the composite shorthand identifying features a good illustrator could turn into a signature series. And then the question surfaced, why couldn't he do the same? A compendium of *Grace & Randolph* books – *Grace & Randolph Learn the Hard Truth About China's One Child Policy*; *Grace & Randolph Get Undercut in the Lemonade Stand Business and Learn Hard and Fast Truths about Outsourcing*; *Grace & Randolph Learn About Derivatives and Futures and Why Daddy Won't Sleep with Mommy Anymore and is Banging his Secretary.*

He knew his main problem had always been having too large a vocabulary and having too much to say. It was anathema for an artist. Maybe he could go with a Chinese Alphabet book, be ahead of the curve in the insipid way parents were now anticipating the reality of what was fast approaching – the decline of the West.

*

Joanne was suddenly interested in an organic quiche and pine nut kale salad. The café had juices starting at $6.95.

A clutch of older women had been quietly assessing Grace. Norman caught their eye as one of the elderlies volunteered that her granddaughter was learning Chinese. She gave Norman an obliging smile. It was obvious they had been disparagingly querying who had the sexual problem, Norman or Joanne.

Norman said, 'It came down to a Bichon Frise, a Shih Tzu, or her. She won out, on account of the prospect that she has a longer lifespan and we might end up living off her.'

It set the elderlies on edge.

A man in a get-up of yellow cashmere sweater and tomato red pants came across to their table in a quiet arbitration of glowing familiarity. He gave off a new car smell. His name was Roger Carlyle. He was in real estate. His face was on his business card. That seemed to be his essential credential, a face.

Norman could see Roger give Joanne the once over. Roger, it turned out, had a tape recorder. He wanted to know if Grace would like to record the Pledge of Allegiance? It was a sales quirk, something he burned to a CD for anybody who bought a house.

Joanne was quietly flustered. Roger had his eye on her. Obviously, she controlled the purse strings, or Roger was giving her the impression he thought so. Norman could see the spark of intrigue Roger engendered in Joanne. This was like someone hitting on your kid sister. It let him understand, too, something deeper about Joanne, about what sort of man she might let enter her life. She was seeking alternatives.

Joanne admitted that Grace didn't know the Pledge of Allegiance. It didn't dissuade Roger. He had a contingency plan, a laminated card, like a prayer card, with the pledge on it. She could read it.

Norman intervened. Grace wasn't, in fact, reading English yet! He said by way of distracting Roger, 'Isn't it true that *The Breakfast Club* was filmed near here?' which, in fact, it had been, at New Trier East, and 'Wasn't *Home Alone* also filmed here?'

Yes, of course it had been, they both had, Roger Carlyle was wildly impressed. Maybe they were in the market for a house after all. Wasn't Norman up on his history! His hands came together in the gathering warmth of a deal.

Norman sidled toward his own interest in the arts, and theater especially, leading toward a reference to his own success in the Chicago theater scene, with the tacit understanding that anything he said could be verified in the surreptitious click of a website. It made lying that much harder in the cast-iron Truth of easily accessed facts. But there was enough to pique Roger's interest in a down-turned market.

Norman rattled on about Second City TV and the great glut of talent that came out of Chicago. Belushi, Aykroyd, Candy, Murray and Chevy Chase.

Well, maybe they weren't all Chicagoans, but they might as well have been. They were associated with Chicago, and that's what mattered. What they shared was a commonality, all involved in the great irreverent classics like *Caddyshack* and *Stripes* and, of course, the lampooning send-up of those damn Nazi sympathizers out in Skokie in *The Blues Brothers*.

The titles, of course, revealed Norman's age, but, then, who wasn't getting older, Roger baited with the good business sense there might be an uncovered treasure here.

Norman turned toward Joanne. He was talking in a way everybody could hear. 'I've always said, if you want to understand Chicago in relation to the politics of Reagan's Trickle-down economics, just think of an incensed Ted Knight in his brass-buttoned, blue double-breasted captain's jacket facing down a bug-eyed Rodney Dangerfield speeding toward him in his power boat in *Caddyshack*. It says something about the driving vengeance of class warfare!'

It didn't quite make sense in how he said it. His voice reached a sudden pitch of hysteria. It was the Feldmans at the root of it. He kept talking.

'And what about *Ferris Bueller's Day Off*? That was filmed here, right, Rog?' He didn't wait for the answer. '*Ferris Bueller's Day Off*, an existential Chicago masterpiece of adolescent disaffection that asks the really hard question facing all of us, "What the fuck will we do with the rest of our lives?"'

They left. Roger Carlyle and the clutch of elderlies looked on, mortified and shocked. It wasn't the sort of language you used around children. It was downright criminal.

Joanne hustled Grace across the road. When they got to the car, she glared at Norman. 'You enjoy making enemies.'

Norman didn't answer. Roger Carlyle was in the street, a cell phone to his ear. He was talking frantically to someone.

They were pulling away from the curb when Joanne said suddenly, 'You don't have a license! Pull over!' just as a police cruiser turned a corner and came at them.

It passed and then in a wheeling turn the police car was behind them, its misery lights swirling and lighting up the interior of the car.

Norman shoved his cell phone toward Joanne, saying, 'Take it. It's got all my contacts on it!'

10.

NORMAN WAS IN the holding cell in Winnetka. During the traffic stop, a quantity of marijuana had been uncovered in a small bag Joanne had packed for Grace. Norman was facing a criminal act of possession along with a charge of Child Endangerment. And there was the matter also of an outstanding bench warrant against him related to a subpoena that he had not complied with in relation to his father's case.

At the Winnetka jail, his fingerprints were run through a database. They came up a match to an ongoing criminal investigation. In a small interrogation room, a detective read from a copy of a letter sent to one Daniel Einhorn informing him that he had been named as a sexual partner of a person who had tested positive to HIV and was legally bound to appear at Cook County Department of Health.

Under direct questioning, when Norman was asked how his fingerprints were on the letter, he elected to take the Fifth. He requested a single call as per his legal rights.

*

Joanne was crying when she picked up. She was out in the waiting area. The car had been impounded. She said, 'I'm so sorry, this is all my fault!'

Norman preempted her saying anything about the pot.

Joanne needed to listen very carefully. He was being transferred to Cook County Jail. A bond hearing was being scheduled for the following morning. He didn't know the exact details. Joanne should ask at the desk, find out his case number.

Joanne's voice was suddenly frantic again. 'Why? I don't understand it... We can just tell them...'

Norman talked over her again. 'Listen to me, Joanne, I want you to call Kenneth! His number is on my cell phone. Tell him they're asking about a letter that was sent to Daniel Einhorn. He'll know what it's about.'

The call lasted two minutes before Norman was cut off.

Joanne took a bus back into the city with Grace, who was still in her new outfit. She drew attention from the other passengers, mostly tired-looking elderly black women. Joanne was dressed in a shabby down coat and moon boots she had retrieved from the trunk of the car, against the protest from the arresting officer who had wanted the contents of the car held. She had waited, insistent, Norman cuffed, her hair wet from the snow and parted in the middle in the way she had worn it in high school.

Joanne felt emotion well up as she stared into the dark. The indignity of it and all happening so suddenly, after all the trouble they had renting the car, when nothing should have gone wrong after that. It was too hard to cope with. She was crying without sound, holding it in and wiping her eyes. How could this have happened? Her thoughts settled on what if Grace had just not thrown up, when she knew the blame lay in her having put the marijuana amidst Grace's snacks.

It was undone, what she had gained with Norman.

'Call Kenneth...' That was Norman's solution, and so quickly arrived at. She was being pushed out. She couldn't bear thinking of it. She had been rash in presuming that anything had been established between them. It had been her hope, her delusion. Anybody else would have seen it!

Joanne let it play in her head in a quiet indictment. There had been so many questions unasked regarding Kenneth and Norman's break-up. She had never even questioned if a court hearing had been held regarding visitation rights for Kenneth to see Grace, or if Kenneth had simply walked away? How could that legally be? It was bound to surface. A relationship couldn't end like this, and now she had facilitated it, ending a détente. Kenneth was being summoned. Where would she go if Kenneth re-emerged?

Joanne felt a deep shudder run through her. She was thirty-nine years old and without prospects. It was the singular, unalterable fact in her life. She lowered her head. She had made some *bad choices*. The expression was on her lips before she could think otherwise, when the greater reality was how chance figured in a life. It came as a revelation, something she would have denied yesterday, and yet it was true.

Joanne reached for Grace's hand to rouse her, to reclaim her, then thought better of it. Grace had become Joanne's single purpose in life. It was what children did, mollified ambition, establishing a reasonable excuse for personal failure. Joanne was accepting of the terms. She had love to give. It took nothing from her to admit it.

Joanne let Grace sleep. She might ride deep into the city. The bus was warm and comforting, a reprieve from the cold and what awaited her. There was Randolph, of course, poor Randolph. He would have to wait their return. She could do nothing else.

Joanne continued to stare into the dark. It was her fault, surely. Roger Carlyle had watched the whole thing from the café. He had acted in the interest of the community after all, cut his losses in seeing Joanne's alignment with Norman. She imagined Carlyle might make the police blotter, inculcating himself further into the community: *Realtor foils drug deal*, or whatever charges the police filed against Norman.

Joanne admitted it against herself. She had found Roger Carlyle attractive. He was one of those professional men full of self-importance who had somehow always eventually passed on her. It had happened when she had been working at a bookshop, before she met Peter. She'd had a succession of relationships that ended most often with men bedding her and leaving her. It was the reality of the modern world.

There had been one among them she'd thought different.

Robert Hoyt, a soft-faced, lanky lawyer who had tipped his head slightly when listening to her, presumably because of his height, when, later in bed with him, he had asked her to speak into his good ear, revealing then how he had suffered a fever as a child that had affected his hearing.

Joanne shuddered and closed her eyes. She saw him as she had first seen him brown-bagging a lunch and paging through a book on Cubism at the store where she had worked. Robert Hoyt who had talked so openly of wanting to be an artist, as though it could be communicated to her alone, when, all along, he had only used her as a foil against the unstoppable influence of good breeding on his life, and understanding it eventually, how no act, no matter how scandalous, could make up for a lack of true talent.

That is what she had been for him, the deciding influence of a flirtatious bad choice that might have ruined him, so that right on the six-month anniversary of unprotected sex, as though an experiment had been completed, he flat-out stopped calling her, swapping her out for a former lawyer classmate with a sparrow's face.

You could drive yourself mad trying to understand it. What Joanne remembered were those times Robert used to stand in the pale light after being with her, the lie of it yet concealed, Robert Hoyt rising to stare back at the city from his skyline apartment, brushing his teeth, the rote up and down strokes and the side to side motion that he had learned in childhood and carried with him, and then back in bed again, reaching and drawing her to him so his breath was on her neck in the smell of mint and good hygiene.

*

Joanne looked into the sullen deadness of the bus. There were events in a life that would never make sense. She consciously blanked Robert Hoyt from her life.

There was something old world about the bus, the yellowish buttery light, almost sepia, so it seemed like a movie set, some compartmentalized scene from the past. And then she had a thought of how it did remind her of a movie she had once seen about a kidnapping, a movie about a GI, down on his luck, who had bullied a girlfriend to participate in a Lindbergh-style kidnapping.

Joanne had watched the movie with Peter, both of them witnessing the disconsolate act of what people, even back then, had been forced to do, when a soldier's service seemingly had not been enough, and nothing was gained in coming home. It had been so terribly sad: a small child of rich parents, a house over from where the girlfriend worked, led to a park by the girlfriend, then taken to an awaiting car, because who wouldn't want to ride with a genuine GI?

In closing her eyes, Joanne let the throb of the diesel engine go through her, remembering how the girlfriend had not intervened in the child's inevitable murder, the kidnapping abandoned with no money gained. It had seemed so utterly hopeless, the dispirited sense of an afternoon so long ago spent with Peter when it was apparent that he would never make it, both of them watching the film in the quieting understanding that something profound was being communicated, and being played for them alone.

Toward the end of the film, Joanne recalled the starkness of the final scene in the small farmhouse, the GI boyfriend seated at a kitchen table. He had a gun in his lap, his head in the fold of his arms, and the child whimpering in a closet. The scene was shot from the girlfriend's perspective, so there was no reprieve for her or the GI – the camera, in the long close-up, revealing in the GI's face, a life being consumed and used up even in sleep.

Joanne took a deepening breath. She was struggling now. An embittered feeling surfaced against her parents. They were at the locus of a point where she might have been saved, when there might have been an alternative, and they had abandoned her. Her shoulders shrugged in the uneasy assessment of her life, and beneath it she felt the unrecorded hum of implication in all that had come before, and would come, and accounted for life, the register of decisions, moments that could never be fully understood or altered.

How often in life was there truly no place to go? She was back where she had been on New Year's Eve, on the precipice of boarding a bus back to Buffalo and landing at Sheryl and Dave's door. She felt the deep rush of humiliation. She had caused this, in putting the pot in Grace's suitcase.

What would they say about her if she tried to return? She used the heel of her hand against her nose.

What she wanted to say to them collectively! She felt a surge of anger. They deserved blame! Not least for the Thanksgiving when she had showed up, bereft of a real future, when they might have said something sympathetic, and offered up hollow words that she was welcome back home, when they knew she wouldn't have taken them up on the offer, but it would have been a show of compassion, or at least concern.

Whom did she hate most? It was difficult deciding, but she laid blame on her parents for their disregard for her in the years after college, when they had actively kept her in abeyance. They had argued that there were no jobs, no future in Buffalo, and yet Sheryl had stayed and had been eventually accommodated after all the grief she had caused in marrying Dave.

Yes, that was the charge she laid against them, their collective indifference. When Sheryl had gone through early menopause and had her hysterectomy, she had the support of a mother meeting the kids off the school bus, supper already in the oven – a casserole and corn bread – and Dad coming on the weekends, sleeping on the pull-out couch and taking the kids to a middle school night football game.

What it had done was allow Dave to continue out on the road, because the money was needed and no opportunity to drive long haul as a contractor could be declined, non-union work, non-negotiable. You served the interests that hired you, put up and shut up, or you weren't contracted again, which led to a survival instinct that calcified around an abiding creed of faith and self-reliance, so what was gained was gained with the Lord's favor, because you couldn't afford enemies, not in this world or the Hereafter.

Joanne knew everything about their lives, the straight truth and the contradictions, what made them who they were. She even had a sympathetic understanding of what it took to survive. It was just that they hadn't extended that degree of understanding to her.

How often did she think of her parents, and of Sheryl and Dave, and how often did they think of her? It was a sobering and hurtful reality. She knew the answer in their preoccupation with their existence, in the reach of Misty's unrealized dreams, and the great resuscitation of new dreams, so a gold medal at the Olympics, or the dream of it, was passed over, eventually, for the love of a guy in a pickup truck who looked like every other guy in a pickup truck.

There was a trick there somewhere, a willful lack of insight, paving over ambition in the sullen settling of life, like a house settled on its foundation in its creaks, groans and cracks. Life, she understood, was a succession of failures, with the oddment of small victories here and there that needed to be cherished, remembered and fanned. They had denied her this.

Joanne felt herself shrug. What her parents had done on Sheryl's behalf was discharge the feeling of loss going on in her life by simply being there – Dave calling the hospital to see how Sheryl was doing, and then calling home, talking to a series of people who loved him, his kids, and then his in-laws. The general pact between them that this was it, what they collectively shared against coming joys and sorrows, and to have it all arriving as Sheryl lost the essence of what she had offered Dave – her womb, her ability to bring forth children – gone, but not her love, nor the children she had borne him. Life moved on.

This was the great difference, the proximity of the lives they shared, when she had left and gone to Chicago.

In those last years with Peter, it was difficult rousing herself – not because of indifference, but because of a genuine fear that whatever foothold she had might be better than what awaited her. She had only herself to blame. She had heard it on the self-empowerment talk shows, the eternal optimism of women who changed their lives, women in far worse circumstances. Evidently, she was not one of those women of great conviction.

Joanne cupped her hand against the cold glass and stared into the dark. She could see a constellation of lights in the palatial old homes. This is where money and success resided. It was there before her and inaccessible.

She turned away, looked vacantly at the black women drowsy with sleep. A dry heat poured from the floor vents. She stared at hands laced over the anvils of old-fashioned purses, the ashen color of black skin damaged by the abrasion of cleaner solutions. They were all domestic staff. It could have been the fifties in the time before the Civil Rights movement, and Joanne realized that for some, so little ever changed.

She imagined them, working in the big houses, collectively removing their wedding rings before the day's work, then tenderizing beef with a mallet, the wet slap of a tenderloin turned and dusted with flour, a roast drawn into a twine stocking, and then, on alternating days, obliged to either change the linens and towels, or bring out a shine in the hardwood flooring, the ironing left until evening, water sprinkled from a cup, pure as a religious blessing. These women surviving admirably in the service of others.

Or maybe these women saw it differently, and most probably did, their self-respect reliant on an indomitable spirit of great religious belief that better explained their revivalist Baptist religion, their full-throated exaltation against what could not be expressed in the dutiful, mute, conscript of domestic work, so that they needed the voice of God in their head, needed to shout his praise at a Sunday service to know they existed, as much as to know He existed.

The bus eventually made its way across a slip of land running between the divide of a cemetery and the lake. On the other side of grandeur, a harder reality emerged. The darkening windows of endless apartments, the winter streets leaking smoke along Sheridan, and a single mother at a bus stop with children clinging to her coat like possums.

11.

KENNETH CAUDILL WAS working the late shift at a gas station when he saw Norman's number come up on his phone. It was close to midnight.

Joanne was sitting at a table in the small kitchenette. When she identified herself, Kenneth was taken aback. He remembered her, or thought he did, then didn't. His voice took on a searching quality.

Joanne filled in the details. She was the downstairs neighbor, the girlfriend of the poet, Peter Coffey. She was separated from her partner and living with Norman as his nanny. She stalled.

Kenneth interrupted. 'Is something wrong?'

Joanne explained it.

Kenneth was guardedly suspicious. 'They locked Norman up for driving without a license?'

Joanne confessed, 'There was something else,' her voice suddenly hesitant. 'They found pot in a plastic bag in with Grace's snacks.'

Kenneth said directly, 'Norman doesn't smoke.' There was a question asked in him saying it. 'How much was stashed?'

'Not much, enough to take the edge off an afternoon.' Joanne took a deepening breath. 'There's something else… Norman told me to tell you about a letter. He said a name, Daniel Einhorn. He said you'd know.'

There was a dead silence on the line. Kenneth walked out from behind the cash register into the night, the fluorescent gas pump awning bright as a movie set.

Joanne asked, 'Who is Daniel Einhorn?'

Kenneth answered flatly. 'He's the guy I cheated on Norman with.'

A silence held. 'And the letter?'

'Norman sent a faked letter from a state health agency advising Daniel a partner he'd been with had tested positive for HIV and that he was required to appear for testing. When Daniel showed he discovered the letter was a hoax. He'd wanted to drop the matter. It turned out it wasn't up to him. Apparently, people did this sort of thing to one another. The department had a procedure. They kept the letter. A few days later, an investigator called asking him if he knew who could have sent it.'

'And Daniel suspected Norman?'

'Norman was high on the list, though Daniel had suspected me at first. I'd been looking for some sort of greater commitment. Daniel was also mixed up in a Ponzi scheme with his father-in-law. It had begun to unravel. Daniel had hidden his sexuality from his father-in-law.

After accusing me, he thought that maybe the letter had been sent by his father-in-law to make him want to commit suicide... I don't know. Toward the end Daniel was looking behind his back all the time. He felt he was being set up as the fall guy by his father-in-law.'

Kenneth trailed off. He said by way of atonement, 'You think bad of me, having sex with a married man?'

It was a question out of left field, yet Joanne allowed a measure of understanding. She said, 'No, Kenneth, I don't think badly of you.'

Kenneth let out a long breath. 'Honestly, I'm not placing you. I'm trying. You lived downstairs from us, that's what you said, right, and you were with a poet?'

Joanne raised her voice. 'Peter, he wasn't famous. You probably never noticed either of us. To be honest, I remember you only because of your looks. I used to say to Peter, I thought Norman was getting the better end of the deal.'

Kenneth let her candor register. He walked a small circle under the flood of light. 'Look, Joanne, this isn't a case of me not caring. I just don't know what I can do.'

Joanne felt a rushing relief. Could this be that Kenneth wasn't interested in returning? She contained the flood of relief. She needed to show continuing concern.

'Okay... but could you call Daniel, maybe do that, persuade him to say that it was a misunderstanding? The letter was sent as a joke. I think it would help greatly.'

Kenneth said flatly. 'The thing is, we're not together anymore.'

Joanne asked against her own interests, 'Do you still love Norman?'

In his silence, she asked again, and Kenneth answered, 'No.' He stepped beyond the icy cube of the gas station and began talking in a way that had nothing to do with what was happening with Norman. The call had evidently affirmed some decision already landed upon.

'I'm standing out here, and honest to God it seems there's no world beyond, just blackness. That is something, right, the way the eyes take time to adjust, to find what's really there? That's maybe how it is with most everything.' In his voice there was a disjunctive quality at odds with the person Joanne thought he would be.

Kenneth hunched his shoulders against the cold. 'To be honest, I never found my place in Chicago. I learned some lines for a play in school. It was everybody's idea I become famous. I was thinking the army, like my brother. I believe I had a sense of myself back in high school. It was just others pushing me to find something else. I eventually settled on Chicago. You could say that external pressures were brought to bear on me that were never my choice.'

He said it in a way so it was the distilled truth of what he had felt for a long time, and to say it with a measure of dignity, in one sentence, seemed enough.

'I auditioned for a short piece Norman was staging. He agreed to give me pointers. I was moved in with him before I was decided what I felt about any of it. I was on his sofa for a month, not paying rent, and, in the day, reading parts that weren't me. Norman helped, then didn't. I was just there on his couch. He wrote. He'd say nothing for hours, then come out of his room and begin making lunch, or invite me out for coffee. He didn't make any advances. He had these great ideas and theories on life. That's how he spent his days, working out what he thought about the world.

'I remember saying to him I had never heard of that as a job, but it seemed like the most important job in the world if you could handle it. It was a lonely life. He gave me money. Women in Chicago were different, or I couldn't find my footing. Maybe you need a sense of confidence and money, something that defines you... I don't know how to say it... how it shifted, my sense of who I was. I began thinking of myself as a potential partner. I was subordinate in the most obvious way. You know what it's like to have nothing, to walk around with nothing in your pocket? In the city you stop making eye contact. It's the opposite of how you might think of city life, of all those millions of people, and suddenly, you're alone...'

Kenneth let out a long breath. He had his index finger and thumb to his head, his cigarette smoldering. He took another long pull. He was settled on giving an account of himself.

'I'll be honest, I never wanted to hear anything again from Norman. One of my major problems has been letting people define me. I'd never been with a man before I moved in with Norman, and then he ended up not being the first. I don't know how to explain it. I reconfigured myself to how I thought Norman wanted me to be, so when it happened, I would be ready, if that makes sense – not the physical part of it, but somehow the emotional readiness. I got in the habit of men buying me things. I gave that vibe at a certain point, the daytime cafés and the transience of a life where I found myself the object of men's advances.'

There was the crunch of gravel underfoot, Kenneth moving out toward the further reach of the dark. 'I think for the longest time, up in Chicago, I was looking at a version of me that was me and wasn't me. Then things changed for Norman. He finished a play about his parents. He attributed his success to me. I was with him at parties. He just reached for my hand. He started wanting it then. I was suddenly somebody else entirely. It was overwhelming. I never loved him, not like that. Sometimes I've tried to explain it as honestly as I can, and the people I've said it to, they've condemned me, and asked, "How could you?" when I don't think it would be said of a woman. They do it all the time. I was just holding onto something, just surviving.'

Joanne felt the trenchant weight of his words, this same life explained, the hallway, the kitchen, the office, all of it re-appropriated and begun again in Kenneth's absence. She said quietly, 'Everything you just said, I've felt – the aloneness, the fear, all of it.'

Kenneth said again, 'I wish I could place you better, but, honestly, I think Norman has made a good choice.'

Joanne closed her eyes at the words *good choice*, her prescriptive, scolding directive toward Grace, the make *good choices* simplicity of assessing the world. It was obvious she had alighted on a life in transition, in the way the Prodigal Son must have returned, not so much changed, but with a greater awareness and deeper regard for the *bad choices* made. She had suddenly the idea of a civil ceremony broaching modern reality, 'Dearly beloved, we are here to join these two, who have made some very *good choices...*' That was all one could hope for, really.

It rescued her from the moment. She said, for the discharge of honesty, 'I wouldn't like to put myself up against you. That's what I feared in calling you, that you'd come back, that I wouldn't stand a chance.' She was trying to contain her emotions still, and couldn't. She was crying. It was better he knew it, better she revealed it, too, to herself.

Kenneth said, as a non sequitur to break the mood, or to offer her the alternative. 'I was baptized last month by an orderly at my mother's nursing home. Thomas Strait, a Christian with liberal views who reads his Bible in how the *Word* is meant to be received. We did the baptizing in my mother's room at the home in the handicapped shower. The shower started, and I felt saved in a way I never did before. Thomas says people don't value what it truly means to be saved, to know that for all Eternity you will live in the light of the Almighty.'

Joanne felt prompted to respond in a way Kenneth felt was testimony. 'Peter, he went out to Oklahoma in the fall late last year and never came back.'

Kenneth made a whistling noise. 'That sounds like the first line of a very long and very complicated end to something that needs the power of Jesus's healing love.'

It roused her, the stark simplicity of the message. It was just beyond her, or it was at that point, but she recognized it in Kenneth. It was enough to know it existed and that it might be accessed eventually.

They talked some more, or Kenneth did. Joanne put the phone to her other ear. There was a threshold beyond which one lost interest or compassion in another human being, Kenneth moving to issues that predated Norman, disconnected from her, and yet there were points and times when it made a difference, not to the listener, but to the one talking. Joanne held a silence in deference to what she might need eventually, this compassion and understanding.

Mercifully, a pickup rolled over a rubber trigger mechanism. A bell sounded like the start to a prizefight. Kenneth's voice was suddenly rushed. 'Look, I got to get this, but you tell Norman, I've accepted Jesus Christ as my savior. I know he'll think it cliché, and I pray for his soul.'

He was gone and the line dead in Joanne's ear.

What was significant, upon reflection, was how Kenneth had asked nothing about Grace. It had passed midnight. She could see it by a clock in the kitchen, the day ended somewhere back in the conversation, in the way time and years can escape notice.

12.

DANIEL EINHORN DIDN'T sleep with his wife anymore. It happened without argument, part of the natural evolution of a relationship that had diverged along the way. Einhorn was in his office. There were overseas markets that needed attention at 3 a.m., in the voracious insistence that capital and opportunity awaited no one.

He stared at the cycle of feeds on the home security system, stopped on his wife's bedroom. A TV threw a shifting light, so there was apparent movement and the faint sound of a laugh track, a rumor of life, when it was just the two of them.

Elaine was asleep. Einhorn zoomed in further. He could see she was wearing her mouth guard. It upset him greatly, in the way Jesus in the Garden of Gethsemane had chided Peter to stay awake and keep him company. She had benefitted from all that had been perpetrated.

He was tempted to wake and involve her in what was to come. He felt it would happen tonight. He was shaking.

There would be no reprieve. He was still the outsider in the family nearly thirty years after marrying Elaine. It hurt, but this was what the great reach of men like his father-in-law Saul Herzog could exact in loyalty; how Saul had come to head the Chicago office of Goldman Sachs and head it early.

They would come for him here, Saul's men, and whatever transpired, he understood Elaine would acquiesce. Einhorn was no match in the pitting of Elaine's loyalty to him against her father.

In pajamas and bare feet, Einhorn was like a penitent on a long and difficult path. He had been called the previous late afternoon by law enforcement. At first hesitant, he had stepped out in the lobby away from Saul, who had looked up and seen him. They were in the endgame of a Ponzi scheme unraveling with the financial crisis. It was only a matter of time.

The call had turned out to be about the fraudulent Health Department Letter he had received months before. His tone registered the halting embarrassment of somebody caught out, but it was not something he could explain to Saul, not the essence of what was ostensibly a gay affair. He was caught in the sullen awareness that this was the end, or the beginning of the end. Saul had watched him throughout the call and at the end, he came forward, inquiring who had called. Under the pressure of deceit, Einhorn had named a client who would not and did not corroborate that there had been a call. It was in this way that Daniel Einhorn knew his life was over, and so suddenly, but it was not unexpected.

For the better part of a decade Einhorn had been watching his back, the secret trysts in hotels in the late afternoon, the complicated sequence of heading to the health club, changing for a leisurely run, and ending up literally running to a hotel room for hours lost here and there. It was a sexual awakening that might have been tolerated and managed under different circumstances. The world was an enlightened place. At issue was not Einhorn's homosexuality, but Saul's essential hold on him. Einhorn didn't conceivably have a life without Saul Herzog. They were in too deep in a fraud that could not see any break in the ranks.

Einhorn knew in his heart that he was a hand-picked scapegoat from the very beginning, chosen purposely three decades ago for his loose-ended family, for his expendability when the time came. Though, at the time, Saul had lauded Einhorn and made an elaborate pretense that Einhorn held a great sway and power within the family, because it would be needed in whatever defense Saul eventually mounted. In this regard, Saul was the most charismatic, sinister and calculating of characters Einhorn would ever know, and yet he submitted to Saul's overtures, when the end was always inevitable.

He imagined now the amalgam of details, how it would end – his disappearance. At first take, it would seem a good, stable life – Daniel Einhorn, married twenty-seven years, husband of Elaine Einhorn, father to four children – a grounding series of facts establishing a life and fidelity in marriage. He had a son with a Harvard MBA who had been on the fast track in New York with Lehman Brothers before its sudden collapse during the Financial Meltdown. There were three daughters married to doctors. He gave generously to worthy causes. His youngest daughter, Rachel, had a son, Noah, with Cystic Fibrosis. He had run a marathon to raise awareness and pushed Noah in a modified baby jogger. He had a picture of the finish line on his desk and in his wallet. This would undoubtedly be the shot against which the enigma of his disappearance would be cast, until the eventual disclosure of the fraud that had been perpetrated. It would be all Einhorn.

His relationship with Elaine dated to a 4th of July party at the Herzogs' during the deregulatory zeal of the Reagan Administration and Trickle-down economics. He was interning at the time with Sachs. Elaine, a twenty-eight-year-old debutante, had studied psychology and was at a loose end. She was not unattractive, but she didn't catch Einhorn's eye in a way where something might blossom, and yet Saul insistently put them together.

Einhorn was no fool and understood that Elaine was part of the package being offered. If Elaine was mindful of it, she never let on. She had seemingly been set up with a series of love interests all aligned with Saul's business partners. She discussed them openly, without indicating that Einhorn was any different. Her sisters had been married off, but to more connected families, life for the Herzogs tied to a series of mergers and acquisitions, so why should love fall so far outside the domain of practical interests?

It was never stated that way, but it was felt and lived by all the Herzogs and their ilk, and if the worst that could be said of them was that none of them fell head over heels in love, then so be it.

In swapping out one existence for another, Einhorn became part of family gatherings centered on tradition and ceremony. They had a rabbi on hand to bless each and every gathering for the equanimity of moral guidance, and their house was always filled with men of notable distinction in finance and industry, willing to invest, and if there were few among them who might have been considered good-looking, well, they were concerned with greater interests, like tradition and purity of stock.

Einhorn was the exception. He had rowed at Yale. He was athletically and academically distinguished, and yet he bore a family secret. His mother, a one-time beauty, didn't know who Einhorn's father was exactly, but she was sure he was one of any number of men, less than five, she assured him of it. She used to count them off on her hand, one at a time, with an apparent history that still tugged at her heart in the baited sense of how in demand she once was. She was defined by her looks. As Saul intuited, good looks could impede one's interest.

Einhorn had advanced against all odds, but the prejudice was there. He was the tolerated guest at friends' houses, regarded with quiet suspicion. He did nothing to incite this, but it was said of him, as he grew into manhood, that other men's girlfriends and wives were always interested in him. Early on in high school he had aligned with how tragic heroes in the Greek and Shakespearean tragedies had irreconcilable flaws that were their undoing, and he had embraced this essential fatalism, not least after confiding in a drama teacher, who had set his hand on Einhorn's knee and then eventually Einhorn's cock, imparting that nothing was gained without courage and risk-taking. So Einhorn submitted, tragedy alive, his thick penis in the hand of his instructor, who explained how in ancient times wisdom was imparted between men and boys. It fucked Einhorn up.

Elaine Herzog was an answer to a question yet not fully answered in Einhorn's heart, but what he had believed in more back then was the genius and prospect of what Saul Herzog was offering him, and so he became a fixture at the house at Saul's behest. In late fall that same year after the 4th of July party, he asked for Elaine's hand in marriage. Elaine deferred to her father. Einhorn should ask Saul. It was how it was done with the Herzogs.

He felt, in retrospect, in entering the pageant of their family, the stirring of a tragedy, and yet he willingly took his place with the understanding that this was the best he could have achieved under the circumstances, and that achieving anything short of this would have been a failed life. He knew the risks, and he had accepted them. It didn't make it easier now, but there could be no denying it.

It surfaced, the wager of what he had agreed to so long ago, the halcyon days of that summer into early fall, the intoxication of luxury such a stark contrast to his growing up in a two-room apartment with his mother, the great ceremony of it, and how Saul had his secretary pre-order two kosher porterhouse steaks and a bottle of 1956 Bordeaux in the advent of Einhorn's asking for Elaine's hand. It was as Saul had planned it, but it seemed all down to Einhorn's good fortune, his persuasion and charm, when it was otherwise.

It was a complicated association. As Saul put it, a hypnotist could not make a man do what he didn't want to, but a hypnotist could call upon what was within a person. And Saul, a reader of the Old Testament, fell upon the story of Daniel and told it to Einhorn – how it was some trick, how the Daniel of the Bible put his head in the mouth of a lion, and that it required great faith, and that he, Saul, could tell Einhorn had come from a people who were used to putting their heads in the mouths of lions. It was decided then, not by Einhorn but by Saul, how the relationship would unfold.

On the appointed afternoon of the engagement offer, Saul was down in the baths at the Union League Club. He had insisted Einhorn join him before dinner, Saul, then, in the company of a gracious Czech named Pavel Matějček, a valet wearing a white smock. Since his arrival in America, Pavel had spent his days folding towels and robes and filling up plastic cups with mouthwash and setting out talcum powder and deodorant for the members of the Union League Club. He was a permanent fixture who affirmed certain truths for Saul, namely that the poor were necessarily dependent on the rich for their livelihood, and the best of them understood this.

It was perhaps Pavel's greatest gift, and why he was still alive when others had been less fortunate under Soviet occupation, and yet, in America, for all his abiding belief in free markets, Pavel Matějček would eventually lose everything to Saul's Ponzi scheme. In fact, it was partly Pavel's money that was paying for dinners and expenses upon which he never would have dreamt of spending his money.

Pavel held a towel toward Saul, who, dripping wet, was pink as a lobster in a mill of men coming and going from the showers in a billow of steam; men of great means, like fat babies, cherubs just born into the world by some monstrous, smoking machinery.

Saul was in the process of a joke. He could and did tell the most subversive of jokes, usually about his own people, which made it all the more scandalous and unnerving.

Saul began again, for Einhorn's sake, and for two other fat men who appeared and were given towels by Pavel.

'Moscow, in deepest winter. A rumor spreads through the city that meat will be available the next day at a Butcher's Shop. Hundreds arrive. They carry stools, vodka, and chessboards. There is great excitement. At 3 a.m., the butcher comes out and says, "Comrades, The Party Central Committee called. It turns out there won't be meat for everyone. Jews go home." The Jews leave. The rest continue to wait. At 8 a.m., the butcher comes out again: "Comrades, I've just had another call from Central Committee. It turns

out there will be no meat at all. You should all go home."
The crowd disperses, grumbling all the while, "Those
bloody Jews, they get all the luck!"'

At the time of the proposal, Einhorn was circulating an
aggrandizing story about an alleged relationship with a
Rockefeller heiress he had dated a year earlier while at
Yale. Saul had the story vetted, he made it his business to
investigate these sorts of claims in the cut-throat business
of Finance. It was key to unraveling the psyche of potential
clients. He discovered it was more Einhorn's dumbstruck
infatuation with a Rockefeller grand-niece he had met at a
party on the Upper East Side.

Saul dropped the grand-niece's name amidst the hum of
dinner, while attempting to pour the last of a second bottle
of Bordeaux. Einhorn put his hand over his glass with a
decided temperance. The evening had gotten away from
him, Saul's eyes flashing anger as he continued pouring,
the Bordeaux drenching Einhorn's cuff-linked wrist, so it
wasn't altogether apparent whether Saul knew what he was
doing or not, but of course he had.

According to Saul, there were only so many people
of means in the world. Einhorn had to understand this,
and there were even fewer Rockefellers, and they were a
damnable breed of bluebloods and anti-Semites, and he
knew every one of them by name, and it was his business to
divest them of as much of their money as humanly possible.

He mentioned the Rockefeller grand-niece by name

again. Einhorn said nothing. It was thus established that Einhorn was a liar, and it didn't matter, just that it was understood between them that he was, in fact, a liar. He was thus chastened. As Saul put it, 'One thing you can't do is to pull the wool over Saul's eyes.'

Saul and his people were old hands at history. They had survived the rise and fall of empires, the Roman, the Byzantine, the Ottoman and the scourge of countless pogroms. They had experienced the best and the worst of times. They had been roused, beaten and dragged from their homes, starved and kicked around Europe, and then they had found America and Wall Street.

Elaine was still asleep. Einhorn thought of speaking over the intercom for the revelation of his voice, but she wasn't his preoccupation anymore. He left his office and stood in the kitchen along the annex to what had been his son's and then his eldest daughter's apartment. They had coveted privacy and independence long before they ever left home. He had been a good provider, but a lousy father. He would submit to this.

He used a pay-as-you-go cell phone to contact his lawyer. He called from inside a walk-in cedar closet with the mordant understanding that this was how it happened in horror movies, so the only option was the closet when the monster was in the house.

He shut the door behind him. He stood amidst his daughters' clothes from years earlier, the rows of imported cashmere cardigans, the Izods in the pastel colors and pop-up collars that were no longer in fashion, along with the obscene number of dresses, shoes, boots, sneakers and sandals, many in their original boxes, never worn, or worn once. In their totality, they suggested a great fraud had been committed, in the way Imelda Marcos and her three thousand pairs of shoes had sparked true moral outrage in a world grown too accustomed to mass graves.

What Daniel Einhorn had to do was not to believe most things that were said about him and his kind and, furthermore, to protect his family by surrounding them with like-minded frauds, in a confederacy of entitlement, in a string of Day Schools where each measured what they had against those who had as much, if not more, so a child could say without reproach, 'Why don't we have what they have?'

They were not easily understood, the feelings of the privileged, but they could and did feel a genuine hurt that at times life wasn't turning out as it should and that there were things as yet beyond their reach, and that $40 million was, in fact, not nearly enough money, so the hurt of a child, no matter how misguided, was still a genuine hurt, and they, the children, were essentially blameless and needed unequivocal protection. They were victims who didn't seem like victims, and, when justice was meted out, they were the ones most often scorned, when they were a symptom and not the problem itself.

He might have begun his defense thus, in the relative comparison to what others had – well, not the majority, but in relation to those who mattered. He could not account for those who had few aspirations and even less drive, for it was an undeniable fact that, despite what it said in the Declaration of Independence, all men were not created equal. He believed this in his heart – not that men *could* not aspire to greatness, but most *did* not. That was a crime in itself. Nothing had come easy.

Einhorn spoke to his lawyer in the whispering voice of someone contemplating suicide, staring through the slats in the porthole window, a cold eye fixed on the desolate expanse of lawn and a covered swimming pool and pump house that had cost the earth, which nobody used, or hardly ever used.

He described the dark, how alone he felt. In the background, he could hear his lawyer shuffling papers. He had the distinct sense a light had been flicked on the other end of the line. It infused the grey where he was standing. In previous confidential talks with his lawyer, he had revealed the nature and extent of the fraud to which he had been party, so it was a matter not only of accounting for the monies, uncovering his complicity and culpability in the scam, but establishing that he was not the kingpin behind the fraud and that it was, in fact, masterminded by his father-in-law, Saul. He had papers to that effect, and tapes of conversations in a deposit box, but in the call now there was no talk of a plea bargain, nothing that suggested that he was planning on living, or exposing Saul.

Einhorn had come to a grander realization about himself. He was ready to assume personal responsibility. This was Saul's doing. But it went deeper, and, if it were not this fraud, it would have been some other fraud perpetrated alongside somebody else equally as reprehensible as Saul Herzog. At best, he and Saul had found one another.

In not acting, in not going forward with the information he had on Saul, he was tacitly refusing to enter the narrative of accountability and full disclosure. His and Saul's fraud was small potatoes really, running into eighty million dollars tops, when institutional fraud in the mortgage sector ran into the hundreds of billions.

If he had come forward first, he knew he could have negotiated a plea, faced the prospect of a white-collar jail that was no jail in the traditional sense of what lock-up could be like amidst rapists and murderers. He might have received a ten-year stretch, served five to six with good behavior. There were always second acts in American life. There was enough life ahead of him. It was an option.

There was the hope again that, in pressing the intercom, in calling for Elaine, she might yet come down, cry, and sit with him and understand that it was a damnable proposition all along, this life, that together they might brave what was to come, and arrive at a clearer understanding of who and what they had been as a couple, in what they had struggled to maintain between them. For there was something between them: the children.

Elaine had been faithful and agreeable, and, whatever the arrangement of their marriage as conceived by Saul, whatever Elaine thought in the cold light of deliberation, there must have been a sense that something held between them.

This, of course, was not the whole truth. There were men Elaine had liked more, men of lesser stature, in particular a gentile of low standing, and a man not open to compromise, or acceptable to Saul. In submitting to marrying Einhorn, Elaine had settled on the least of all terrible options. If she had a hint of what was slowly unfolding, if the demise of the family was at hand, she never let on. She never broke rank, never offered succor to Einhorn. Elaine was doing what she had always done. She was watching out for her interests.

It was Einhorn who was presuming too much, and, at the back of it, there was the great shame of Kenneth Caudill, what Einhorn had resorted to, so it was, in the end, his own undoing really. Kenneth Caudill had called him hours earlier, looking for money. Einhorn couldn't tell if it was a ruse on the part of the FBI. It seemed so convenient, such a set-up. Kenneth wanted $50,000 to keep quiet. Einhorn had simply hung up mid-call.

Einhorn looked up. A light shone at the gated entrance to the house, then died. A shadow emerged. A car moved across the crackle of the loose stone drive. He was at the window. A door opened and then closed without sound. It was happening as though it had been planned for a long time, which it had.

He decided the closet was an ignoble place to be found hiding. His office was a far better place. Let them find him in the act of uploading or downloading a file, doing something suspicious and unnerving and deserving of his fate. Let Saul's men make a mistake and kill him in his leather chair. Let Saul's plan backfire. Let the forensics put together the last moments of his life, so it would be tragic, but, by uploading an incriminating file, it would be determined that Einhorn had found a decency and humanity to come forward before he was shot in the face.

13.

THERE WERE PEOPLE in spandex working out in the fitness center at five fifteen in the morning. Nate passed them. The breakfast buffet wasn't open for another fifteen minutes.

The center had a galactic feel of self-improvement. An infinity pool floated in an effervescent shimmer, a bead of mercury advancing the idea of space without boundaries, auguring how home in the future would most probably be experienced in a float of unmoored space aboard interstellar vessels crossing the void.

Nate saw existence better in the moment, what true history revealed, deep emptiness, so there was something to Ursula and Frank Grey Eyes' way of seeing the universe.

It stalked him still, the quiet assessment of his time back home again, the inlaid memorial plaque out at the graveyard recessed into the grass for the unimpeded run of lawn equipment, and his house out there and now owned by somebody else. It seemed strange you could be so dissociated from your history that the recording of a deed could preclude you from ever returning, that your rights could be thus terminated.

He remembered Ursula telling him about what Frank had said, that the world was not owned, and that this was the great mistake the white man made that had caused so many wars. Of course, this opinion made Frank a bum in the eyes of everybody else, but Ursula believed it, and it was why she loved Nate too. He had walked willingly into the wilderness, away from possessions.

Ursula described a night in downtown Toronto when Frank had stood in the middle of a traffic island, dangerously drunk, shouting that the cars were salmon in the late crush of evening spawn. He kept shouting it to everybody around him. All you had to do was close your eyes and you could see it, the other life beyond the immediate one. Things died and were reincarnated as something it was not always possible to imagine, because that was the creator's great trick. All was concealed, and it was the job of men like Frank Grey Eyes to go out and uncover it.

Frank wanted to just scoop up the salmon the way his ancestors had, to stand in the flowing, throbbing stream of life. Ursula held him back. She said that the salmon had not completed their journey. Frank stopped. He said that he had been wise finding someone like Ursula. She saw the salmon like he saw them.

They stood amidst the shoal of life as it passed around them on a traffic island in downtown Toronto and, together, they discovered where the salmon had gone. It was beautiful to know that nothing ever truly disappeared, that they were there, as Frank Grey Eyes had said, and that Toronto wasn't the mistake everyone had said it was when he'd announced his departure.

Nate remembered how Ursula told him the story, the beauty of it, when it was nothing but a struggle with a drunk in the middle of an intersection, but she could invest herself with the spirit of another, and so it was about what Frank believed.

There was that pain in his abdomen again. He called to Ursula in the way he did when he was alone at the cabin, gave voice to her name like a soft incantation. It was almost enough to bring her to him.

He tried to call on the great strength of the great Per Ingebretson, that figure his father had so valiantly conjured to know that a man could continue alone.

He had talked about Per and his journey to Ursula. She'd smiled and imagined how the squaws would have found him strong and capable. To the First Nation's people, the first incarnation of the white man was not feared. They were of a similar spirit, making their way without possessions in the world.

On the ground she had drawn a circle around Per and around her people, and then another around Nate, and around herself, and then a greater circle around the entirety of circles so it made sense of life in the way she lived it.

In taking him in the circle of her arms and the girdle of her hips, she created another circle, so he felt the pulse and twitch of energy, the give of her insides in the gentle pulling oneness, letting him find his way back to a place of first origins. This is how love should find two people, conjoined as one.

Nate was on the road by five forty-five. He passed the graveyard where his father was interred, the hoary frosting on the lawn so it looked, not so much a graveyard, but a golf course.

It was strange, the converging landscape of places. He was seeing life through Ursula's eyes. What he remembered of his father was a succession of afternoons at the Winnetka Country Club, a mid-morning splash of soda and dash of Scotch poured from a flask in an allotted recklessness essential to confronting life, his father smoking in deep pulls, a smokiness that blued the air, then waving his way out of the smoke in the sheer act of remembrance, as though he had come from a distant front, which, of course, he had.

His father had returned from the war in the South Pacific as an atheist, a hero, though he hadn't felt like one. It was a disaffection that beset many of his generation, yet it never found a name like it did in Vietnam. Medication was self-administered from a bottle.

His father had favored golf as the modern incarnation of hushed containment of how the world might yet be recouped. He was deadly serious. Golf came closest to the dignified reach of what American greatness could maintain after the turmoil of two world wars, a refinement of the wild links courses of Scotland, re-envisioned as a more attenuated game played along the sunbaked peninsula of Florida, and up through the swelter of Augusta, or in the dry desert of Palm Springs. This, his father believed, was how you reoriented a society, set the quiet bounds of restriction within the greater illusion of a democracy. You set a man like Arnold Palmer out there, Arnie's Army!

His father liked Palmer best for his expansive vision, for the far reach of his firmly hit tee shot. A ball sailing along the fairway, the entire gallery following its course with hushed admiration, knowing it should, or would, land, and most always did, within ten yards of what was expected.

His father was proud that America could offer the world a man of such distinguished character and grace; Palmer, a man most comfortable in the bosom of the great democracy, walking calmly among enthusiastic spectators. The British Empire had fallen because of snobs and bores with a great imperial condescension of its subjects, and here was Palmer, a new man for a new age; a man among men.

What his father liked was the keen sense of the predictable: Palmer, deferential, genteel, nodding to his club-laden caddy, conferring intent with simple eye contact, suggesting a six or seven iron on the approach shot, and then proceeding with a striding advance along a flush of fairway, and arriving at the velvet texture of the green that called for a more deliberate, more thorough read of the way the lines broke, the wide arc of Palmer's putt improbably breaking toward the hole along a line of sight only Palmer could read. And then the tempered applause, while, in the offing, the prospect of a well-made drink awaited, poured by a good-natured Negro at the clubhouse, where neither Negroes nor women alike, were ever going to become members. There were simply bounds that needed to be kept.

It was easy to analyze history, to see a grave and assess a life, when the dull stuff of everyday life disappeared, leaving the subconscious to decide what was worth keeping.

Nate was not guiltless. There were other reasons beyond his relationship with his father that had kept him away, reasons connected to what might have been conceivably criminal acts. Nate had done something awful before he left for Canada.

In its most poetic terms, he had taken down the fawn of innocence, or that was how Frank Grey Eyes might have put it if he had known about it. There were legal terms, though, for what he had done, statutory rape was one that fitted with the way he had pushed himself on his best friend's kid sister Janice Marsh, compelling her to give up something that should have been cherished and preserved for someone truly deserving.

He kept nothing back from Ursula. She had quieted him, told him how she loved him and to stop. It was enough. She told her own story over his. When she walked, she had a slight limp from when Frank had kicked her and broken her hip. Each time she walked she felt not her pain, but the dull ache of Frank's regret, so it was completed, in the way everything was completed. When she limped, she did so with the memory of Frank, the bone wove his anger and love and frustration into her hip.

Nate thought about it as he drove in a slow circle through

his old neighborhood before heading back into town, the way the circle might be closed.

He checked the digital clock. It was not yet quite six in the morning. In looking up, he nearly collided with a Lincoln as big as a hearse. It was his fault. He made eye contact with the driver to acknowledge that he had been in the wrong. There were two men sitting up front. He saw the red pulse of a cigarette glow in the dark orb of the driver's head, and a soft glow showed the pair of eyes of the passenger, but just for a moment.

14.

DANIEL EINHORN GAVE his lawyer the location of a deposit box and where a key was hidden for his Chicago Union Club locker. There was a stash of money, along with bonds and securities that could be accessed and that, with discretion, if his children adjusted and spent wisely, if they stayed below the radar of the IRS, if the sum of their purchases was not too extravagant – they might find helpful, and, in the long run, when the IRS stopped looking, when the present scourge of accountability passed, they could resume life in the natural order where there would always be a separation of the rich from the poor.

Einhorn was not a snob in believing this, more a realist, aligned with how even Jesus conceded the poor would always be among us, so the Almighty could live with around 7 per cent unemployment, the best that could be hoped for in an imperfect world.

He was deadly serious in his general assessment of the economy and life in general. Nothing was a given, nor could anything be taken for granted. It was all earned. You were as good as how far you could stretch a lie, reel in expectations, and deliver within a margin of agreeable return.

Yes, there was the grim understanding that it had all been a great cash grab, the millions stashed in the deregulation of markets that allowed and damn-near sanctioned fraud when circumstances might have turned out differently if expectations had been tempered, if the realities of a flattening of growth and wages and the demise of what was formerly known as the middle class had been acknowledged. But expectations had not been tempered. It was not just the Wall Street fraudsters, but greed spurred by those insufferable alleged victims, who, in demanding upwards of 20 per cent minimum return on investments, simply looked the other way as financial shenanigans were set in place to hide the truth that there were no more good paying jobs, and that what had existed in their parents' time, a true and honest middle class, was long gone.

What Einhorn believed, if he were truly pushed, was that there was a point just before the grand deception of his and Saul's fraud, when there had been Vision and Hope. He had worked with special interest groups related to gaining eminent domain along a corridor running through three contiguous states for a Wind Farm along Tornado Alley. They had a prospectus drawn up, the facts and returns. It was a legitimate venture. The valuation ran into the billions. It would have covered all the losses, reconciled the Ponzi scheme and made it right. They were ahead of the curve on Thinking Green. This was good for America, for sustainable homegrown energy and domestic jobs, a win-win along fallow tracts of land that could easily have been used, and yet, it proved an insurmountable legal undertaking tied to absolute bureaucracy at the State and Federal levels.

There had been an abiding patriotism and a great outlay of cash that included the savings of Pavel Matějček. The first monies were spent judiciously, until it was understood there would be no corridor, and funds set aside to influence the election of candidates who might vote Green in future elections were not guaranteed. Politics was like pissing against the wind, so, eventually, said monies were syphoned off for personal use.

What Einhorn believed anathema to the system was faithlessness. Faith required a willful commitment to that which might never be fully explained on a balance sheet. Or, put another way, what Daniel Einhorn needed was more time, and, during his more prone, vulnerable and sanguine moments, he imagined himself a disconsolate Moses stopped by some shortsighted Rabbis who wouldn't give eminent domain to part the Red Sea. He had planned on using the line under oath to make those accusing him understand the monumental will that Creation demanded.

Einhorn was about to exit the walk-in closet when he saw on a shelf a series of small boxes tucked away and tied with a coarse, old-fashioned string. He smelled a dank musk of animal oils, a water-repellant greasiness of worn woolens, sweaters, socks and scarves still redolent with a whiff of a crystalized sea salt from the winter his youngest daughter, Rachel, had spent along the Brittany coast under grey clouds and unassailing winds.

It stopped him cold, how some of the money spent could never be fully understood or explained, how it had played in the coming-of-age of his beloved daughter Rachel, who on a semester abroad program in France had come under the sway of Philippe Rotheneuf, a rugged Breton with big weather-hewn hands and a Roman nose, a Spartacus or an Argonaut look-alike.

Einhorn searched the driveway again. He was sure he could hear a noise at the front door. He moved further toward the back of the closet.

What he rallied around was the memory of Rachel, how she had made her appeal to him, and not to Elaine, when she got into trouble in France. It was no small comfort to find his youngest, the brightest of his children, needing him, so there was an act of generosity and kindness bestowed along the way. A life had been saved. The money had mattered. It had made a difference!

He held his breath. My God! To have it end like this. He thought of calling Rachel, but it wouldn't have been fair. She might be the only one to mourn him truly, or maybe, with his death, a great secret would be ended, and she would be left assured that only she alone would remember. It was difficult deciding which way she might see it.

At the time Rachel needed him, she was in the flush of a

radiant emergence that was all from his side of the family. She had inherited the looks of his ill-fated, beautiful mother. For Einhorn, he had a feeling that here was a reclaimed beauty resurrected in the world, and that this time it could be made right. Rachel was the envy of other girls, and often had to appeal to boys for friendship. As with Einhorn, her looks had worked against her.

There had been much resistance on Elaine's part to letting Rachel go abroad, but it was Einhorn's gift to his daughter. He insisted. In his heart, he knew his life would end horribly, and that if he had lost his elder three children, he would make amends with Rachel. She deserved this much.

She had a boyfriend at the time, the son of a notable family who had funds tied up with Saul, so the boyfriend felt sufficiently secure in taking advantage of Rachel. It was tacitly endorsed, if not promoted, by Saul. This was the essence of big-time fraud, the swagger of familiarity, the intersection of lives and family, so proper accounting procedures were not adhered to, because Saul worked a sort of magic that needed a measure of faith, and, though everyone knew Saul was most probably a crook, he was their crook.

It turned out in the end, for all the elaborate planning and application letters and references, the boyfriend had also been accepted into the program, so a freedom gained was suddenly taken. Einhorn saw it in his daughter's eyes, the shock and the awareness she had been caught out. She was her father's daughter. He was deeply pained by how it was made known to his daughter just how calculating the world was, but he was insistent that she learned it early. The boyfriend sprung it like a surprise, so, in a calculated maneuver, he had a continent between Einhorn and Rachel.

Einhorn kissed Rachel and told her to live life and to call often. He saw her off at O'Hare, as you might see an immigrant off to new lands. He hugged her, his lips on the crown of her head, so she was embarrassed, but he was entitled as a father. It was ending soon. Rachel reached up and touched his nose.

There was culture over there. She should try every cheese and wine. She should know her options. He was shouting 'Run' without actually saying it. He believed she understood. Saul accompanied them to the airport. He didn't like the exchange rate. That was all he said.

Einhorn drew further into the closet. He regretted now not having a gun. He heard noises downstairs. They were, of course, fucking, this boyfriend and Rachel. At the boyfriend's insistence, they boorishly wore matching college sweatshirts, hoodies, and high-tops and toted knapsacks with attached water bottles to the airport.

He received photos through email. Part of the process of parenthood was coming to terms with stomaching the shit-eating grin of a guy banging your little girl.

At the time, Philippe Rotheneuf was the proprietor of a stall at the Bird Market at the Ile de la Cité. He was selling domestic parakeets and finches, but also exotic parrots and cockatiels. For Rachel, the contrast was so shockingly glaring, an out-of-body experience, the sum of her life revealed in a damp market in early November, the beautiful alternative, the vagabond intrigue of Philippe. He coaxed a finch onto the crook of his index finger and, reaching for the tips of Rachel's fingers, the bird hopped from his finger to hers, the black drop of its eye staring at Rachel before it hopped back onto Philippe's finger. He reached into his pocket, gave her posies, and explained as best he could the nursery rhyme 'Ring Around the Rosie', and its connection to the Black Death.

The boyfriend, quietly seething, had a map of sights circled like a general. They were to meet friends in the Latin Quarter. He said it petulantly, and what had passed a moment before, the intensity of a touch, suddenly ended in the conspiracy of a shower that had threatened and finally opened in the heavens.

She had acted like a whore. They were headed toward the Left Bank. The boyfriend had trouble with the map. He hated the warren of goddamn streets. He could pronounce none of them. The French were all assholes. He couldn't wait to get back to America, the study abroad program affirming, not a tolerance and acceptance of other cultures, but rather his Americanness and American greatness; this, the undisclosed truth about pretty much all study abroad programs.

Notre Dame loomed as an afterthought in the grey slant of rain. Pigeons roosted in the crook of gargoyles and the beseeching outreach of saints looking heavenward, Parisians everywhere just then stopped under the awnings of cafés in an accommodation of the weather, the women in stockings and heels, and all smoking. By contrast, Rachel and her boyfriend were in North Face expedition jackets brought for the contingency of rain. There was the whispering whoosh of espresso machines and the boyfriend's voice in her ear. She was fucking him, and she felt absolutely nothing for him.

The next day Rachel returned. She had a bottle of champagne. Einhorn knew this. It was credited to his Visa card. A week later, she and Philippe traveled in a medieval pageant of caged birds on a rural train line to the fortified city of Saint-Malo. Philippe had aspirations of opening a culinary school and raising any number of babies. He was a peasant through and through. It became apparent to Rachel, not what she wanted, but what she didn't want.

Einhorn flew to Charles de Gaulle six weeks after it was discovered Rachel was no longer at school. The call came not from the school, but from the boyfriend's father, who called Saul, who immediately challenged Einhorn. The boyfriend was upset. He had accompanied Rachel to France to protect her, and beneath the revelation, Einhorn swelled with a secret pride that Rachel had done what she had set out to do and had found true love.

An investigation turned up a phone number that led to a series of calls. It was not exactly as Einhorn imagined. Rachel was hesitant. She thought he should come see her. There was concern in her voice. Her mother wasn't to know. It was agreed she and Philippe would meet Einhorn off the train at Saint-Malo.

It drove a wedge between Saul and Einhorn. Saul contended that the French had let the Germans march right into Paris. He held the country in the greatest disdain possible. He hated, equally, existentialism and a faithless disregard for God. It was almost too much to stomach for Einhorn, what they were doing between them, the lives under ruin, and to talk in these terms, to deliver such a sanctimonious assessment of a culture and a people.

Einhorn took the precaution of securing a driver off the flight from Charles de Gaulle. He had the driver drop him at a station before Saint-Malo, so it seemed the most natural of arrivals, when he had the basics of the escape plan established. The driver would await instruction. He worked with embassy attachés and was professionally accustomed to quick getaways and absolute secrecy. His rate was $1,700 a day.

Philippe was everything Einhorn expected, his hair pulled back in a ponytail. His face had an equine quality of strong peasant breeding. There was no awareness of what would happen in the coming days, or why Einhorn was there. Philippe was pleasing and hospitable and believed in his heart that Rachel loved him. He called Einhorn, *Mon Pere*.

It would have been easier if Philippe's motivations were less obvious, but Philippe embraced Einhorn in the way the peasant French greeted, slapping Einhorn hard on the back, kissing him on both sides of the cheek. He was like a great statue, say Michelangelo's David, who had stepped down from a pedestal and set about life in the ordinary world.

Einhorn felt in his loins the flicker of what his daughter must have felt, and he had the most disconcerting thought, that if he could swap out his life for this life, to be in the company of Philippe Rotheneuf, he would have done so.

They drove in an old Renault borrowed from a neighbor, Philippe scattering sheep with the horn. He used his fist like an anvil. The car could not accommodate his size. He negotiated a series of blind turns run along hedges that made the road dark and patchy with a black ice. He talked in his broken English, his head touching the roof of the car.

The seaside village appeared around a bend, sudden and complete, the fierceness of the Atlantic pulling smoke from chimneys against a sky hung on a shroud of grey mist. The smell was so insistently strong. It was in their nostrils, the charred wood, the coal and the salt, all of it mixed and defining a life by the sea. Further on, a crescent of beach was garlanded in a tidal swell of shifting seaweed.

The proposed location of the culinary school was halfway down a steep decline to a horseshoe pier that boiled in a chop of waves breaking over an ancient stone, while black-clad fishermen looked up momentarily, stitching and repairing nets in a fingering spool of filament like earnest spiders.

At the establishment, the one in question, for it was hard distinguishing it really, since the houses were all part of a long grey façade running toward the pier, they saw it, or saw chairs upended on a table. It was desolate, empty and cold. A laced curtain hung like a veil. Rain fell out of a grey sky.

They looked at it a second time. They might see it tomorrow. It was Sunday. It wasn't going anywhere. The owner, a devoted Catholic, observed the Sabbath, Einhorn, aware how a marrow cold morning might pass in medieval devotionals while a roast cooked in a sizzling fat and how, afterward, against a pull of windblown storm, an afternoon might be given to a roaring fire and a read of papers with a well-deserved plug of tobacco.

They passed the house going down the hill a third time. Philippe pointed through the streaking rain, the throated gurgle of gutters spluttering in a glazed runoff, whitewashed walls stained a sanguine iron-rust. Philippe spoke of a recipe that he had learned from his grandmother for mussels cooked in a white wine, served with a goat cheese garlic crouton. He would prepare it later.

Einhorn listened in a quiet betrayal, inventorying Philippe, infatuated by the immensity of his knowledge, Philippe's muscular hand on Einhorn's thigh in a familial familiarity of peasant closeness. It was evident, Philippe believed in the singularity of fate and could see no other reason Einhorn was here other than to sanction this union. He wore a cravat around a muscular, veined neck and emanated a hot ripeness of stale sweat in a layering of shirts with worn collars.

In the rear-view mirror, Einhorn averted his eyes from Philippe. He caught sight of Rachel, her mouth curved in the vague expression of resignation. She was already pregnant and fearful and wanted to be home again. She had bouts of morning sickness and looked grey as the landscape.

Philippe wanted Einhorn to see something. Rachel should stay. Philippe kissed her hand with a subtle intimacy that only the French could affect, the bud of his lips on the back of her hand. They proceeded down along a ragged coastal road against the pull of wind. The bay churned in a pewter swell. Against Philippe's advancing strides, Einhorn tried to keep up. He had to eventually trot, until they arrived at a series of caves where Philippe explained how, during the Neolithic age, man first committed his history in the simple story of the hunt. It brought Einhorn close to tears. This was everything he ever wanted, this life, this apparent freedom, this man.

It took three days before Einhorn could execute the escape. The professional driver, who had seen his share of intrigue and who had spent the three days a town over, syphoned the gas from the Renault, so it was a great consternation and uproar as a towering Philippe appeared in his nightshirt, like a mythic Cyclops, raging against the night.

They flew home Business Class. They stayed at a suite at The Plaza, looking out on Central Park. The next afternoon, Rachel emerged from a clinic on New York's Upper West Side. She was pale and disoriented, but on the other side of a great mistake. She held her father's arm. He hailed a cab, and they were gone toward the bustle of mid-town, while the Rotheneuf legacy, what was left of it, the bits and pieces, the flesh and blood, made its way along East 91st Street, toward the funneling sewers along the East Side

River, rounding the Statue of Liberty before being carried out to sea.

Rachel was a better mother for it, years later, when her mind was more determined. She married a doctor with the conscious understanding of what she was doing. Einhorn took her hand and gave her away in an extravagant affair that he paid for because this was how a daughter in some circles was still passed on, in the last shouldering of expense before she became the property and charge of some other man. She would never work a day in her life. It was a great accomplishment, not to have to want for anything of a material nature.

A check Einhorn had left for Philippe was eventually returned, along with the box of woolens Rachel had left behind, in what was the thoughtful evacuation of an American dream and an American girl. Philippe wrote a note in broken English that was heartbreaking. Einhorn read it and tore it up. Some things could never be explained, not by the deceiver, and not by the deceived.

They found him – that is, Saul's men found him – in the closet. It took a matter of an hour, a search methodically conducted room by room. He could hear their voices getting closer. He wet himself and felt a great shame in doing so.

15.

IN A SMALL interrogation room, Mr Ahmet, Walter's former legal counsel, stood in a threadbare suit with a missing button.

Mr Ahmet directed a guard to set a box on the metal table. As the guard did so, Mr Ahmet kept his hands midline with his body, assuming the grim prosecutorial aesthetic of a minor bureaucrat within a Kafka novel. In the folds of softer flesh around his eyes, an inky darkness showed the color of tea leaves. He was of some indeterminate immigrant stock, the Middle or Far Eastern, anywhere from Turkey to Uzbekistan. His receding hairline revealed a high, shiny forehead the color of walnut.

When the box was put down, Mr Ahmet thanked the guard. The door opened and closed again. When Mr Ahmet sat, he drew close to the table and introduced himself. He had been legal counsel to the officers accused in the alleged murder of two drug dealers. He had known Walter Price very, *very* well, right from the beginning of the case and on through the years.

It turned out that it had been Mr Ahmet's longest and most complex case, a watershed case when the city was beginning to change in its view of how policing was conducted. He explained it, how he had been hired because of civil rights advances and affirmative action. He was of that generation just past the great sweep of change and all those who came before. It was what interested him in the law, how righteousness could eventually prevail.

He was given to a moment of self-reflection and, shaking his head, said how the years had passed, and so quickly.

Mr Ahmet continued talking. He had made a great many friends in defending those who needed defending on the force. It had been his honor, advising and helping with the case. He stated it like he was giving a sworn testament on the record. He was, in some respects, the most unlikely of allies, his swarthy figure, his diminutive presence suggesting the tokenism of the era, but he took men as they came.

The system, yes, it was corrupt, or had been, rife with a demoralizing cronyism. He understood it. This was not akin to conceding one's lack of awareness of all that went on around him, but they were the times, and a man had a right to survive as best he might and to make compromises. He was, he declared, without prejudice. He understood the ways of the world. It was important to understand a man's motivations in all matters and proceed from there. He talked like legal counsel.

His long index finger touched the desk as he enumerated points along a history of his career and his own principles. He was a communicator, but, equally, a listener. His voice held a directness that suggested English was not his first language, not for the paucity of what was expressed, but in how he expressed himself. He came upon words, chose them. He was forthright and direct and spoke in complete sentences. It was a soothing sort of voice that could lull children to sleep.

Mr Ahmet stopped abruptly. He rattled a wet cough, dislodged something, which he turned in his mouth and then swallowed. His eyes were glossed. It took a moment. His breath was a pant. It was obvious he was sick. He recovered and, apologizing, raised his hand, then searched his inside pocket. He retrieved a pair of wire-rimmed glasses, put them on, the wire around the left ear and then the right, his eyes so magnified that he looked like an insect.

He seemed intent on sifting through the box, though he said, without looking up, 'I must tell you, I just learned this morning that the Daniel Einhorn you contacted with your letter, he is missing.'

Mr Ahmet stopped a moment, his hand on a file in the box. 'Mr Einhorn's lawyer, he called 911. The situation, I believe, was quite desperate. Federal prosecutors were ready to indict Mr Einhorn for a Ponzi scheme running into tens of millions. Regrettably, these are the times we live in. There are many like him, these swindlers, but of course, so many more victims. The police are not long arrived from what I gather, but Mr Einhorn is gone. The police interviewed Mrs Einhorn. She was at the house but she alleges that she heard nothing.'

Mr Ahmet shifted and leaned back from the box and, in so doing, removed his glasses with a slow deliberateness as he looked directly at Norman. 'Can you imagine, Mr Price, living in a house so big your own wife does not know where you are? My wife, she would love a house as big as this Daniel Einhorn's. But everything comes at a cost, I tell her, and yet she would have it anyway if she had the chance.'

Mr Ahmet held Norman's stare. 'I am almost certain this Mr Einhorn has come to great harm. There is a story there somewhere. Maybe you can write it?'

Norman said curtly, 'I don't write crime stories.' Then he qualified his remark. 'I don't deal in bodies... in a body count.'

He might have stopped there, but there was something grandiose and blusterous about him, and despite the situation, despite knowing why Mr Ahmet was actually there, he added, 'As a writer, I am in search of a suspicion of happiness.'

The remark seemed to delight Mr Ahmet, who smiled and said, 'Ah, yes, I am aware of your *talents*.'

Mr Ahmed's myopic eyes were still fixed on Norman. His eyebrows moved of their own accord. 'If I may suggest it, Mr Price, you should meet my sister-in-law at some point. She is the one in the family with the brains, and she will make a thing complicated when it need not be. She is a Mr Woody Allen fan. She likes the sort of movie you describe, where there's "a suspicion of happiness..." She likes unease. She has been through two husbands and many more lovers. She is a scandalous, beautiful and very independent woman. It seems little satisfies her, but I have said to her that I believe bad conscience is always tied to bad acts.

As proof, I said to her, what this Mr Woody was alleged to have done, sleeping with his daughter, or the adopted daughter of his wife, whatever, something quite despicable. I said to her what I sensed about Mr Woody, this man with the twitching face of a watchmaker's son, that if you can make your pathology and insights into something others want to pay to see, that's a definition of a kind of art. There are many ways to proceed in life.'

Norman flushed. 'If this is about me being gay...'

Mr Ahmet laughed. 'Please, Mr Price. In my homeland, we invented the fucking of goats. It was our national pastime. You cannot scandalize me, but this is the problem your father talked about, your perception that the world is against you. I will be honest with you, if I may. I went to see your show for myself, and what I believe is that all artists should know the story of others as much as their own. As legal counsel, this is what I am tasked with every day. Where are your sympathies for others, I ask you, Mr Price? I am not a critic, but you cannot dig half a hole. That is what I suspect you have been digging all these years! We must have the entire story Mr Price!'

The accusation had the sting of truth, the second time in a few days that Norman had been chastised for an apparent shortcoming, his lack of understanding of life around him.

'Your father, I will tell you, was a friend. We discussed you often. If I may have your attention a moment, Mr Price, this might be of use to you in your writing. I might tell you about real discrimination. It will take but a moment.'

He didn't wait for Norman's permission.

'My parents and I, we are immigrants. When we arrived first in Chicago, we found the Irish, the Italians and the Poles had it sewn up between them. The Irish and their famine, it is known the world over what they suffered, yet they held power like they had never known hardship. America was not what my parents had expected, but they had lived through the alternative. We left our country on the backs of donkeys, Mr Price. I swear it.'

Mr Ahmed crossed his heart. 'By the time I got to high school, I was ambitious. I wanted to be a lawyer. My parents said, "Ahmet the lawyer, ridiculous!" They had their religion, their community. They kept to the old ways. They were Christians, a minority among minorities. They had endured Stalin and the purges. The Child of Prague visited our Chicago church for a week of devotionals when I was young not long after we were arrived in Chicago. I remember it still, the bitter cold, and yet we went for the absolution of our sins and prayed to a doll in an ermine coat. Such extravagance! The doll set in a gold tabernacle. Oh, to see it, Mr Price, this doll ferried cross-country in what I learned later was a school bus more commonly used to transport those with mental retardation.

'My point, I am getting to it. I was ashamed of my heritage, Mr Price. Everybody wanted to touch the doll. This is how they gained access to heaven, and I thought, years later, when I was better educated, how I was all the more satisfied with Karl Marx's explanation of the world. Alas, I became a high priest of a civil law. This is what my education did. It liberated me, but it also robbed me of a greater salvation, perhaps, but I am happy, Mr Price, in my own way. This is what counts, what the heart feels, is it not?'

Norman said, as though he was essential to the continuation of the story, in the way a listener is, 'So you became a lawyer?'

Mr Ahmet nodded. 'Yes... thank you for kindly listening. Yes, I became a lawyer, first a night court clerk and then, much, *much* later, Law School, at the prompting of a woman who supported me. I was in love, but there was a catch. The woman was divorced with two boys, a second-generation Romanian with hair black as coal, a stenographer at the county courthouse. She kept her hands in gloves like a pianist. "The Gypsy", my parents called her when they saw her. The sacrifices they had made for me. I hid my education. I went on supporting my parents after my marriage. At forty-four, I was the oldest graduate. I was a laughing stock. I was the one laughing the loudest, Mr Price, I can tell you. I have no use for irony or any of the mechanisms of self-deception. I know what I was, and what I became.

'My parents, they said again as they always did, "Ahmet the lawyer, ridiculous!" I was in a cap and gown and in a great amount of debt. All my parents wanted to know was what money I might have made if I had just worked and not studied and not married the gypsy. They were, of course, right, but money is not everything. Dignity and satisfaction count in ways that cannot be measured. They could not appreciate it. You stop learning, or your understanding of the world ends at a certain point. I was their son, and not their son. I became a married man, a husband, a father, and then a lawyer. My father, regrettably, he remained all his life a goat herder, or, more tragically, an ex-goat herder, and my mother, the wife of an ex-goat herder. It takes a generation perhaps. I believe this. They had found the courage to leave, but the language was a great obstacle. In the end, I broke free and had my own life. It is the same already with my sons, and now my grandsons. It begins with the music they listen to. That is how you know when life has passed you by.'

In this appraisal, there was a connected sense of why Mr Ahmet was here, that it connected to a view of parents, or it was the best Norman could assess. He simply waited.

It wasn't established why so much information had been gathered in the box related to Walter's suicide and his killing of his wife. There could be no case, and yet it was evident a great deal of time had been given to establishing a timeline related to Walter's last day alive. The writing was all the same hand, a looping cursive. Norman understood in viewing it that this had been Mr Ahmet's work alone.

Mr Ahmet set the glasses around his eyes again. He was more direct. He began with a review of Helen's movements on the day of the accident, captured in still photographs by a series of street cameras. Both Helen and Walter's cars were circled.

Mr Ahmet pointed. In a photograph, Helen's car was in the turn lane. Then, she pulled out again. 'You see, how she changed her mind.'

Helen, at that point, was ten minutes from her appointment. She had been charged for the no-show at the appointment. 'Office policy,' Mr Ahmet said, without looking up.

There was testimony, too, regarding what happened much later at the hospital. Mr Ahmet sifted through folders in the box. He produced a piece of paper. A nurse had spoken with Walter minutes before he went into Helen's room. She described him as in deep shock. A security camera shot caught Walter buying coffee from a vending machine. Nothing indicated what would happen minutes later.

Mr Ahmet set the shot back with other photographs. He took out another folder. After the original trial and acquittal, the District Attorney's office had continued following Walter and the others. There had been talk of money being spent extravagantly. Corruption was endemic. It was the order of business, how the city was organized. Extortion rackets were generally accepted.

Mr Ahmet leaned forward again. He said pointedly, 'Nothing was linked directly to Walter, but it emerged that Helen had purchased a fur coat for over two thousand dollars. She had paid in cash.'

Mr Ahmet thumbed through the invoices. 'The coat triggered a deeper inquiry, challenging the veracity of sworn testimony and alibis as provided by Walter and the other officers in the original case. The families of the two victims got the support of a bombastic community activist preacher who challenged the impartiality of the judiciary. A young district attorney with rising ambitions entered the picture. Suspicions were aroused about Walter. This was the underbelly of how the system worked. It was known and accepted, and then, of course, it wasn't. Times change, Mr Price.'

Mr Ahmet stopped for a moment in the quiet assessment of the statement.

He began again. He had interviewed Helen at the time. She had refused to explain how she had come to spend more than $28,000 over a number of years at a variety of upscale stores. Much of the evidence gathered was from sales clerks who were familiar with Helen. She had a reputation for being disdainful and for always paying with cash.

Helen had despised Mr Ahmet. She had called Mr Ahmet an ant.

In her non-cooperation, Mr Ahmet conceded, 'It was, of course, the most indelicate of situations. I approached Walter with what I felt was at issue. There was a witness at the company where Helen worked who suggested improprieties and favors gained between certain parties. There was allegedly an affair going on between your mother and her boss, Mr Feldman. Walter ended up shouting at me. It could not be discussed. It was difficult terrain to navigate. It was so very complicated, Mr Price. Your father was a friend of mine.'

Mr Ahmet shook his head at the memory of it. 'I will tell you, I sided with your father always, because there was, in fact, systematic extortion going on in the South Side, and I thought, "Let it be uncovered in another way and not mixed up sorting the wheat from the chaff of Walter Price's personal life." What I can tell you, in looking back on it, your parents, they were preoccupied with a crisis in their own lives, and quite beyond the reach of reason. Regrettably, when two drowning people are locked in a struggle, inevitably, they will take each other under. Both will die.'

Mr Ahmet was quiet a moment. He then came back to certain points like a lawyer at the end of a long trial. He laid out a sequence of shots taken from camera footage along Lake Shore, essential to establishing a better understanding of Helen's emotional state. Walter's unmarked car was seen with its lights flashing. Helen was just a car ahead of him.

A magnified series of shots showed her head turn, looking back before she abruptly changed lanes and advanced across the six lanes of Lake Shore Drive. Her foot had not, as was initially theorized, inadvertently slipped in a moment of confusion from the brake to the accelerator pedal. Helen had deliberately changed lanes.

Mr Ahmet pointed, the steering wheel turned in a hand-over-hand manner. It was caught on a sequence of shots, the deliberateness of her action.

Helen Price had actively attempted suicide.

Mr Ahmet gathered the files like a dealer gathering a fold of cards at the end of a long deal. He said, without looking up, 'Maybe, sometimes the secrets we withhold reveal more about us than what we ever say. It is perhaps better understood by greater minds. Maybe you can say it better, Mr Price. I am simply a gatherer of evidence.'

His smile was consolatory. As for Norman's laundry

list of judicial infractions, it had been discussed with a number of authorities in a position to advocate on Norman's behalf. Norman could plead to a series of misdemeanors, and serve a two-year probation on the drugs charge with the guarantee that all associated criminal records would be expunged if he stayed clean. The deal had been vetted through the District Attorney's Office. They were amenable to the terms proposed, cognizant of Walter's service. The entire family had been under undue pressure.

There was, however, the aggravating and regrettable circumstance of a Mr Kenneth Caudill. Mr Ahmet proceeded. 'Apparently, this Mr Caudill called Mr Einhorn in the early hours this morning. The FBI had an injunction to tap Mr Einhorn's phone. There are incriminating remarks, possibly a count of blackmail. I have not read the transcript.'

Mr Ahmet clarified the situation. 'It will, of course, be established it was not Mr Caudill who killed Mr Einhorn. As I told you, Mr Einhorn and his father-in-law were going to be indicted, but it is an unfortunate coincidence that Mr Caudill did call. The police, they will get to the bottom of it, I am sure, of why he called.'

There was the charged sense in so saying it that Mr Ahmet already knew Norman had gotten word to Kenneth about his arrest. Joanne's call from Norman's phone to Kenneth would surface, if it had not already.

Norman advanced no explanation. It would have demanded too long an explanation and an admission of guilt in having sent the original letter to Daniel Einhorn. He remained silent.

Procedurally, there were terms of the agreement to be formalized, papers to be signed. Mr Ahmet would take care of it. Norman could expect to be out before the hour.

There was also the issue of the box. Norman felt the compunction to do the decent thing, and, clearing his voice, he settled his hand on the box and said, 'I might yet make something of all this if you wouldn't mind?'

Mr Ahmet was accommodating, agreeable and generous in his comment. 'You might yet write something great, Mr Price.' In rising he moved the box slightly, so it was closer to Norman.

Amidst the exchange, Mr Ahmet called out to the guard and, turning again, said quietly, 'They will have the box up front. It is for legal reasons, you understand.'

He was then gone and so suddenly.

16.

WHEN JOANNE WENT to the jail, a Cook County clerk told her that Norman had already been released, and then wouldn't tell her anything more.

Joanne checked her voicemail immediately. There was no message. In the echoing vault of the courthouse around her were prosecutors, defenders and witnesses. At the entrance was an airport-style security in full operation, voices echoing in the municipal vault of the tall ceilings. It added to the confusion in her head.

In her manic state, Joanne checked again with the clerk, who then asked her to produce ID and state her relationship with the accused.

Joanne turned and walked away.

The day had turned to a mixture of snow and sleet, a continuation of the same cold front that had descended the previous afternoon. Throughout the early morning, on no sleep, Joanne had trawled in a cab for a *Check-into-Cash* outlet to advance money against her credit card so she might have sufficient funds to make Norman's bail.

Joanne stood looking out on the street at a clutch of immigrant drivers talking among themselves. She held Grace's hand. They had argued, Grace defiant and tired. She had demanded a McDonald's. Grace looked at Joanne with hardened determination. She said, 'I want Daddy!'

Joanne was on the verge of tears. She said, 'We're going to find him, okay?'

Grace was still dressed in the same godawful outfit from yesterday. She looked like something from a pervert's wet dream.

The sky opened in a stinging sleet as they clambered into the furnace of a taxi. The driver hit the meter without acknowledging Joanne. She gave the address, toppling back into the seat as the car lurched forward.

The driver had a single ear bud in his ear. Joanne felt his eyes in the mirror locked on her, then he looked away. He was talking about her to someone in Iran, calls a cent a minute, detailing the great damnation of what he was forced to do here in Chicago, USA, drive this woman, who had committed a multitude of sins against Allah that would see her flogged or beheaded under Sharia law.

Joanne was determined to get through this, to make it back to the house without crying, and then, in thinking of not crying, she was crying. She raised her hand up to her face and turned to the window to hide her tears from Grace.

*

Joanne had not been honest with Norman about the reasons she had left home.

It had begun with Dave when she had lacked the perspective or insight to even process what was then happening. She squeezed her eyes shut. She would blank the world out, and yet it was alive in her head, all that had happened, and how it had happened. It accounted for why she was here now in this cab. She believed it.

Six months after Dave had started dating Sheryl, he had begun picking Joanne up from band practice so Joanne didn't have to take the late bus, an ingratiating kindness to get in with the family. Sheryl had endorsed it, promoting Dave's big brother familiarity, Dave arming himself against Dad and all his resistance.

Joanne was a pawn in the conspiracy of their love.

Dave had always had an over-familiarity about him. She should have seen it. He wasn't as stupid as he seemed. This is what groomers did. They talked about it on daytime TV, the obvious signs: Dave sitting at the kitchen table with a tall glass of milk and peanut butter sandwiches, talking to 'Jo', a name she hated that further made her less a woman and just a kid and incited her in the way someone like Dave better understood; Dave making it his business to be out in the open in his dealings with Jo.

This was again how a groomer groomed. She hardly showed in her chest. She was conscious of a slow change that could not come fast enough. She was her own worst enemy. She stuffed with cotton wool. Sheryl made a point to tell Dave this, because Sheryl was a bitch, and her gain always had to be Joanne's loss. These were the trenches of family life, of sibling rivalry. Dave, in taking Jo under his wing, was seen to be seeking a mediating peace.

He took Jo out for a sundae at a roadside ice-cream parlor. He was sympathetic and not given to taking sides. They would work it out between them. Jo was a rare beauty and he told her the story of the ugly duckling, which should have raised five alarm bells about his intentions, but he knew what she wanted to hear. There was any number of things a person could say to another person in a shared intimacy that could never, or would never, be repeated in the light of day.

Who didn't love Dave? Dave, familiar and funny! Dave, all hands, taking the truck the long way home, wresting the last of good fortune from an Indian summer, because he loved drives and aloneness, something he revealed as he stopped smiling, which suggested suddenly a greater depth of understanding and caring. He had the power to see in Joanne's heart. She understood, in looking back on it, how it happened.

He had money in rolls and paid at a small window at what was ostensibly a summer shack for hot dogs and ice cream – Dave, licking his thumb, peeling off notes, and Jo on a picnic table in the last of what had been a long hot summer of first awakenings. He was a loser if she had looked close enough. She hadn't. He incited an underlying pathology and fear in younger kids. He was the Fonz in that arrested state of early manhood, come of age early, when there were kids with acne and no facial hair, or no hair where there would be hair eventually, and Dave made it known, pushed his advantage. He was a bully, and maybe understood already, that, in the long run, these lesser kids would eventually run his life and make it a misery.

They were headed back from the ice-cream parlor when Dave reached and wiped whipped cream off her upper lip. He put it to his own lips and tasted it. Did Jo taste that good, or was it the sundae? He had a cassette he had made for Sheryl – all love song tracks – power ballads. He loved Journey and REO. He wanted her opinion. What turned her on?

She liked the drives along roads with harvested corn: the land worked and prepared in the fall; the U-pick apple orchards; the fermented tang of rotting apples along the roadside; Dave getting out and taking an apple and giving it to her, polishing it with the sleeve of his denim jacket, getting in again and simply driving, the cassette playing, and his eyes drifting toward Jo, giving her the once over with an appraising smile. So it was built-up between them. It would define a life she would look back on.

On a third consecutive Friday, he picked her up and smelled a perfume she had on. She had worn it especially for him, and admitted it, so, after ice cream, on a circuitous road home with few cars he unzipped and, taking her wrist, placed her hand there until it grew into her hand. She felt such a racing feeling of sudden panic. He went for her chest. She had not taken the precaution of removing the tissue and was so mortified. Dave, in his way, paved over it, removing the tissue, saying it was like opening a present in the crepe of paper balled and hot against her heart.

It took a matter of weeks until she did it of her own volition, looking straight ahead. Dave shifted to accommodate it. There was the occasional oncoming traffic, the brim of baseball caps and deferential nods. She kept her eyes straight ahead with it in her hand, feeling its pulse. She had experienced nothing like it before, that it went on like this between two people and she had never known it, or never experienced it. It became her life.

When it was not enough, and she felt a sudden wetness below, with the pressure of Dave's hand at the back of her neck, she disappeared into his lap, and, when it was done, Dave smoothed strands of hair around her ear with a tenderness she had never experienced.

It became something she looked forward to, taking him in her mouth.

It continued, Dave taking 'Jo' with him on errands, when Sheryl was already entrenched in a domestic future of what her life would be like with Dave, and it was okay, until there was eventual penetration. Dave wanted to be inside her. He made promises he could not keep and didn't. For a time, during it, in the midst of his strength, the scent of him, the hotness he emanated, the pulse of it, she wanted to become pregnant, in the way she had heard girls speak of in school.

It was how she would usurp Sheryl and her full rack, aligning her life with a man who came so close to perfection. She had won a great prize. She had it in her head, a man arrived into her home, and, finding her preferable to her sister, chose her, like in bygone days of *Little House on the*

Prairie, where a man might seek a woman early, because it took so much to survive, and where it wasn't uncommon for a girl of sixteen or seventeen to be God-fearing and simultaneously sexually active in a marriage. She had anticipated the advance, the realignment of Dave's heart and his appeal, with absolute sincerity, standing alongside her, like some adolescent pairing of American Gothic, this love that would not be denied.

These were the dreams of youth, the reach for the improbable when it wasn't improbable, and all Dave had to do, really, was to assert his love for her. She would feel the thrill of vindication, big-breasted Sheryl beginning to snort like the pig she was!

What she remembered of that fall, her sophomore year, was the time alone with Dave, the way she learned to straddle him in the pickup, her back against the steering wheel, the slight tear when he entered that she would never really know again. She wore no panties, Dave running his tongue along her clavicle and down under her raised arm, into the cup of armpit, biting her hardening nipples, and, after it, semen running between her legs. She loved it more than anything and understood why the body was made the way it was, when she had known nothing of the experience before.

She remembered Dave staring across the harvested stalks of corn, the great bounty of what had been yielded from the land, lamenting that it was not as it was earlier in the country's origin, when land was there for the taking. He would have built her a homestead and filled it with children and chickens, and so, in the lurch of want, she felt his seed again, if one could feel a life force finding and attaching itself in a great yearning and reach for life.

In compensation, in the brooding sense that this was not possible and that Dave was, in fact, a factory worker, she reached and touched his face and said she could imagine him before a plow, and, in saying it, touched him, so there was enough in him that he could take her again, but with more effort, his head against her sternum, in the place where there should have been cleavage.

It persisted, the way he took her, the hard grind of his teeth against hers, her head in the growth of hair on his chest afterward. This was a joy and a love that would not persist. All that came after would pale in comparison. She knew it then, the imminent danger of it.

On the way home, near the end, she could sense the malevolent grin of pumpkins everywhere. Sheryl was dressed as Dorothy and Dave as the Cowardly Lion, heading out to a Sadie Hawkins dance. It pained her, all that she could offer ignored or not acknowledged. She was Cinderella. She thought it, against her own better judgment. She felt it between her legs, the surge of something awakened, the great swoon of adolescence breeched, so it would never be the same again. She would have killed for him!

A week later, Sheryl and her mother were scooping out the innards of pumpkins and going about roasting seeds for Dad and Dave's lunches. Dave was at the table, drinking milk, Jo sitting across from him, and wanting to be compared to Sheryl. There was a rise of ass on Sheryl that she had in common with her mother. It was there for comparison, the mother and daughter in the kitchen by a countertop. This was what was in the cards thirty years down the road, and it filled Joanne with a great sense of warmth that what she did for Dave was enough, and that he could not do without it, when it was otherwise. Dave was fucking both of them.

Before Christmas, she went a month without her period. They argued. She said she would keep it. Then she got her period. Right after it happened, Sheryl announced, while their father was on swing shift, that she and Dave had set a date for their marriage. Dave had bought an engagement ring.

Her mother relayed the message over the phone in the dark to the roar and hammer of machinery in the background that could be heard from the kitchen.

It had so ended without explanation, without even the kindness of an excuse, Dave continuing with the temerity to call her 'Jo', to push innocence on her after all they had been through. It made her suffer a great agony.

Joanne looked up, reconciling it again, how a chance had been lost so long ago at the very beginning. She had loved Dave.

She remembered the end, the Thanksgiving she had gone back to see Dad, Peter smashed out of his mind and pitching the car into a snow bank not far from the house, so Dave had to drive them to their motel, Peter in the back seat moaning, Joanne up front with Dave staring straight ahead like the night couldn't end quickly enough.

He was then pulling down more money than Peter ever made. Maybe it was what had made him feel the way he did, insolent and proud, and, despite his impervious indifference, Joanne conceded at the time, she'd thought about what it might have been like to be with Dave, to swap out her life with Sheryl, to submit to him, to feel his bigness between her legs again in the comfort of a home, and in the morning, rising to cook breakfast in housecoat and slippers, knowing that their daughter wouldn't amount to a hill of beans, and to have it not matter, for life to continue where nothing worked out exactly as planned, and that it would be just fine. What she had thought at the time, against her own judgment, was it seemed the best of all possible worlds.

17.

NATE TRIED TO book in early at The Drake. It wasn't possible. There was a convention in town. The meeting with the lawyers was not until eleven. The concierge could, of course, store his luggage.

There was immediately, in looking around him, the tug of nostalgia. The hotel was redolent of a bygone era. The heavy cornices, the vases of flowers, sconces and oil paintings hung discreetly in alcoves. He glimpsed an ornate marble powder room glimpsed as a maid came out with a roll-cart of cleaning supplies.

This was the Chicago he remembered. He had booked into The Drake because this was where his father and mother had first met. To understand the past, Ursula had told him, it was best to go to the origin. He believed her, but he felt a gathering tiredness. It was hard carrying her memory with him.

He had not been up this early on a succession of days in a long time. He could very well have slept in advance of his meeting with the lawyers. Yes, he conceded, it had been unwise getting up so early, and yet he had wanted to be here with the pressing need that Ursula should see everything through his eyes, that she might know the extent of his existence. He was that alone in the world, or that contained, speaking to a dead woman. He was undecided. He suffered her loss more fully in being away from their home.

What he could tell Ursula was that, without The Drake, there would have been no Nate Feldman. That was a cosmic fact. In discussing his parents, he had always begun the inventory of his life with a quiet defense because there was blame to go around and he had never taken sides in the frigid affair that had been his parents' marriage out in Winnetka.

What he remembered of his adolescent awakening was not the house in Winnetka. That was a part of his life, but more so the trips down South into a Southern Gothic tradition of WASP entitlement that better defined his mother. She had been sent North in the time of Southern ruin, in the days leading up to the rise of Martin Luther King, before Selma and the march on Montgomery. She had never settled right in Chicago. Of course, she had kept this desperation from his father during their brief courtship.

Of a lineage dating to the first holdings of plantations in Virginia, she had descended from those who had thought it a good idea to enslave another race for their own end and then laud their Bible with a divine right to what was done. Racist in the most absolute sense, she had asserted on more than one occasion while passing through the Chicago ghettoes that the complex racial politics of the city, if one looked deep enough, was connected to the Civil War, to the great tidal waves of unshackled Negroes, who, in rising out of the Deep South, had re-settled in the industrial rim of the Great Lakes, so it was eventually understood that this was what the prospect of freedom really looked like, that the killing fields of Shiloh, Antietam, and Gettysburg had only dislodged and shifted a greater discontent into the North.

And yet in saying so, she had cared deeply for Negroes, or certain Negroes attached to the house, those who knew their place. She held scandalous opinions, arguing how freedom so suddenly earned brought on the reality of not actually having a job. There were many Negroes who never left the land or the houses, Negroes not so much moved by Lincoln and The Emancipation Proclamation. What she thought of race relations was that the North had just asked the wrong Negroes what they wanted. She believed it.

There was the divining sense, in so describing the full aspect of her character, that she had maintained an absolute commitment to a history that would define her the longer she stayed away from the South and the more her looks failed her.

Or, to put it another way, she would become a caricature of the South.

Nate's memories of Virginia were of the godawful

Southern drawl of genteel manners, the strange affectation of men with a peculiar aplomb for drink and silk neckerchiefs – men like his grandfather who held onto tobacco too long, the South becoming decidedly conservative as the mania for a healthy lifestyle took hold – people wanting to stay alive as long as possible at the expense of actually living when the obvious truth was, there were those who died, those who survived, and then those in between. It was by then a great hardship to find tobacco, the surviving crop that, beyond the abomination of cotton, could be the new scourge – the South, twice damned.

His father had explained it once in defense of his mother, the fierce pride of the South, how the South became more and more extreme and looked eventually to a distant past and their Bible so they truly believed the world was approximately 5,000 years old. When you began fighting science, when you went down that road of fanaticism, when you defied facts, you ended up believing God put the dinosaurs down on earth, alongside the first humans, so the world was configured like a passable episode of *The Flintstones*.

Against his better judgment, Nate ordered a whiskey at the bar in The Drake. He was looking for evidence of a past, of some sense of a presence. He knew the outline of his father's history. He was telling it to a ghost, Ursula beside him in a small booth.

It began over drinks, his father's courtship. *Teddy* is

what his mother called his father when recalling the good times. She had been dining with a gentleman at The Drake.

His father described having been captivated by her advancing and then dismissive stare, watching her eyes follow him. There had been a brazen charge to the occasion, his father, drunk in the mediating company of fellow recruits in a carousel of what the war years then allowed – a fraternity of men in a trawl of bars, in advance of the hell that awaited them.

Nate looked to the sepia light of the bar. It was there if he looked closely. The afterlife of what happened was left, its essence. All he had to do was see it. As the story went, his father, struck by the loss of so much in life and determined that each opportunity must be seized, had begun walking back and forth against a great paned window, affecting a Nazi goose-step. Then he waited round front.

Shelby Pettigrew showed with a haughty independence, smelling of mint julep and tobacco. She wore mink stoles and pumps. His father learned that the man she was dining with was her distant relation and that she was from the South, the latter fact betrayed by her accent.

At the time, Shelby was in the countdown of a dwindling allowance. She had been sent North to secure a Yankee Republican husband passable to a Confederate father looking to hold onto the past. Yet, for all the apparent deceit behind it, his mother carried his father through the war, or, more exactly, he carried her.

Before he shipped out, she gave his father a picture of her taken on a tobacco plantation, her hands on her hips in riding jodhpurs that accentuated thighs that had held him in a gallop of a lust experienced just twice before his deployment because he felt compelled to know what awaited his return.

He kept her image against the shrapnel of Dear Johns, those letters that found their way into the Pacific before the assault on unnamed beaches, responses written within the hull of a ship, or a bunker, letters reaching home long after events had passed and, in many instances, taken the lives of those who had penned them.

Shelby Pettigrew was pregnant. She had informed his father soon after he shipped out. She lost the child eventually, but it made a great difference to his father's survival.

Across the great distance that separated them, it was enough to know she loved him, but, regrettably, in reconvening in a time of peace, when there was less at stake, what they could not bear to lose – at one point, one another – seemed less important, less necessary to their mutual survival.

Nate looked up in the stream of light from the world emerging beyond. Day had broken into dense clouds threatening snow. He pinched at tiredness between his eyes, the day not yet begun, and there was so much yet to accomplish.

Nate drank again. He felt the burn in his throat. Drinking was ill advised in his condition. He caught up again with the story for Ursula's sake. There was a part left out, the intervening years of his parents' life. It was not explained fully. He had the story in his head.

Ursula said it didn't matter, though it mattered greatly to Nate. He was agitated.

The barman came over and asked if Nate was okay. He was apparently talking aloud. He apologized. It mattered little. There was nobody in the bar, yet Nate set his drink away as a measure of contrition. He announced that he had arrived in from Canada.

The barman stared at him, vacant as a spoon, then left.

Nate was then suddenly quiet. He felt Ursula awaiting him in the way she must have navigated the petulance of Frank Grey Eyes.

Nate closed his eyes to catch up with the story, at the point where it had gone wrong.

There was the cofounding influence from the very beginning of Harper Delacroix, the Southern gentleman Shelby had dined with the night she had met Nate's father. Delacroix had harbored designs on Shelby that had always lurked in the shadowy murk of a sexual longing that most probably could never have been quite fulfilled. Delacroix was portly and dandified and twenty years beyond Shelby's age, and yet he confused the hell out of Nate's father.

Delacroix became a perennial presence at the house, or he arrived to take Shelby to tea at a club in the city. He was known simply as 'Dear Cousin', his stout figure centered over the knob of a cane. He carried a pocket watch. He maintained an interest in the Kentucky Derby. He advised Shelby on what hats and dresses to wear. He had certain affectations and standards when it came to women. He was not beyond reminding her of the innate beauty of her shape.

He used his cane to poke her calves and mid-thigh, lifting her hemline with a sanctioned impropriety because he had an eye for style and he paid for everything. He plied her with sherry and other aperitifs served in small crystal glasses, so she gained a measure of how a day of ease might have been so enjoyed before the shifting influence of change and a spurious democracy. They were decided between them that they were living in terrible times.

The truth was that if Delacroix had been anything but what he was, maybe Nate's father could have intervened. Nate's father stayed at the golf club, recused from any definitive judgment. Shelby was lost to him anyways, with or without Delacroix.

This entrenchment of Delacroix in their lives continued and with greater frequency during the legal suits against the tobacco industry. There were by then, hearings at the state level, and then eventually at the Supreme Court. Delacroix's practice was center stage in the Southern defense, and, though it was a losing proposition to be on the side of tobacco, it paid handsomely nonetheless. It mattered little which side you were on when you were at the top. There was money to go round for all involved.

Delacroix represented not so much a legal presence, as a fast-disappearing world of genteel manners. He puffed a redolent, sweet tobacco, so the scent of his presence lingered long after he was gone. He took Shelby to Washington DC for a series of congressional hearings, maintained decorum by calling her 'Dear Cousin' to the great interest of hotel and congressional staff alike. Shelby took a five-minute egg, wholegrain toast, orange juice and black coffee. The waiters knew her by name. Theirs was a life in great ruin, yet between them, they maintained the allure of something grand and dignified.

Nate's father suffered the indignity. Shelby had all but left him. They had separate bedrooms, separate lives. He had been the future once, young and handsome, then, suddenly a silver-haired alcoholic with a great mistrust of everything he had once held close.

He had money. That was never the issue. It was just that he didn't spend it with the lavish excess Delacroix spent it. It took a special talent, when, to Nate's father, much of what was purchased was unessential. That was it, eventually, a profoundly different worldview, no better, no worse.

Nate ended with the impartiality that nothing could ever be charged against another, and that there were ways of seeing around all sides of a life in the equanimity of how Ursula would have seen it. She influenced him still.

He might have had another drink in advance of going to the offices of Weatherly, Sutherland, and Saunders to steel his nerves. There was time yet, but he thought better of it. The barman was not a friend.

Instead, Nate checked his phone to see if Norman Price had responded. He hadn't.

It left Nate undecided what he should do. He felt a diffuse

hurt in the subtle rejection of such a benign and considered request to meet. Surely, Norman Price could have politely excused himself with a prior engagement, anything but simply not answering.

Nate was resolved to try again when the pain in his side made him brace and set his hand against the table.

Before leaving The Drake, he crafted a brief, non-committal email, more a courtesy note without the suggestion of any intentionality or favor begging, a note not dissimilar to how one might have in days gone by sent a telex: *Arrived safely at The Drake. Taking Dinner at 8 – NF.*

18.

NORMAN WAS COMMITTING a great infidelity in his heart. He was downtown in the Loop and hadn't yet called Joanne. He was considering calling Kenneth. He had the pretext that he had learned what the police believed had happened to Einhorn. He would like to apologize. He had in his head an opening of quiet contrition. Enough time had passed that they might talk civilly. He deeply regretted how it had ended between them.

Norman checked his email from an Internet café. He figured that maybe Joanne had emailed by now in a general alarm over what had happened to him. She hadn't. But Nate Feldman had.

Norman read in the single line the overture of Nate's persistence, asking and not asking Norman to dinner in that subtle, condescending smarm that was so patently Feldman. Norman decided that at times the only way to compete with prose like that was to not respond. Silence spoke volumes to anything he might have written.

Nate Feldman would be back in Canada soon and that would be the end of it.

While Norman was deciding what not to write to Nate Feldman, an email arrived from someone called Thomas Strait. He identified himself *as a concerned friend* of Kenneth Caudill, and went on to explain that Kenneth had been interviewed in connection with his allegedly attempting to blackmail Daniel Einhorn, but that everything was being handled. The email had the peculiar feel of an intercept to keep Norman from contacting Kenneth.

Norman waited, considering how to respond, and then, as with Nate Feldman's email, he understood that to not respond was the better option, though he continued to look at the name, Thomas Strait. It had a rural, puritanical literalism that incited a quiet interest in Norman, so he wondered, what the hell had Kenneth become mixed up in?

For the effect of indeterminacy, shame and humiliation, Norman called Joanne from a pay phone under the rumble of the L track.

Joanne was home and alarmed. Norman prepared himself for the onslaught. It came, and in a way it was all too easy. Norman was forthright, humble and apologetic. He explained how Mr Ahmet, legal counsel to his father, had intervened and called in favors so the charges were dropped, and how, in view of the extraordinary allowances made on his behalf, Norman had not wanted to simply hang around the courthouse. He said it all in one breath.

It was no excuse for not waiting or not calling sooner, but Joanne forgave him, as Norman knew she would have to. At the back of it was the issue of the pot that Joanne had hidden, her big screw up.

Joanne said in a kindly, disarming tone. 'I would have liked to have met your father.'

It stopped Norman for a moment, the reach of her caring. He was on the verge of saying he was coming home when Joanne said, abruptly, 'Is Kenneth with you?'

It was the out Norman had been seeking. He said flatly. 'I'm a liar, is that what you think?' A silence hung between them. There was the sound of traffic, and a train on the L.

A coin fell through the slot in the payphone, validating the fact that Norman was indeed at a payphone. He said, 'Wait!' He fumbled for another quarter and fed the phone and then continued contentiously, 'Look him up on the Internet, Joanne. Mr Ahmet, defense lawyer.'

Joanne, chastened and submissive, said, 'I don't need to look him up. Just come home, okay?'

Norman didn't answer her directly. There were conditions to his release. It was not as cut and dried as he had explained it. He had the name of a lawyer he had to see. There were legal documents that needed to be prepared to have the outstanding subpoena against him 'quashed', a legal term he pulled out of his head to add credence to his explanation.

And there was the issue, too, of the rental still out in Winnetka. Norman asked if Joanne had called Alamo since they had not returned the car. She hadn't.

Norman said, 'You should go get it. It's in your name.'

Joanne let Norman finish and then she said it against herself. 'Grace is mad at me. Earlier I wouldn't get her McDonald's, and you know what she said? She looked me right in the eyes and said, "I want Daddy!"'

It almost stymied Norman, but not quite.

Mill Shoals was a three-hour drive by Greyhound Bus into the isolated southern reaches of Illinois with its small white chapels.

Norman sat low in his seat. He had not showered in two days. He had the box from Mr Ahmet on the seat beside him like a man intent on spreading the Word with small pamphlets of righteous damnation. Whatever he was thinking of his fellow passengers, he realized they must have been thinking the same of him. Who traveled Greyhound anymore?

Every other row was left empty.

Norman had emailed Kenneth via Thomas Strait, asking Thomas to pass on the message that he was arriving via Greyhound. He gave the estimated time of arrival.

He would advance on an explanation with Joanne later. It was heartless and cruel, but there were times when the heart was set on what it wanted, what it needed.

Joanne wasn't going anywhere. She could do nothing else but wait. In so setting Joanne aside, in admitting it to himself, Norman felt a sudden raw cold in the after rush that he was on his way. It was decided. He was on a bus.

Sleep dogged him. He was out minutes later. In sleeping, he encountered almost immediately the flash of Mr Ahmet's face, the sifting images of photographs he had been shown, the grainy tableau of what had been the final sequence of his father and mother's lives, and then the stark instance of Walter pointing a gun to the roof of his mouth.

He awoke some time later and, clearing the window of condensation, stared into the grim façades of old factory buildings running alongside the bus. He was seeing and not seeing them. His mind was still elsewhere. He was processing a life long passed that still played in his head in the way his early work had been communed, distilled in the first awakenings where he had so often left the warmth of Kenneth behind, evinced that the singular truth to all great art was simply showing up. It had been an unencumbered life. He quietly assessed it against what he had with Joanne and Grace.

If he had to make a determined judgment of absolute truth, Norman understood in his heart that Helen had not been needed in the years before Mr Feldman committed suicide, or not in the way business had once been convened. She was left idle with her dead shorthand language and spiral notebook, sequestered in her office fronting Mr Feldman's office.

Norman had observed it, what he didn't understand fully then, but what he would come to understand years later – the fall off in numbers at the office, the cull of staff in the downsizing of mergers and acquisitions that had begun to trim the largesse of what had once been the great flagship of American dominance. It was the great fear of Mr Feldman's come upon America. It was in Mr Feldman's eyes, in his unease. He said the word *Imports* on more than one occasion when Norman was quietly oblivious to what was being announced.

In looking back, Norman understood how there were less perks, less decorum, less allowances made for the two martini luncheons. There were no longer secretaries, but administrative assistants. New hires were required to type their own reports.

Through those unsettling years, Mr Feldman had put on a front of congeniality, his last stand against a miserable and advancing age. He called Norman 'Fauntleroy', owing to the get-up of blazer and slacks Helen had insisted Norman always wear when he went into the city. Mr Feldman liked snappy dressers, while Helen, always in the offing, never failed to make mention of Norman's grades, 'straight As', Mr Feldman quipping, 'I dare say Fauntleroy here will have me out of a job if I'm not careful!'

The name Fauntleroy burned a hole through Norman even now. The condescension of it! The grades were always an overture to a traditional toast, Mr Feldman pouring a measure of Scotch, and another for Norman, and for Helen, too, so they could make a toast, 'To Fauntleroy!' Mr Feldman downing his shot, then swooping in and drinking Norman's shot, and what remained of Helen's, before bustling them to lunch at his club where the report card was set out on the table as evidence of a great and burgeoning mind, and at some point in the charade, the general manager always arriving on cue, whereupon he proceeded to hold the report card up to the light to make sure it wasn't a forgery, and, satisfied it was not, dutifully notified Fauntleroy that when he came of age, there was room for him at The Club.

It came again, a surging memory of something long sublimated, these emblazoned days set against the reality of that impoverished home life: Walter arriving home with a Dutch Apple Crumble picked from the discount rack on the occasion of all As, the goddamned sticker announcing, 'Day-Old!' when it might as well have read, 'Don't Give a Shit!'

It was always there, the abject comparison of this pathetic celebration set against the realization that there was another way, a better way, and that a man from the middle of *goddamn* nowhere, from Saint Cloud, Minnesota, had gained it, and that nothing had been granted him that hadn't been earned.

Norman pissed into a chemical swill of aqua dye that sloshed with clots of shit and toilet paper. The mirror was a distorted sheet of metal, not a mirror in the real sense, because nobody on a Greyhound bus could be trusted to see the real self.

The bus turned onto a county road, meandering through a series of abandoned storage buildings along a curve of river. In the distance, Norman stared as the arm of a giant silo swung out over a glint of river the color of mercury. He had his face against the warmth of glass.

There had been a bustle of trade here once. He was aware of it. At a point in the distant past, those who lived here had stood on the side of the Union, when the issue of slavery and the rights of men held, when great sacrifice had been called for and blood had been spilt and families torn asunder in the cause of Freedom.

It stirred something within him. He sat upright. Yes, minds here had settled important issues, because places like this were more vibrant and alive a century before.

Of course, progress was not uniform, and what rose in one place caused a death elsewhere, so, here, the prospect of a livelihood gained from a host of associated industries – barrel making, a forge for making plows, fixing wheels, a feed store, a barber, a general store, all the necessities of life – disappeared. It was sad to give witness to its death.

At an intersection, a pickup truck pulled alongside. Norman could see a rifle mounted across the rear cab window, and a hunting dog sentinel beside its owner on bench-style seating. It accounted for a way of life, as much a part of the American experience as its greatness.

19.

IN THE GREY dark of his hotel room, Nate was inclined to understand how a Holy War, or the idea of a suicide bombing, its conception and then the commitment to it, might be better sustained by staying in a hotel room, in a bewildering disorientation with a minibar charging six dollars for a bottle of water.

He regretted the thought. He was not thinking straight.

Nate had the film reels. He had received them at the Law Office of Weatherly, Sutherland, and Saunders, all three present at an office skyrise with varnished trim, leather-back chairs and an ornate throw rug.

Collectively, all three had looked like the three pigs had finally gotten it right and forsaken the shoddy construction of straw and stick houses. Their names were embossed in gold lettering across the entrance. A glass elevator soundlessly arrived on the floor and opened. Nate stepped out onto the tiled expanse of a marbled floor.

In coming south he felt a greater awareness of distance and how time imposed itself that he had not experienced in the hideaway of his life with Ursula, where the seasonality dictated an easier, more rote existence, perhaps no less tied to time, but there was a sense now he was moving against a clock.

He had a time-stamp from the garage where his car was parked. The first hour was thirty-six dollars, and it went up from there, – this on top of the valet parking fee at The Drake. The car was gathering a great expense in just existing.

He didn't like the feeling, how money was made while nothing was being created, how an empty space could account for so much on the ledger of some accounting book somewhere, but it could, and did.

A beautiful Latino secretary with almond-shaped eyes reminded Nate instantaneously of Ursula, her skin tone the same, her hair similarly long, but she wore too much lipstick, and she was in high heels and a short skirt.

She was a great distraction. She looked past him while he waited, while the lawyers, in the custom of selling their time, talked among one another, checking their watches before the appointed time Nate was expected. He was ten minutes early, so Nate waited, and they waited, as though he didn't exist.

The secretary might have been an incarnation of Ursula, but, in this life, Nate didn't matter in the way he had previously. It struck him how a life moved through cycles, the realities of what you might have, what you had, what you lost, and what you would never have again. He felt a stabbing pain where it hurt nearly always now.

The three lawyers had a decided opinion about Norman Price. Helen Price's last will and testament had been harder to execute, given Norman Price's unwillingness to serve as executor. A small fortune was lost on associated legal documents.

It seemed a quibble and strange that any one lawyer, let alone all three, Weatherly, Sutherland, and Saunders were concerned with what was a minor legal matter, given the grandeur of their office and the clientele they represented. The reels were the last disbursement associated with the will.

It had taken time to track Nate Feldman. According to Weatherly, the law office had hired a private investigative agency. It was through documents connected with the sale of Nate's organics business, specifically, the uncovering of an outstanding IRS bill for unpaid capital gains that led to Nate being located in Canada.

The law office prided itself on its thoroughness and professionalism. They had a facsimile of the bill from the IRS and Nate's social security number printed in block lettering. Weatherly went about handing the facsimile over. Nate had the presence of mind not to take receivership of it. He knew enough about the law.

It was apparent then, Weatherly, Sutherland, and Saunders, all three, were Nate's age. What they wanted was to have it known that they had served with distinction in the US military during the Vietnam War. It seemed principally for the benefit of the Latino secretary. Perhaps she didn't fully understand their collective sacrifice. Their military pictures were mounted alongside their law degrees and an American flag.

There was an IRS statute that all American citizens living abroad were required to pay US taxes. Sutherland pointedly asked, 'Are you a US citizen still?'

Nate politely refused to answer. He felt a grave and sudden danger that this had been a grand trap to bring him back to America. It turned out not to be the case. Weatherly, Sutherland, and Saunders were just asserting their collective history. It was that simple.

The terms of Helen's will as pertaining to him was read, the minutes taken by the Latino secretary. The lawyers dispersed to their various palatial offices. Appointments were lined up. Each office was almost identical. Each looked out on the city in the great expanse of glass and light amidst the upper-reaches of the other skyscrapers.

It proved a powerful and evocative sight, reminding Nate of his father's office, and how hard it was to scale to such heights, and that, after the day schools and the great promise he had shown early, he lived now in the shadow of a hill by a lake six hours northwest of Toronto. It was not so much a lament, as a fact.

The Latino secretary executed the release of the reels as Nate went about signing the forms, but then hesitated. He first read the disclosure statement with the distinct fear that, if he didn't do so, he might have been signing some document of admission, some legal statement of guilt.

The Latino secretary was on the phone. Moments later another Hispanic woman, less pretty and older, appeared from a back office. A conversation, the entirety of it, was conducted in Spanish, so Nate was a stranger, twice removed in his own country.

It would be a few minutes longer, the Latino secretary advised him. He was obliging, cordial and enamored with her. He recalled again the same breathless anticipation of how he had used to sit in advance of Ursula serving him, before she had arrived at his cabin with her rhubarb pie.

It was strange, how a history went two ways, this Latino's run for the border, a history she might tell her children and grandchildren, while he had escaped America. He might have told her about Ursula and his own life, or how a beauty like hers shouldn't be cheapened with lipstick, stockings and heels.

Nate Feldman might have left Chicago. There was nothing that held him, but he had been up since 5 a.m. He knew he should rest. He would leave at first light the next day.

He looked up in the rush of emotion and tried to set his mind elsewhere. So much was lost to him. Nothing was as he remembered really.

The room, for instance, hadn't the luxury he had anticipated. The windows lay in the shadow of other buildings, in the slim margin of a reduced and angled light.

The largesse of what he assumed had been there before was now gone. The attached suites and a bar area had been swapped out for the confinement of refurbished rooms cut in size from their original grandeur to boxy rooms with a king size bed so Nate had to literally walk over the bed to get to the small bathroom comprised of a stand-up shower, sink and a toilet wedged against a towel rack radiator, hot as an iron.

This had happened, these changes, since the Vietnam era. When he had left, there had still been the Playboy Mansion facing the Lake, and an understanding that certain women might spend their best years in rabbit ears, bunny tails and heels, toting trays of cigarettes and cigars, and that neither the city nor the country, nor the women for that matter, saw any contradiction, subjugation or irony in any of it.

His father had subscribed to *Playboy*, kept it within reach on a nightstand. What he could say was that there was no Playboy Mansion anymore. It had disappeared from the skyline. Not that it was undone, the baser instinct that kept the species going, these instincts confined now to a rougher sexual content percolating just below the surface, to a place off of center – so, on the Internet, there were sites where it was not uncommon to see a girl eating cum from the gaping asshole of another girl. It was a search word away.

Nate stood in the grey dark, yawned and then checked his email. He was waiting for something without acknowledging he had been waiting for something, waiting for Norman Price's email.

Norman Price had not replied, so Nate was reconciled that there never would be a meeting. He let the fact settle amidst the dispirited sense that there was no going back ever.

Life moved on.

He was tired and yet he could not sleep. Minutes later he was back online. He did a search for an old-fashioned reel-to-reel projector. The reels were of that vintage. He searched Craigslist and found a projector offered by someone in Chicago. He might yet view the tapes before leaving for home.

It was done, the search and bid in less than twenty minutes.

In the stand-up shower, under the high-pressure water, he tried to release a memory of what Ursula was like. Disconcertingly, her face refused to show itself. What he saw was the Latino secretary, so it was hard to hold on to what was then and what was now.

Nate reached for the blankets, drew himself into a ball on the bed. He felt the smallness of the room around him. He thought of the lawyers in their prejudicial assessment of him. What did they know of his life really! Those early years of a new beginning where nothing had come easy or been granted him. He could say that in all honesty. The organics business had begun as a means of subsistence, a supplement to the wages he had drawn at the mill.

The work at the mill was then new to him, but in the act

of physical labor he had grown strong and confident, and, though it had put him on an equal footing with those who had worked the mill their entire lives, he had quietly taken a correspondence course with an agricultural college.

He was with Ursula at that point, the quiet insistence of her presence compelling a great and earnest want in him to do better, to make a home for her. They had savings in a jar, wads of bills with the picture of Queen Elizabeth, a decree of royal patronage that somehow subtly denied the present its absolute hold on life. He believed that, to achieve great things, you had to move outside the influence of yourself, that you had to spin in the vortex of a space you created that let you be within and outside what you were.

In this belief, he shared a truth with Frank Grey Eyes, that, in all traditions there had been the presiding influence of a psyche, be it a guardian angel or a modern day shrink. You had to distance yourself from the self.

In that process of self-improvement, Ursula had brought him scones and flat cakes and black tea sweetened with honey and watched him study, so Nate was conscious of the act of the act of watching her watch him. Their lives grew in a deeper soil.

Ursula had kept the doors in the cabin open out of native habit, the world alive with sound. This was her world and she would not be dissuaded. She listened to the purling throat of the falls at the edge of Grandshire. She could identify the cry of osprey, geese and loons. She called Nate's attention to the insistent tap-a-tat-tat of woodpeckers, and the far-off whine of the sawmill. She could read the seasons in the cry of animals, in the directional shift of winds. She was a student in her own right.

Nate had followed the advice of provincial government pamphlets received through the mail out of Ottawa. There was help in the way the federal government in the United States had once been a friend to the farmer, to the rugged individualist. He used a potash fertilizer as a hold against a depleted soil, grew a cold hardy root crop of beets, rutabaga, squash, yams, sweet potatoes, parsnips and carrots. He tapped a line of trees for maple syrup, ordered a colony of bees from Prince Edward Island and planted a winter hardy grape vine and apple trees. It became a homestead slowly.

He worked on his studies early in the morning before leaving for the mill, and late in the evening after work, by candlelight in the advancing fall when the sun fell early and there were not enough hours in the day.

When he did so, Ursula made a habit of approaching, spectral as a ghost, and without a word, she simply blew out the candle, so there was an absolute and sudden darkness and the day was done.

Nate shifted and turned in the dark. It was there again as it had been, just the two of them alone in the world. He said Ursula's name aloud.

When Ursula became pregnant, Nate had heated water in a tub, buckets drawn from a piebald cobble stone river, the flashing ribbon of it seen through the gaps in the trees in late evening, the rushing force of it almost always toppling him.

There was the outside, and then there was the two of them, alone in the world. And out of that love was born a third, a child. Ursula said this was how love was divided and shared. He had felt the heel of a foot in the universe of her womb, a child in the watery sack beginning life the way all life began as a oneness, which was not a fanciful, native myth, but a biological truth readily revealed in any middle school biology textbook.

What he recalled of those days was the bite of the axe running up along his arms, the centered sense of a life so contained and the hungry mouths of the traps that snapped unseen in the finality of a sudden and merciful end. There was that much bounty to be received from the land if one sought it.

They delivered the child at home, without real under-standing, just instinct. It was enough. Nate brought Ursula leavened bread with honey as she sat before the fire and bled between her legs while the baby suckled.

Nate awoke to an alert on his phone and from a dream where the world was again restored, where he had dreamed, not of the Latino secretary, but of Ursula, in the way she had existed for him alone.

In checking the phone he saw his bid on Craigslist had been accepted. For a fee the projector could be expedited and delivered by late afternoon.

20.

JOANNE AND GRACE ate a Happy Meal downtown because sometimes McDonald's was the right choice.

Back home, Joanne smoked a joint and felt the slow release of tension, resigned that her fate was being decided elsewhere. Randolph came and licked her hand.

From the doorway, she watched Grace asleep in her bed. She could see, too, in the living room, the disconsolate tent set up over her heirloom table. The joke was long stale. Norman had been right about almost everything in her life. The heirloom table had not sold. In Norman's office, she looked at the board of *The New Existence*. She was just glad she was on it.

Peter Coffey told a series of lies and some truths, not necessarily in any order, when Joanne called him. She had done a very bad thing for a nanny. She had left her charge alone, slipped out and rented a movie at the convenience store that made its trade in more illicit, pornographic movies, though, there was still the clawing nostalgia for faded cassettes like *ET*, *Jaws*, *Poltergeist*, and *Close Encounters*. She had seen the box sets on display on her walks with Grace.

She was gone a matter of minutes.

She stared at the cassette boxes. Youth still lived within these films. The great genius of Spielberg's *Poltergeist*, reconstituting and making innocuously entertaining the genocide mass burial of Indians, rising in a California subdivision, when the Jewish holocaust must have been alive in Spielberg's soul. There were histories allowed or disallowed, or that was not it exactly. It was not a matter of censor, but rather that there was great fortune to be made in the quiet distraction of a lesser, apolitical history, and those who understood it, they were the new historians of a sublimated and complicated history.

Joanne had some preamble in mind like that, something that might appeal to Peter. It was said in a rush of words. She didn't even announce herself. She came up on his phone, her name. She was in his contacts still. He said that somewhere into the conversation. It augured a faint hope. She was not erased from his life.

She mentioned the convenience store specifically, for a frame of reference. They had rented movies, or Peter had sent her down for porn on the occasion when there were insults flung that she didn't know what she was doing. It was a life of injury and sustainability, or it had proceeded along those needful lines. That was how she might yet describe it. At that moment, she would take it.

It was four in the afternoon when she called. Peter answered on the second ring. He was working, grading papers. A silence hung between them.

'What is it like, Oklahoma?' Joanne asked, when nothing else came to mind. She had heard they were called *Sooners* but never looked up its meaning.

Peter obliged. The *Sooners* were so-called because some jumped *sooner* than the official start time for the race to claim a part of the American heartland.

Joanne said innocently, 'I suppose the others are called the *Laters*?'

Peter turned a paper validating that he was indeed grading papers. Joanne heard the sound paper makes.

Snow was heavy and thick. Peter took up the conversation. There was longing and desperation in his voice. The snow was a far greater burden here, what with winds that blew unimpeded. Whiteouts and drifts were a way of life. Roads could disappear just like that and did. He clicked his finger.

Joanne closed her eyes. She could see it then, the vastness – the emptiness.

Peter explained how the Board of Regents was investigating an online program where nobody would ever have to show up. The most desolate places were often in the most need of the greatest advancements. If you were injured there, chances were you would be flown by helicopter to a regional facility, and your scans would be read by somebody in Oklahoma City or Tulsa, or, maybe, not even by an American, and not even read in America. The Great Plains was a great contradiction of patriotism and pragmatism.

It was all monoculture and great machines, robotic harvesters controlled from satellites. They kept the rodeos alive for a sense of nostalgia, but most rode a mechanical bull in the bars on a Friday and Saturday night.

In simply speaking, Peter pushed an alternative reality on her. He didn't say which was better. He did the majority of the talking. He didn't say if he liked it or not. There was little to stop him talking.

He was, he intimated, living with the widow of a farmer who had died while riding atop a great combine harvester that had covered near twenty miles of planted wheat after he died.

The husband had been found a county over, in sheaths of wheat so high that they had to follow the trail left in his wake and work backward to discover where he most probably died, Peter pondering if, perhaps, God had simply forgotten George Farmer was dead. It was worth considering, God's assumed culpability in being responsible for all living things. It seemed incomprehensible one being could bear such a burden. It was, Peter maintained, felt more fully in the vacuum of distances, in the great divide of time and land.

'Farmer' was the farmer's name, which was suspicious and indicated there was less truth here than might have been initially granted. It seemed like such a desperate and incredulous overreach of any apparent legitimate story.

Joanne might have said this to Peter, but she didn't. His life was not her life anymore. There was no mention of the graduate student with whom Peter had left, and there was solace in that fact alone. It was a marvel Peter had found somebody at all, if he even had, which she doubted, but then the world was truly a big place.

Peter set about reciting a poem he had written about the death of George Farmer. The poem, titled, 'Silo...' was spelled, 'Sigh Low'. He was playing with some literary effect. It was a poem, not for the page, but to be read aloud, with a lot of alliteration and onomatopoeia, or some such literary inventiveness Joanne was not entirely sure she understood, but it kept Peter happy and content. It was what counted in the end.

They were talking over forty minutes, and nothing of substance had been said. Her ear had a slight ache. She said, in a vexing way, just to suddenly know, 'This widow, does she have a name?'

The widow's name was Jessie – Jessie Farmer. Peter elaborated. She was decidedly younger than her husband had been and marked by an indefatigable spirit of the early pioneers. She had left home at fifteen. He described her as a spirit akin to Annie Oakley.

Joanne sensed the imaginative reach of the desperate. She was turned to the TV, her mind already distracted in the cleaving awareness that they were done. None of it was true, but she had brooked a dam of emotion in Peter. It was her obligation to stand in the deluge of regret.

Poltergeist was on auto-replay, rolling through the credits, and had been for close on five minutes. It was a great wonder how a movie was ever made, how each found their calling. She meant to look up what exactly was a Key Grip or a Best Boy.

Peter was still talking about Jessie Farmer, how she had come from a long line of ancestors drawn by the Forty-Niner Gold Rush, and how she was sure there was whore in her some ways back. It was inevitable, men drunk on whiskey, men laid up in tubs of grimed water in advance of services rendered. It had been a quarrelsome business, those pioneer years, where there had been no long-term options and where each had survived by their wits and sense of fear and, in the West, how well they could handle a firearm. This was how the West was won and lost and won again. In his explanation there was a preternatural sense you could enter and understand another's history better than your own. There was something good happening out in Oklahoma. Joanne believed it.

Joanne checked on Grace. She felt the far cast of men in her life at a great distance. She was alone but contained. Randolph roused. Joanne hushed him and went back into the long hallway. She was listening and not listening. There were, according to Peter, communities where Jessie came from out along the Pacific Northwest along the island chains, on Whidbey Island, who were preparing for the apocalypse and believed it was fast approaching.

Joanne had the insistent idea to bake something. She gathered ingredients in the kitchen, while Peter talked in what proved a yawning chasm of intersecting histories, Joanne understanding that the act of movement was essential to life, Peter describing further how Jessie Farmer met George Farmer going east, while passing through Oklahoma City's Greyhound station. Jessie had stopped by the Federal Building, where Timothy McVeigh had killed all those people. George Farmer had been there and had handed Jessie a book of psalms, then asked her to pray with him for those lost. She had. George Farmer was in a black suit, like a scarecrow. His ankles showed over white socks. He was worth over two million dollars. Jessie learned it later. It didn't change her.

Joanne said, 'You should write all this down now, Peter, not to forget it.'

Peter didn't get the underlying jab that she knew it was all made up. He was, he told her, lifting bales of hay in a regimen that started at five thirty, when the cock crowed. He was living the most salubrious life imaginable.

Of course, to verify any of it, Joanne might have asked simply to say hello to this Jessie Farmer, but she didn't, because it was worth not knowing for sure. There would be, eventually, the break-up, the climax and bitter end of what had started with such promise.

It gave her an understanding of the sketched details he would pawn off on her if she called again. Instead, Joanne said in a quiet appeasement, 'You make Oklahoma sound like it might be the answer to a great many troubles.'

Saying it stopped Peter cold, or Joanne felt it, her perceived gullibility emboldening within Peter a belief just then that he could conjure anything from make-believe.

He had determined, he told her with a rising truth, that you could scream at the top of your lungs and nobody would hear you for tens of miles, the snow on the plains, its blanketing monotony such that you could watch from

243

a window, see the demarcation of the drive, and then the road, your escape to the outside world disappearing before your eyes in a matter of minutes.

This was suddenly the greater reality of his life. His voice was filled with a stark melancholy.

He began his poem again in earnest, fleeing from an apparent and glaring truth, so the poem was dead of whatever spark it ever contained. It was characteristic of Peter's work and tied to his essential failing as an artist, his misconception that true genius was only ever uncovered in throwing up barriers to absolute happiness, when the opposite was most always true, and that, without a sense of openness, without love, all remained hidden behind words, or built around the fortress of poems.

Joanne said nothing. She rolled out her dough, used the depression of a cookie cutter shape to cut gingerbread men. She made a sad-faced gingerbread man, an effigy of Peter. She could almost transpose what was being said in her ear as something communicated by the gingerbread man. It made her smile, and then she thought, what might it be like to pull an arm off, one, and then the other, and the legs, too, anything to stop him?

The poem was so absolutely horrible. Were there in other professions, say in architecture, architects who couldn't handle a protractor, or who didn't know the basic elements of trigonometry?

What she thought of was the paunch of his belly, the way he used to advance with it between his legs. It was all a great confusion in her head, the alternative to Peter, the

Robert Hoyts of the world, the self-aware, Hoyt making accommodation for a great and undeserved success that would be granted him, and, even before Robert Hoyt, the Daves of the world, those hypersexual Fonzies who would see the flare of high school notoriety pass them so quickly and who would eventually become the paranoid, hyper-religious, in their unironic *Promise Keeper* fidelity to Faith, Family, and Guns.

Joanne had read about them after her encounter with Dave, these *Promise Keepers*, who prayed before fucking, who went down on their knees and thanked God before they got a hard-on, praising Jesus through the act, and praying right after intercourse.

It seemed they were everywhere now, this fearful, vengeful stock, these reformists, those who wanted saving, so that even someone as preoccupied as Peter could not help but land upon a vague societal disaffection with his imaginary Jessie Farmer come inland from a white supremacist enclave on Whidbey Island.

Peter, she was sure, was tapping what he had witnessed in Upstate New York, Dave and Sheryl living with the confirmed belief that they were living through the last days in a world come undone by socialists, niggers and *A-rabs*, and that a legitimate alternative might be for Dave to pump a round of ammo into Sheryl, Misty, and the boys' heads and then off himself with an abiding belief that life might resume under better conditions in the afterlife. It was an alternative reached by more people than anyone wanted to admit.

Joanne set the phone down eventually. What Peter said was not up for debate, speculation, or open to response, but a string of words spoken down the line and into the void where everything was a deep silence in the end.

Peter was still talking, and probably continued for a long time, when it didn't rightly matter. Joanne balled the gingerbread man so he was without form. He was there if she needed, and that was enough to restore a strange confidence that all was not lost, not yet.

21.

GRANDSHIRE WAS NOT, for Nate Feldman, the Paradise Found it had first seemed, but rather a Paradise Lost, for the leach of unseen heavy metal contaminants from the mining of the nineteenth and twentieth centuries. Most notably trace elements of zinc, cadmium, lead, manganese, nickel, and arsenic, released into stream-fed aquifers by abandoned tailing pool toxins and acid rock discharge, in the overgrowth of reclaimed operations deep in the wilderness.

The details were contained in government reports – soil analysis, evidence of contamination sources as best could be identified. For the victims, the effects were slow to manifest, but pernicious, cumulative and irreversible, leading to organ failure. Medically and legally, it was a complicated matter. At issue was the absolute causality of the associated illnesses. Lawyers and experts were lined up on both sides of the argument so it was apparent there would be no justice for the immediate victims, and little, if any, for the surviving family members.

In the interim, the witnesses were simply to put a face to a story of human tragedy. This was Ursula's opinion. Cynicism, she said, was a white disease, and now they were going to add this injury to all that had come before. She would not allow it.

Ursula spoke of a mushroom grown in the fetid dark that allowed one to speak with their ancestors. They should know and be ready for her arrival. Death should be nothing hidden in the palliative care of a hospice on Toronto's outskirts.

What had befallen her was better understood by the tribal leaders of old and more recently by men like Frank Grey Eyes. A disruption in the land always registered in the depletion of fish stock or the bitter taste of game when a sickness could imperceptibly slow an animal, and if caught in too great a number then the species should be left to recover.

This was generationally observed, these signaling events, and told in any number of stories of how, in ancient times, the lakes and streams and rivers sometimes churned in the turbidity of waters in a choke-out by non-indigenous grass or weed, seeds carried on the wind so a balance was upset, the soil silted so it was hard for the salmon to find their way and lay their eggs in what had been the clear pooling of once undisturbed waters. What they attributed to the Gods was not a naïve understanding of nature, but a keen observation of nature, a balance where their own temperament, their own actions connected to a cosmic harmony. Nativism was not aligned with ignorance, but a willful submission to direct observation.

Ursula spoke of it. It was preserved in the oral history, the demise of the great Chinook spawn along the Saint Lawrence, a lifecycle disturbed by the presence of outsiders. It was carried with the natives, the memory of fish, in song and story.

What you had to do, in your most solemn appeal, was pray to the wolf, the bear and the eagle, seek alternatives, abstain and let a species recover. In so doing, you nourished the inner spirit, humanity following nature, and not the other way around, for it was not mankind who first uncovered the ice bridges and the vast new interiors, but the vast herds. The tribes simply followed. This was a great lesson forgotten.

Ursula talked of the First Nations people who bore witness along the Saint Lawrence, in the aftermath of the demise of the salmon, to the arrival of a great spawn of a new human misery, the portal, wide-eyed coffin ships, unloading a grim discharge of Europe's flotsam. The Irish, most notably, those awful, pale-faced, skeletal wretches, ragged in the embattled way salmon rushed headlong against the current in a death run for the spawning grounds to seed the next generation.

The deplorable famine ships, still remembered in legend, blighted with cholera and typhus, all stopped short of Quebec, at the outpost quarantine of Grosse-Île, so it was wondered among the First Nations people what this Europe of Kings and Queens was like that undertakings so perilous were embarked upon. It was thus understood that all things migrated along a route, a life meridian, first the fish and then the people, sharing a same history, or so Ursula believed.

In their time, toward the end, as Ursula faded, Nate added remote and distant histories. He ordered a history book of Canada, traveled to town for a brief reprieve. He stood in the cold vestibule of the post office. The books arrived wrapped in a crinkle of brown paper.

Ursula was taken by the story of the Basque whalers – the Basque, who throughout the sixteenth century had sailed along the Americas, fishermen more intent on concealing their hunting territory than claiming land.

In between the facts of the nautical coordinates, in the margins of the book was a sketch and tale of a fisherman who hauled up a three-foot-long cod, common enough at the time. What was astonishing, the cod spoke an unknown language. It spoke Basque.

Ursula drowsed and woke again, Nate, mindful, covering a history again, in the way a bedtime story was told time and again for its cadence as much as its details, where all strands led to the liminal depths of sleep, where there was no differentiation between fact and fiction, and all was a sound.

Nate read the account slowly, this history of exploration, surreptitiously and only recently uncovered in the archives of legal documents in a Lisbon library, when it had been there all along. There were, he told her, doctoral candidates, modern scribes who earned little, but who set themselves apart from ordinary concerns. In this instance, a doctoral candidate had uncovered legal documents concerning reparation for a ship lost some five centuries past in a place that was deciphered, from scant and purposefully hidden details, to be along the Labrador coast. Upon investigating these old parchments, a whaling galleon was discovered submerged in Red Bay, in a harbor deep enough that the inhabitants had sailed over the ruins for centuries, unaware of its presence or what had come before.

Ursula ran her fingers over the images and words, the Basques in the grey swell and kick-up of whitecaps, harpoons at the ready, and, a page later, the dead-eyed whale, pinioned and hoisted, belayed to the side of the whaler, in advance of the quiver and shudder of blubber flensed, the content of a belly let spill in a great effulgence of its precious oil.

This, Ursula, believed, was how you lived. She did not shudder from the hunt in the way the environmentalists would have. Their interests were divergent.

Ursula would not have made a very good witness in court, not when she held such opinions, and she might better have been embossed on the back of a coin with a papoose, and not set before the courts to topple the growing opinion of her resuscitated, noble people.

She was a contradiction, or the others made her into a contradiction, when life was more complicated. She was on the Organics logo. It defined her in a way neither she nor Nate understood it would. Nate could be charged with conjuring this innocence, capturing her so, but it was done out of genuine love, in a moment of apprehending her, a literal moment in time, so he could be forgiven. Ursula had forgiven him. She cherished what he saw in her. But it was also why the business had succeeded, because of her image, captured in the honesty in which Nate had come upon her so long ago. It was their shared truth, uncomplicated.

People corrupted it, tied it to all manner of opinions and ways of organizing a life. She was the essence of a Truth others sought, but did not fully understand, so she was a fraud, too, for knowing this, and letting it perpetuate, for letting her hair grow longer than it might, for being perhaps more native than she might have been.

She had become trapped in an idea of the idea of what she represented. She saw the image of herself as the image of one staring into a stream, and never seeing the actual self, when even that explanation was too native, too given to nativism and primitivism.

They got rich. That was the essence of what befell them, if befell was a word you might assign to becoming rich.

They were, in the end, trying to recuperate a hidden and remote Truth known only to them, and not to their daughter, who grew to hate the wild, rejecting the silhouetted figure of her mother, a silhouette that grew to resemble her, so she hated it more and more.

What Ursula said of her daughter was that she had suffered from a lack of love. In certain bonds, a child could feel a loss from the strength of a union unavailable to her. It was so with Ursula and Nate.

Ursula spoke at times of how a mother in the wild will

risk her life, give of her sustenance to an offspring, but, at a certain point, the bond dissolves, and the yearling leaves, or the mother eventually drives it away.

It happened with their daughter. She did not figure in their lives. She was committed to the fundamentalism of her Pakistani husband, but it reflected, in a way, Ursula's mania, her reach for someone beyond the immediate tribe of her own. There were, Ursula said, discontented Eves among the tribes, women who bore the seed of nations and took up with other tribes.

She had done so with Nate. Every generation had such daughters, and they made the world a magical place of convergence; they bridged the divide between tribes.

It consoled Nate to a point. It made Ursula angry that Nate saw, in her death, an end to all that they had shared. She pulled at him and insisted he not forget her. She could hear him always if he had the strength to listen and hear her.

Ursula's death took a long time. Nate made the mushroom recipe as he was instructed. She had been to the other side. They were making ready her arrival. It was not her deciding, when to leave, but theirs alone above, so she waited.

Her heart rose in her chest and lines formed on her face in the sudden consternation that she had deserved none of it, the good fortune. She never thought she would die rich. It troubled her suddenly. What good was money, what did it represent in the way you might leave something woven, a blanket or a basket behind that might be used and be a touchstone to your craft and skill?

She was not angry with Nate, but something was lost, something to her and him, and to a generation. She might have gone further north. It was determined she would have, if it were presented again, her life as an eagle or a wolf. Too many years had been lost somehow. She was the logo and not the person, and she had let that happen, her alone.

She touched Nate's face. She wanted, again, solace in a study of accumulated history, histories he conceived as important, factual, and literal, because there was a great difference between them, her and him, and for this she loved him.

He completed a part of the unknown world. A mixing of blood was never troublesome to her people. Women had a status and were sent along with the early settlers to help them with new discoveries, women left to fend for themselves amidst the spirited restlessness of men who had not experienced the company of women in months, if not in years.

It was managed somehow. Women were a miracle shared, and there was no shame in it. They could walk as far and carry as much as any man, and, in the taking of pleasure, they were not demur, or filled with anxiety, and they took as much as was given, and, in the morning, they resumed their place, and nothing was lost in the act, and the great measure of a woman was how long she could walk between resting, just the same as a man, no different out there in the wilderness.

She wanted to die in the solitude and isolation of a single love, in proximity of the roar of a fire and a view of the lake in the natural light of the season. She reached for his face. Her hands, near the end, a collection of sticks, like kindling, brittle and dry, the swan of her neck giving in a sudden keel and slump of gathering sleep when a minute before she had been talking, so he was made ready for a coming sleep that would not end.

In the day, to appease and remind her of their past, he would sometimes play the fool and dress in the early Elmer Fudd cap he wore on arrival in Grandshire, which Ursula said made the men laugh so hard behind his back, they pissed themselves, but it was a hat that made her yearn for him so much more because there was so much improvement needed about him, and innocence, too, and yet a depth of great knowledge and compassion.

He was the opposite of Frank Grey Eyes in so many ways – the one going, the other coming. She had found them both here at the edge of nothingness. How was she so lucky?

To the antecedent history of the newly discovered Basque, Nate added a history preserved in the Viking Sagas, the banishment of Eric the Red, a fierce and flaxen-headed warrior, who, along with his followers discovered Greenland. His son, Leif Erikson, pushing ever west, arrived eventually into the far reach of the north, making settlement briefly in a new-found-land, where a grape particular to the land grew. He called the place of new discovery, Vineland.

And somewhere into that mix, in the trawl of stories and interests, he came upon the feat in an open boat of a Celtic monastic named Brendan, who might or might not have reached the Americas.

Ursula said Brendan was a name she would have chosen for a boy. In her native way, she pronounced it Bring Dawn, so its essence was unlocked and understood better. A name meant something. She could unlock a history, a hidden meaning, in the way there were men who spent a life cracking open rocks, discovering a great and distant past.

In the approach of death, all she wanted to hear was the consoling voice of Nate. The business was sold with this in mind when her sickness was apparent and how it would end. She did not want to die with the phone ringing, with someone wanting something of her, checking on a backorder, or making complaint, someone demanding a refund. With her death, so would go much of his life. He was at ease with it.

Ursula eventually slipped from life in his arms in an absence felt more than anything ever gained.

22.

THOMAS STRAIT'S DAUGHTER, Lee-Ann, was all rural good looks with three kids under twelve who had taken nothing from her figure and filled her just right. She got out of the front seat while the bus was stopped, presumably at the mild reproach of her father as she got into the back of the car.

Thomas Strait quietly advanced with a dignity and hitch to his step of someone who had marched in military formation. He raised his hand as he walked toward Norman, beaming a smile, his face unshaven. He had on a medical orderly's smock, of a pale blue starched material, stiff as cardboard, his hair, a steel grey and thinning, combed off his forehead.

Thomas Strait drove a first generation Saturn, a car Norman immediately recognized, and commented on for a conversation opener. There were no formal introductions. Norman remembered what he called the ballyhoo of patriotic commercials, a factory somewhere south, if he rightly remembered, free of the shenanigans of the UAW. He talked a mile a minute, the Saturn, a company his father had touted as part of the rebirth of the American automobile on the right side of organized labor this time, though, in the end, for all the soft pitch, for all the happy employees smiling and waving, for all the American flags, it didn't make a damn difference because the cars were crap and cheaply made.

Thomas said, 'You remember Saturn. I'll be damned if you are not enlightened! God knows we need every good idea that's out there. The Saturn, I'll be damned if you don't remember it just so.'

There was the preacher in his voice and issues of salvation never far from his mind. Thomas took Norman's box, set it in the trunk then he went round his side of the car.

Norman got in. All the warning lights on the dash were lit.

Lee-Ann was piled into the back of the car with her three kids, all shoulder-to-shoulder. Her knees showed, her dress pulled around her thighs showing the white of her panties. She wore no wedding ring. These boys were single-parented. It was self-evident. They had that watchful, wary look of protectors.

For lack of anything to say, Norman commented how well mannered they were, which led to the eldest punching the middle one. The youngest, Sherwood, had his eyes locked on Norman.

Thomas said quit it to the two older kids. He looked in the rear-view mirror.

'Sherwood, you have something to show Mr Price?'

Norman was half-turned in his seat. He smiled encouragingly. 'Something to show me?'

Thomas added, 'In honor of your arrival, Mr Price!'

Sherwood was all giggles and shy at the same time, while Lee-Ann said impatiently, 'Well, show him then, will you, go on!'

Sherwood said softly, 'It's a drawing for you, Mr Price!'

The picture was of a stick figure man and a round-bellied cat that was holding something in its paws that Norman couldn't quite make out. They were framed, the man and the cat, in a window near the top of what was obviously the Sears Tower.

Thomas Strait ventured, 'Where you live, Mr Price, right?' so Norman feigned incredulity and, looking at the kid, said, 'That's exactly where I live.'

Thomas interjected. 'Kenneth told Sherwood all about you being famous, Mr Price, and about Mr Whiskers, your cat, who rides the elevator all day long, pressing all the buttons, and how he opens cans of food with an electric can opener.' He added parenthetically, 'That's how you were able to come visit, Mr Whiskers being self-sufficient and all. Sherwood was concerned about you coming down and the cat not having anything to eat. But you had it figured. Mr Whiskers is no ordinary cat, right, Mr Price?'

Norman played along. 'Mr Whispers is a whiz with the can opener.'

Sherwood corrected Norman with an exuberant shout. 'You mean, Mr Whiskers!'

He was giddy with a child's glee, the car alive with his presence.

Thomas had his eyes again set in the rear-view mirror. 'That's Mr Price's way of testing you.' He lit a cigarette from the car's lighter. He handed it back to Lee-Ann, then lit another for himself and said, 'He got all As, Mr Price!'

The sudden sense of déjà vu struck Norman. He felt himself forming the words and let it happen, despite himself. 'He's a regular Little Lord Fauntleroy!'

Lee-Ann blew smoke out the side of her mouth. She nearly choked with laughter when Norman said it. She coughed and coughed some more, and then said, with her eyes still watering, 'That's what we'll call him, Mr Price, "Little Lord Fauntleroy".'

On second look, Lee-Ann was not the prize she had first appeared. Lines showed around her mouth. She stopped smiling as she met Norman's eyes. She was aware he was appraising her. She pushed her hair off her forehead. Despite her embarrassment, she rallied and kept on talking for the sake of the kid. 'I guess it's big up there, huh, Mr Price? We never got round to getting up to Chicago yet.'

Norman kept looking at her in a quiet appeal that he thought nothing bad of her. He said, 'Well, now you have no excuses. You've a place to stay when you come.'

Lee-Ann smiled. 'That's mighty generous,' while Thomas tempered the offer, erasing the lie of the Sears Tower. 'At your *other* place, if you might, Mr Price, at your apartment, and not your office at The Sears Tower. We are all sufferers of vertigo.'

Sherwood piped up, 'What's vertigo?'

Lee-Ann said, 'It means we can't take heights is all.'

A sense emerged that this third child might steer fortune elsewhere in the reach of his inquisitiveness.

Thomas Strait had trained as a phlebotomist in the army. He offered this information as a form of credentialing. There was a faint indigo tattoo of a snake around a woman on his thin arm, suggestive of a former life of corruption, drink and sin.

He worked now at the care facility where Kenneth's mother lived, a 'small time' operation, but Medicare and Medicaid were a sure bet, and social security might see a person through a dignified end. He was suddenly more serious.

He had finished his education at a community college and was a certified Nurse's Assistant. He had read every *Reader's Digest* going back a decade, read every funny. He could remember names like you wouldn't believe, names of relatives and cousins and family trees that meant something to the dying. He kept a roll of stamps in his locker, just for the occasion a letter might be sent, if the spirit took a patient, and he had very good penmanship, something that went back to his school days, and it was a wonder what you needed in life, when it was least expected.

While Thomas talked, Sherwood kept his eyes on Norman in the kindest way, smiling all the time. It was a blessing. Norman hoped only the best for the kid.

Lee-Ann, in deference to her father, waited. She was in the process of trawling for a husband. She mentioned it when the opportunity presented itself, the name of a schoolteacher whose house they passed by. Lee-Ann turned her head and looked toward the house. They were out a great distance in fields, heading where, Norman didn't know, nor did he ask.

Mr Tobias Rash, the schoolteacher in question had lost his wife to breast cancer and had three girls of his own. Lee-Ann sang it in the theme of *The Brady Bunch*, how it might be, if she could swing it. She had three boys of her own. Life could convene and settle like that out here. It was an option and opportunity that might not be passed on.

Norman corrected Lee-Ann. 'The man in *The Brady Bunch* had the three boys, right, not three girls?'

Lee-Ann responded, 'And the father, whatever his name, he died of AIDS in real life, right?' so it might have been an insult, when it wasn't. It was just a fact.

Thomas Strait interjected and shook his head. 'She knows every fact not worth knowing. If you can remember facts like that, and school is nothing but facts, then, *ergo*, it should be easy, right?'

The question was directed at Norman.

He said, 'It's a matter of aligning your desires with your talents, and then things come pretty easily.'

Lee-Ann held a mouth of smoke. Her eyes widened. 'You a licensed school counselor, Mr Price? Cause that's exactly how they all sound. What I always want to ask 'em, if they're so smart, why are they still in high school?'

Thomas Strait smiled and was given to a natural paternal love. His gums showed. He said, 'That's deductive reasoning. That's a genuine gift.'

There was love and concern in this man who couldn't keep a set of teeth in his head.

Lee-Ann bent her wrist, her index and thumb opening and closing in a yap, her lips barely moving, ventriloquist-like, repeating what her father had just said. It got the kids to bust out laughing and Thomas Strait, despite himself, bust his gut, and suddenly Norman was trying to catch his breath, caught up in a fit of laughter he had not experienced in a long time.

Lee-Ann and the boys were eventually dropped off at a ramshackle house at the end of a dirt drive.

Sherwood came round to the front passenger side.

Norman lowered the window.

Sherwood asked politely, 'Can you send me a picture of Mr Whiskers opening a can of food for show and tell?'

Norman was at a sudden loss.

Lee-Ann intervened. She crouched next to Sherwood and exhaled a secondhand smoke that was all but criminal. She said, 'You know how many people would be after Mr Whiskers if his secret powers were revealed? He couldn't ride that elevator no more. Somebody in China would steal him, and all day he would be made to open cans for the Chinese to figure it out.'

Lee-Ann met Norman's eyes. 'Isn't that right, Mr Price?'

Sherwood was going to be called a liar in school if he didn't bring a picture. He had told the class about Mr Whiskers, but he said with the firm resolution of a child, 'I can keep a secret for Mr Whiskers. I don't want the Chinese to get him.'

In that moment there was a cat and the greatest menace in the world, the Chinese.

Thomas Strait wanted to show Norman something. They left the car on the rise of a dirt road because of the warning lights and a problem with the oil. They started to walk. There had still been no reference to Kenneth. Norman now accepted that what passed would be determined by Thomas Strait.

Thomas was conversant in literature, specifically Steinbeck. He had sought answers in books, then discovered Steinbeck was more socialist than he liked. He was not reconciled that a man could be overly concerned with this life without forsaking the hereafter. This was his decided belief.

Norman listened quietly. Thomas Strait was an honest man hiding a secret – bottles of booze under his bed. Within him, all the incongruities and inconsistencies of life, damnation and salvation fought it out, and somehow kindness and understanding emerged. He was a man who could give advice because of his foibles, because of his shortcomings.

Thomas Strait had got his schooling because of time served in the military at a community college with just enough communists to make it interesting.

He smiled knowingly as he said it. Sherwood, his grandson, was named after Sherwood Anderson. Thomas had read *Winesburg, Ohio*. What he believed was that a deeper knowledge of all things was not such a liberating gift. It left you, more times than not, alone in the world. He put opinion out there as a matter of guiding principle. He was open to debate, to seeing around an issue.

Thomas Strait was simply establishing a level playing field in the eyes of Norman, without ever overtly announcing his intention. He had that nascent gift and worldly comport of a man who could befriend a stranger in the way so few could in a world gone cold and calculated.

His eyes flit between Norman and the emerging landscape.

He continued. 'In European literature, they are always in fear of becoming invisible, I mean up here, in the head. *Inchoate* feelings, Mr Price, that's how I described it in a paper. My professor, she just about shit herself when she read it. The professors, they couldn't give advice. They were trapped, and I was tending toward something of substance. I wore a stethoscope around my neck like a religious cross. It was salvation in a way. I had short-term and long-term goals.'

They were near the apex of the road, the land in shadow and colder, though the sky was still a clear, empty blue. This might have been how the apostles talked in the quiet remembrance of Jesus, in the distillation of what was said, and why it was said, and how it would form four gospels of a varying life, but a singular message.

Thomas said, 'I could take your blood pressure now, Mr Price, give you a good indication of your general health and a prognosis of how you might spend the next twenty years of your life. You want me to tell you?'

There was a question behind the question. Norman had his eyes on the dirt road.

Thomas stopped with the tacit awareness that they had come to a point of obvious impasse. He said, 'Why don't you ask why we came and met you?'

Norman answered. 'I might first ask myself why I came.'

Thomas acknowledged it. 'I guess that is another way of asking it.'

This was all new to Norman. The terrain and the essential freedom of being somewhere he had never been before, and to be in the company of Thomas Strait, a man who talked like Tom Joad, and Norman, aware that Steinbeck, on his travels, he must have happened upon these straight-talkers of distilled truths, men who understood the essence of life and knew it since birth, against all the inducement that understanding and knowledge came only from books.

Off in the distance, Thomas pointed to a brown-bricked building fashioned in the clay of the river's bed. It was a former Tuberculosis Hospital. Thomas explained, his voice reverently solemn. 'We can only imagine the capacity for suffering people had in the past, when losing a child in birth, or to disease, was almost a certainty, and nothing lasted. Religion served its purpose. I see God as a way of allowing us to ask the right questions. I don't think religion was ever about answers. That's where modern philosophy got it wrong.'

Thomas kept staring across at the hospital on the hill. 'They were so scared, everybody in town. You don't know what fear is like until it takes the form of illness or plague.

Compassion dies, and fear sets in. Supplies were just loaded onto carts hoisted up to them by a mechanical pulley. Patients went up there and died for the most part.'

They were further down along a run of fence line. In the emerging clearing, Thomas pointed to mannequins of a vintage dated to the thirties and forties. It was apparent as they got closer, each eerily lifelike, and yet of another era, the mannequins hewn with a gaunt leanness that defined a time of want and scarcity.

They were clothed in sundry outfits, coats and dresses, in sweaters and skirts, a man not unlike Mr Feldman in a long trench coat and black unlaced shoes.

The mannequins had come from a store long closed in downtown Saint Louis. Thomas explained it. Someone had the idea to use them as scarecrows, truckloads of them delivered out to the surrounding areas, and then, mysteriously, over time, they began aggregating at the base of the Tuberculosis Hospital, and then there were mannequins of children, gathered in among the adults, a community of dead souls. It just happened all of a sudden. It was never decided.

Thomas Strait shrugged in staring out at the hospital. He was arrived at some point in his head. 'To tell the truth, Mr Price, I'm looking for something sustainable. In a Composition Text at the college they had a chapter on a Business Proposal, how to apply for grants and federal dollars. What I'm proposing would be a regional educational center where we would make up a biography card for everyone who died at the hospital. They kept copious records.

One of the victims, Marshall Ames, was a confidence man who was said to have inspired Herman Melville's *The Confidence Man*. This Ames made a livelihood aboard the great Mississippi paddle steamers when plantations were lost in the roll of a dice, and all that went with them, a holding of slaves, a wife and family made destitute.'

They were stopped, looking at the sun falling on the distant brownstone building.

Thomas Strait continued. 'Aside from the bio cards, I have a script of Ames's life and on some others. I got Kenneth reading the life of Marshall Ames for me right now.'

Kenneth's name was dropped without the slightest hitch of unease or qualification.

Thomas Strait kept on talking. 'Like I said, this would be a living history of a region, maybe actors dressed in period costume coming forward and announcing themselves, like ghosts. I see the dying in beds, and a clutch of infirm in a room under the salubrious warmth of light, just playing cards, talking after the times. I have in my head how it might all work.'

Thomas Strait turned and looked at Norman. 'That about how you come upon your stories, Mr Price?'

Norman said, 'I like the idea of ghosts, and the fluidity of decentering any one story. It would be better than a play letting people form their stories.'

Thomas Strait smiled. 'You see now that's what I was thinking, like you said, a decentered story that don't occupy any one place. I think that's the American story, Mr Price, I really do.'

*

Norman was still unsure what was being asked of him, or if something was being imparted and nothing was being asked of him, but something given him, a way of seeing life that was up to then not immediate and obvious.

Thomas got round to it slowly, how injurious it would be for Kenneth to go back to Chicago. Kenneth had a gift for drama. He had been active through high school. People said he had the looks, but sometimes one's greatest asset could go against you. That's what drew Kenneth to Chicago, acting.

Norman knew the story. He had fallen on the abject spectre of Kenneth: a man with looks and little else. Kenneth had read so hopelessly for the part, coming to the awareness that nothing was going to work out career-wise, as he had anticipated.

Norman had met Kenneth in that awakening vulnerability. There had never been real love, just an intense attraction, and maybe not even that on Kenneth's part, and only the promise of shelter, the quiet reprieve against going home without fame or fortune.

For Norman, there had been the salve, the presence of observing a beautiful failure, seeing the quiet injustice of God's creation, seeing how such splendor could be sent out into the world, and that it counted for naught. It was apparent over the time they had been together, the luminescent sheen of Kenneth coming from the shower, the singular vein run along his cock, the taper of his thighs, his inherent beauty, Kenneth's inventory of his assets – what of this plated chest and abs, all of it amounting to nothing.

Thomas Strait was still talking. He had a way of shoring up questions unasked and offering alternatives. He knew why Norman had come down here. In the subtle persuasion of an alternative for Kenneth, Thomas made his case. They were on a dirt road, and it might have been Jesus laying out some plan of redemption and reform, some way back that wouldn't involve miracles, because there were no more miracles anymore.

They were again stopped and looking at sun on the distant building. Thomas pointed. In the glint of light, in the breeze, was a movement and a communion of people gathered below, or it seemed they were, in the way clay was gathered and breathed life into, so the universe gained a consciousness.

Thomas was talking, in what were tongues of fire, but, when Norman listened, it came out as something ordinary.

They were in Chicago by seven o'clock, in advance of Norman's meeting with Nate Feldman. Norman emailed and accepted the invitation. He showered out at Lee-Ann's house in a claw foot tub, a genuine antique and allegedly worth a fortune, Norman sanguine enough to understand the interchangeability of so many lives, so many convergent hopes.

He might have put Lee-Ann's claw foot tub on his board right alongside Joanne's heirloom table, run the calculation of perceived value against its eventual purchase price. He was sure it would come out to $pv < pp$, or more likely $pv \ominus pp$.

It was there again, his underlying cynicism, and yet the world got along, and people like Lee-Ann kept on living and dreaming of comforts and contingencies that weren't worth a damn, in the empirical sense that there would be no sale of said item, and yet a delusion could be upheld, or put another way, a belief could be maintained, or a hope. That was more probably it.

The great miracle was the reach of the Saturn with its yellow warning lights that never went out and somehow didn't amount to anything of real consequence, so it was not the car at all, but the electronics, the warning lights that had to be simply ignored.

Thomas Strait read the signs that mattered. He said that on the way up. He and Norman were aligned along a revelation of converging truth. Perception was one thing and reality another. They talked about the Saturn like it was a great metaphor. Thomas Strait was on that level. He could talk and not talk about something. It was a gift seeing it in its nascent form in a man like Thomas Strait. He felt in his heart, that here was a friend found when the heart had begun to close off and that it mattered again that he proceed onward through life.

The kids, too, were in the car, alongside Lee-Ann, because people like this would have it no other way. School or the structure of life could be abandoned, if need be, if opportunity presented itself, and these were the Joads, or a variant of them. They would always survive.

Norman was glad they had come. He felt the weight of a gathering influence of how a connection to others was essential to a greater understanding of life. As for Kenneth, he didn't push it. What they had shared between them was passed. This was the general nature of modern relationships, or so he believed, a person, or a series of people, footholds on the edge of a moment that might be eventually navigated. He thought of the apparatus of belay ropes, the piton spikes, the contingency of a bivouac, the sheer face of life's quest that required the nuanced read of flaws and weaknesses essential to the ascent but, equally, to the descent.

He had sold the idea of a once-in-a-life time road trip, offering it on the spur of the moment, because he had wanted out of Mill Shoals.

Regrettably, though, Norman could not accommodate a meeting with Mr Whiskers, not right then, or the next day, for that matter. Mr Whiskers was tied up with meetings.

Thomas smoothed it all over. There was enough to occupy them with the swimming pool and the buffet breakfast and the pay-per-view movies and room service. Then there were the museums along the Lake Shore that they could visit.

The room, and whatever they ordered, it was all on Norman's credit card.

Down in the Loop, Norman went to an ATM to withdraw money for incidentals. Thomas's expression was one of abiding thanks as he accepted the money.

There was a deep-dish pizza they should try and a Chicago-style hot dog. There was so much Norman might have advised them to see – a pair of beluga whales at the aquarium, circling ghosts of strange discontent, alive and without hope, these creatures that once ranged oceans.

Norman's head was partway in the open car door before he left. Lee-Ann was holding Sherwood. He was in her lap still, smiling, like this meant everything in the world to him, which it did at that moment, and Norman thought this was perhaps the rush of what Mr Feldman had felt on the occasion of his kindness, and that Mr Feldman had done what he could, in the damaged way his life had turned out, in the loss of his son to war, and probably so much more that Norman would never quite know or ever understand.

Lee-Ann reached and shook Norman's hand. She leaned so her cleavage showed. It was purposeful and intended. She smiled in so doing it. She had a sex men yearned for, and she could torment a heart for a number of years yet. It was her true essence, no matter the prevailing politics or attitudes of political correctness. She had on the same dress and flip-flops, and this city would see something so rarely seen anymore, a woman of no prospects and rising spirits intent on enjoying life.

23.

Down on the street below his hotel window, Nate could hear the sound of traffic. There were people everywhere. He had lost a certain perspective, an ability to see in the way one loses a sense of depth perception on the tundra. The Eskimo compensated and learned to see the world through a slit in a piece of bone. He was doing it through the split of blinds. His eyes hurt and adjusted. It was snowing.

The projector was a heavy gunmetal grey contraption with a dead weight not found anymore in objects. It had once been the property of the Elgin Public School System. It said so on a metal tag, a projector undoubtedly used to address and educate a conflagration of life's great conflicts in the fifties – Sex Education and the Cold War.

Nate set the projector on a chair. A length of cord ran to a wall socket, the projector pointed to the interior of a closet wall into a maw of darkness. A light glowed, a smell of scorched dust illuminated in a scattered beam. A label cautioned the bulb had to warm and cool in the vacuum tube apparatus, its filament visible to the eye.

Nate followed the instructions. He had the box of reels on the bed, the dates labeled. They were in chronological order. He had dates in his head, certain years. He moved them accordingly with some calculus of events running through in his head.

It was the saddest he had been in a long time. He was aware of it. He had hoped for a sequence of mishaps, a border crossing where he was denied entry into America and turned back. That would have ended it.

He would be lying if he said he didn't know why he had come south again. In Grandshire, on the Internet, he had seen pictures of Norman Price, the jawline of the Feldman family. He went searching for it not long after the letter from the lawyers.

He knew a dark secret was being revealed, one long suspected. It was still a great shock, even across the span of years, this disconnectedness to a half-brother, a relationship that could never be repaired, and yet the letter from Helen Price had arrived in the immediacy of a need, his own illness, in how this might actually work out.

He felt a shame in having conceived the idea. His kidneys were failing. He had been poisoned as Ursula had been poisoned. How best might it be explained? Did he dare ask for a kidney?

He was thinking, how Frank Grey Eyes might have asked. Perhaps in the apparent poetry of some grander, cosmic story, referencing a shared life source of a great headwater, the attendant tributaries of two life streams run to remote and distant regions, two waters diverged in the babble of different journeys, then rejoined in the brackish estuary of a great watershed, some opening to the sea, where all was one again. This was how Frank Grey Eyes might have put it, but much better in his grand and overarching theory of everything. It was hard to speak with the conviction of Frank Grey Eyes, because that was Frank Grey Eyes' undoubted gift and truth.

It sounded wrong appropriating what was not his understanding of life, when he didn't believe in everything Frank Grey Eyes believed in.

Nate checked the public records of births and deaths. It was all there on the Internet, the year and the date of Norman's birth. Perhaps Norman already knew this secret, but Nate doubted it. This was Helen Price asserting her hold over the Feldmans.

It was how he saw it, a cold indictment passed down. It was cruel, sending him these reels. She was asserting her influence in death. It suggested the sort of woman she was, or had been, calculating, reaching out in death to stab at him.

Nate looked up. His head was not clear. He needed to voice what he was thinking. He made his appeal. 'You see, Ursula, what this woman has done to my mind?' He was standing in the half-light, the curtains drawn in advance of viewing the tapes. 'This is the trap she set for me.'

The tapes had all been recorded at the office. The ones he was interested in were taken post Norman's birth, in a lapse of almost two months when Helen Price was not there to run the camera. It was easy establishing how Helen had filed the tapes.

The reel rolled in static-filled black and white in contrast to what was, back then, a glorious day of brilliant light and cut shadows. His father stepped into and out of frame, a series of out-takes that had never been edited. They had simply been recorded, labeled and stored.

There was no narrative, no purpose and, eerily, no sound. The tapes simply existed, a contrail of memory, evidence that survived the act itself, eclipsing time, this the sort of evidentiary material St Peter might be charged with reviewing in the great assessment of a life, in advancing one's destiny toward Heaven or Hell.

There was the single sequence at a certain date. Nate fed the reel in a blurred advance and arrived at a scene. Helen Price's gloved hand adjusted the lens. She emerged, walking away from the camera, this woman, now dead, the spread of her hips betraying what had happened and so recently. Nate held his breath. He cared little about Helen Price. She was there in the historical record. To get to his father, he had to go through her.

Her hair was combed in a wave off her forehead. She was drawn, her eyes sunken, suggesting a period of convalescence, her lips a shade not identifiable in black and white, and yet he observed the exercising control she maintained, an influence and presence that would not be dismissed. It was communed in the quiver of her hold in the crook of his father's arm, this the first time Helen Price had appeared alongside his father, his father suffering through it, and left holding the baby. There were sayings that literal.

They both looked stunned. It was recorded without sound. It went on longer than it should. His father's lips began moving. He spoke out of the corner of his mouth. He was saying something. It added a solemnity and underlying mystery to have his father speak and not hear it.

He remembered far back with Ursula, how she had quieted him on their first night after the act was done. She had wanted to hear his heart and not his opinions. Words meant so little and he had quietly caved to a love that would sustain them. It was the opposite in this instance, the silence so sharp in the insistence of an underlying rage barely contained.

In releasing the child, there was opportunity for some show of affection. His father was a head taller, his lips near the crown of Helen Price's head. He did not kiss her, when, at one point, there had been an act and an intimacy that begat a child, and Nate felt a deepening sense of her pain, for the betrayal of what had happened.

Nate stopped the projector at the moment the child was surrendered and they were suddenly out of frame. In their absence, he could see the shrouded relief carving of a giant Egyptian and Indian cradling time aloft out over the city.

It was 4.46 p.m. by the clock, deep afternoon in late April 1963. April 22 to be precise.

279

Nate checked the historical meteorological records. The mercury read sixty-two degrees at two in the afternoon in what was described as a week of glorious weather, a high pressure front of blue skies. It was a point of no importance, but a fact, nonetheless, that could be accessed on the Internet. The Cubs were playing well out of the winter pen in Arizona, in advance of what would be their first winning season since 1946. Jack Brickhouse was making the calls on WGN.

Nate spent another hour screening reels in the way an ad man might audition actors for a part. His father wore his pants cinched above the hips. He had a figure not dissimilar to Clark Kent, as played by a vintage George Reeves, the original Superman, when vainglory and heroism were not necessarily aligned, the glasses worn such a weak conceit. It was, he understood, less Lois Lane being actually duped, as her wanting to be duped, to permit normalcy to proceed alongside valor as it did, or had, in the lives of so many who had served during the war effort.

Nate fed another spool, unraveling unremitting hours of tedium, his father at his office window, his gaze drawn to the camera like some desultory God.

At some point, a tripod had been purchased. Helen appeared in one sequence, smoking at his father's desk in the fashion of James Cagney. He thought her so fundamentally ignorant. Her misconception of how men of power acted, when she had evidence to the contrary, when at certain moments, there must have been confidences gained and succor sought, before eventually, and without ceremony –

like mild-mannered Clark Kent – his father had taken his leave, not up, up and away, but to his death below.

On his laptop, Nate opened a site from the Philippines. You could buy a kidney on the Internet, or begin the brokering. He stared at a line of bantamweight men, all smiling, fathers with their arms raised revealing stitch marks running beneath their ribcages.

They were all healthy success stories, each having willingly agreed to sell their kidney to pull their family out of poverty. They were posed against a non-descript Manila slum of corrugated shacks. Their lives were not changed so much. It was no different when you overdrew on a credit card. Extended credit, or pawning something, was never tied with absolute freedom, or to a definitive change of fortune. It bought the illusion of a certain respite from crushing debt. It let you luxuriate in things you did not need.

Nate's cell phone beeped, a declarative one-liner email. *In the lobby.*

A minute passed, then five, then ten. Nate waited. The reel kept playing.

Theodore Feldman had done Helen Price a great harm. Nate believed it. It had taken a willful act to exert his improvident influence over a woman so fundamentally lost. She had a lazy float to the left eye. It gave her expression a flattening quality. She had never been good looking, and perhaps it was this that had made her susceptible to his father's advances.

It had taken the two of them in their mutual foibles. Nate would make this conditional assessment, not to relieve his father of a great wrong, but to apportion how it happened, the ease with which Helen Price fell under his father's influence.

She had represented a reprieve from the war, an endearing faithfulness, distinct from the underhanded affectations of Harper Delacroix, who as an incessant presence had foisted his Southern sensibilities on Shelby Feldman, who, in a desperation in coming north, was never truly comfortable there, no matter what Theodore Feldman or any other Northerner might have offered.

Nate could discharge their relationship as simply as that. He understood better what they never shared, but for a brief flicker in the intensity of the war.

Whatever about his mother, in those rare instances when Helen appeared on the reels, there was a strangeness of her general disposition, a stiffness to her movements. She pulled at her skirt and jacket, all of it managed, but not with any assuredness, so she was forever an amateur negotiating a bit part, a woman caught in some far cast plot she couldn't finally manage, so her world, what she sought, had disappeared, and had long before she was born.

Nate was turned toward the door, caught in the beam of light. A tape was still playing, his father at his desk, the camera rolling in a stultifying omniscience God must have endured, watching over this man, this hero, determined to persevere as best he might a life, when his best days were behind him.

Nate closed and opened his eyes, his thoughts landing on the awful circumstance of Walter Price's suicide. He had given absolutely no thought to the man, to this cuckolded man. What a terrible word! "Cuckold!" that it even existed in a language, that it had a name.

Did Walter Price know it?

Another email arrived, a single word, *Here!*

It had been a mistake summoning Norman Price. It had troubled Ursula greatly that Nate had come upon the idea of approaching Norman. It was a betrayal to her, extending their natural union in death. She had settled like a bad conscience.

He whispered, 'Sorry' into the grey dark.

Nate let out a long breath. In light of what he now knew, the meeting seemed pointlessly hurtful. How could he explain the reels, when he had come upon them so recently, and he had yet to come to terms with something not yet fully understood?

He would not presume to assert any influence as a half-brother, or as a half-not-brother. They were bound, but not in a way that should be pushed upon either of them. There could be nothing gained. He had been rash and too mindful of his own circumstances, when there was Norman Price to consider.

At some point in the future, he would forward the reels to Norman and let him configure his own understanding. It was decided.

He sent a cursory email, abrupt but deferential, ending any chance of their meeting. 'Regrettably, due to unanticipated circumstances, I am returned to Canada. I beg your forgiveness.'

Of course, Norman Price, if he wanted, could have checked the desk to see if Nate was checked out. In fact, a minute later, the phone in the room rang and rang.

Nate held his breath, waiting for it to stop, its insistence in his head, the shrill ring. Norman Price knew he was there.

A minute passed, then another, and then five minutes.

Nate heard voices and footsteps along the corridor. He sat staring at his father, the tape at the end of the reel, the last tape. He purposely played it last, this the day he died, the quiet meditation of a life coming to an end. It was different from the other reels. The date was written in his handwriting, not Helen Price's.

His father had set up the tripod. He walked toward the camera and away, sat with a conscious stiffness that his destiny was decided, and had been for a long time. He did not look up or drink in the way he did on other occasions.

He put his signature to a series of letters or statements, the flourish of his hand raised at the end of signing his name. At a certain point, his father simply stood, and, adjusting his tie, he was then out of frame. A sheer curtain billowed a moment later, a ghost passing, his father gone to his death.

The reel went on a good while longer in his absence. Fifteen minutes or so, until it was uncovered, who had jumped, because there was no identifying the body from such a height, a search conducted floor-by-floor, until there was the frightful desperation on Helen Price's face, her hand raised to her mouth, upon entering the office. She was caught staring at the camera, the absolute horror of it, the wide-eyed stare and her mouth open in an awful bawling that he heard in his head, when there was no recorded sound.

The phone rang again, a shrill ring from another era, the inherent alarm in the sound itself when a phone was never at arm's length, and it took a breathless rush to reach it. It kept on ringing. Nate had his hands to his ears.

Norman Price had the tenacity to knock on the door. He called Nate's name, and when he was done knocking, when Nate was sure, when the persistent shadow from under the door was gone, when he heard the elevator door open and close, he unplugged the projector, let the bulb cool.

Standing in the sudden dark, he lifted the projector for its dead weight, to know he still existed, to somehow anchor the present.

PART II

The test of a first-rate intelligence is the ability to hold two opposed ideas in the mind at the same time, and still retain the ability to function.

—F. SCOTT FITZGERALD

24.

THERE WAS ACTIVITY on the house, as the realtor described it, a tentative cash offer by a family of Mexicans.

The outstanding issue not yet managed was their legal status. The family had been to the house three times already. There was nothing easy in real estate, and it was made more difficult in the tightening of credit. An intermediary, a legal immigrant, might front the offer. It was done within their community. The realtor sounded unsure. She had not worked with this community before.

Under better market conditions, the house might have been a starter home for a young couple, a law grad, accountant, a medical intern, those of upwardly mobile means, starting out, the house close to the commuter train. A house, until recently, meant equity in soaring market values, monopoly money, a recoup against unrealistic student debt and credit cards. Accommodation had been made within the system.

The projected tentative offer would be lowball, his

realtor warned. They had a number in mind. He should be prepared to counter. He magnanimously declined. They were hardworking immigrants, and, if they could swing it, he wanted the deal closed.

Norman was in the post-shock of Nate Feldman's retreat, in Nate's decision not to meet. Something had been decided at the last minute. He couldn't figure what it was that so suddenly changed. It mattered, and did not matter. His life was elsewhere.

The realtor called on a daily basis. It was the new preoccupation, the new distraction. Life had a way of intervening. The family wanted relatives to do another walk-through before making their offer. The realtor advised of further rumblings. He should brace for an even lower offer, or they might want a land agreement option, a variant of renting with an option to buy.

Something dropped in the pit of Norman's stomach. The house might not close. If these buyers walked, he was looking at a mounting investment of retrofits if he was going to compete in a buyer's market, when a house might now be lived in for a very long time. His only solace, he held no note on the house. The question was put two ways: How much was he willing to lose in a sale, or how little was he hoping to gain?

Joanne arrived bare-footed and unannounced before Norman's office door on the morning they had a car rented again from Alamo to visit his home in the suburbs. It was still dark, but there was shading in the East, the days lengthening. Spring was in the air.

Joanne asked quietly, 'You were up all night writing?'

Norman nodded. He didn't take the opportunity to explain. He said, in an almost whisper, in deference to Grace sleeping, 'I might write for an hour.'

Joanne was turned and gone into the kitchen. She poured coffee. She repeated the minivan pickup time – 11.30. She was back at his office door, her chin set on the lip of the cup. A minute later, she slipped along the hallway. She was on a hideaway bed, in with Grace. The conceit of the tent had passed. She was here more permanently, but it was yet decided how they might fare. It fell under the category, Platonic.

In the quiet indecision, Norman looked at the box from Mr Ahmet. There were files on all four of the officers related to the gangland-style murders. Each officer had his own personality, his own history, but Mr Ahmet centered in Norman's mind. He had a chart on the wall, the intersecting histories, the birth records and marriage records of the varying characters, their ethnic origins. Mr Ahmet was the outside perspective that might better comment and understand what needed to be explored and explained. All points of inquiry went through him, what could be known ostensibly, within the bounds of reason. The legal brief, the officious nature of his position, might allow Norman to exercise a variety of voices. He had a working title, 'A Grand Indictment'.

*

A half-hour or an hour passed, some allotment of time. Norman looked up. In the bathroom, the door was ajar. He had been looking for some time. He was unaware of it, and then he was aware of it.

Joanne was working a washcloth along her extended arm, her head angled so it appeared she was licking her arm with the earnest resolve of a cat. She repeated the process with her other arm and then began on her legs, each leg in turn. He could see between her legs. He closed his eyes.

She approached minutes later, in a wraparound towel tucked at her cleavage. Her hair, gathered in a bun, revealed the sweep of her features, clear to her high forehead. She was of strong German stock, high cheekbones particular to northern regions, eyes blue, lips full, and, yet, she missed being exactly good-looking, second chair flute, always present, amenable, but generally overlooked, at home with Sheryl, and later in school, and with Dave.

She had revealed what had happened, why she was the way she was, as she described it, 'So fucked up!' And yes, she had called Peter, and, if he would have taken her, there was a good chance she might have left. She couldn't be sure, but it had seemed an option.

Norman held nothing against her.

She smelled of cocoa butter, a hydrating ritual religiously adhered to since high school, Palmer's Formula, bought at a fraction of what it cost for more expensive lotions. She told him this. He was aware she was talking. She had a way of saying 'Ka-ching!' when she beat the system, the sound of an old-fashioned cash register.

'Eleven-thirty, right?' she said eventually, looking down at her wrist, at a non-existent watch and then at Norman directly.

He was caught staring at her a second time, an assessment of their chances, their odds. He was unsure. He was deeply preoccupied. There were things and moments that held his attention in a gathering of ideas not quite ready to make their presence fully known, but they were everywhere, in the way one courts and invites revelation, how one must be open to what is fast approaching. It was a feeling he longed to inhabit.

It was enough enticement, his look, for Joanne to know she was being watched. You were in grave and present danger in emoting even the remotest interest in her life. She hung on an appeal of any human kindness. She was off on one of her stories. It began as a non sequitur. It could not be stopped, in the way you could only board up against a hurricane, brace the sustaining winds.

She informed him that he could use any of her stories free of charge. In fact, she would be insulted if she didn't appear somewhere within his work.

Time slowed in the way only a family can weigh down life. At the small kitchen table, Joanne explained the term Recon to Grace. That was what Joanne was calling the trip out to the suburbs. She posed, James Bond style, her hands clasped and her index fingers extended in the shape of a gun. She made the sound of the Bond music.

Grace was bemused and eating a waffle drowned in maple syrup. She had not seen James Bond. It was obvious, but Joanne was determined that Norman play the bad guy, Auric Goldfinger, to elaborate and teach Grace.

Norman made a cackling laugh of evil, advancing on Joanne, who said, 'Do you expect me to talk?' and Norman answered, in his best evil German voice, 'No, Mr. Bond, I expect you to die!'

It alarmed Randolph, who roused, his legs skating out from beneath him on the tile flooring, his bark sudden, determined, a distant memory of how Peter must have been aggressive and might, or might not have, struck Joanne. There were secrets still.

They were forty-five minutes behind. It wasn't even referenced that there was a schedule, the excitement deflated somehow. Randolph skulked as Norman packed the dishwasher, and then he was gone.

In the hallway, Joanne, in pantyhose and a bra, put her finger to her lip.

Norman overheard Grace say the word recon. He edged to the door, a game already in progress, a circle of dolls around her, Grace ensnared, trapped. She imitated the Barbies' shrill Chinese voices.

There appeared no way out, then she got into the Bond pose and, turning slowly, with each shot, kicked and toppled a doll.

It was curdling, the depth of her psychological issues. But there had been healing, if he could call it that. In the configuration of her language, the dolls were identified with

China. They were on the side of Evil. Randolph represented American experience, his head angled, his ears perked. They were allies.

The dolls were all dead, or in the process of dying. Grace grabbed and spoke harshly to a Barbie, shook her in the act of interrogation with an authenticity that betrayed this was lived experience. She still wet the bed.

Randolph was up on his haunches. He wanted in on the action. Grace put the doll close to her face. She said roughly, 'You want to finish her off, Randolph?'

The word Randolph was understood, and Randolph barked, his tongue a long sinew of hot affection, all slathering kisses, Grace modulating between Chinese and English. There was no presumption Randolph could speak Chinese. English closed round their relationship.

Grace was done playing minutes later, the Barbies heaped, the collection of them, in the carnage victors are never obliged to clean up. Norman would, but later.

It changed slowly, life. A dog called Blue on the TV needed help finding clues. A bilingual girl, Dora, with a backpack, found it easy to mediate and move from one language to another. She needed help find things as well, with Grace, pointing and shouting in an alliance with Blue and Dora, her circumstance, perhaps, not so out of the ordinary.

The Sanchezes arrived in a pickup with a trailer of equipment, most notably a wood chipper. There was no concealing what they were, or how they earned a living. The name

'Sanchez Lawn Care' was written in big letters across the side of the trailer's wooden slats.

A husband and wife and a grandmother exited the pickup.

A second mini-van pulled up. A squat woman emerged with the same thickening middle as Sanchez's wife. Both wore embroidered sweaters. On the side of the minivan, it said 'Sanchez Daycare'.

Joanne watched the Sanchezes go up the drive. She turned to Norman. 'They seem genuinely interested.'

A Cutlass Supreme arrived with alloy rims and music booming. It was evidently the son. His presence, on exiting the car, conferred an immediate menace to the Sanchez wood chipper.

He walked with a rolling gait, gangster-style, up the drive.

Norman was brazen in ringing the doorbell to his own house, but then the realtor had never actually met him. He identified himself as a drive-by interest. He was in the market.

He pointed to the sign, while introducing Joanne and Grace. In doing so, he advanced into the hall without the realtor having agreed to it. The realtor seemed on the verge of protesting, but it would have been too awkward and disruptive to try explaining it to the Sanchezes.

From what Norman could evince, the Sanchezes were definitely interested and disbursed to various quarters of the house.

The father – Miguel – his name embroidered on his shirt, was fiddling with the thermostat. His son was alongside him. The father communicated something in Spanish and then the son interpreted in English and said to the realtor that they wanted to see the heating bill.

The furnace was on full blast. The bathroom sink and the tub were all running, the bathroom a microclimate of billowing steam. There was a vent the realtor evidently wasn't aware of. Norman resisted saying something.

The Sanchezes didn't care about the dining room, a box off the kitchen that had been much maligned by previous buyers. It was left unexplored.

The Daycare sister-in-law was down in the basement with Mrs Sanchez and the grandmother. Norman went down. They were apparently taken with the spaciousness of the unfinished basement, but there was a fetid odor of mildew. It was discussed in Spanish and then English, and relayed to the realtor who arrived and wrote down notes on a sheet attached to a clipboard.

The son followed and tapped the faux wood paneling Walter had installed to disguise a poorly installed drywall. A chalky dust powdered the baseboard. The son bent and ran his finger along a line of fine dust in a manner Norman prejudicially aligned with a dealer checking the quality of cocaine. Evidently, the Mexicans had their own plans for the basement, a remodel.

In the unfinished laundry room, Norman turned on the only tap not running in the house, just to show some genuine and competing interest.

The son had an industrial-sized yellow tape measure. He took a series of measurements. The conversation continued, conducted in Spanish, then in English when the realtor was asked a question. There was talk of a daycare unit, or that is what Norman gathered, the realtor unsure of the legality of permits. He thought she was scuttling his prospects and again, he had to refrain from saying anything.

The grandmother fingered rosary beads, her mouth moving in a prayer of providence. She said the word, 'Daycare'. Seemingly, there was no word for it in Spanish, or maybe the concept only existed in English.

It appeared that the son was planning to take care of the remodel himself. He made some more provisional measurements and wrote them down in a spiral notebook.

Norman stood amidst the dank limestone drip of unfinished walls in the laundry area. A smell of bleach clotted the air. He could see, across the basement, the crawlspace. He was mindful of what was still there – his bundle of porn magazines.

He felt a great shame in all that had passed. The basement would now become the center of a daycare business, this basement where he had jacked off and where Helen, too, in her failing years, had faithfully watched *Judge Judy*, becoming an expert in small claims cases, fence line disagreements and overhanging trees, in the likelihood that you could sue and win over a bad haircut, and affirmed in her belief that you should always take pictures and bring at least two legitimate estimates to court. This had been the end of her days.

With his mother, Norman conceded that there had always been the sense of a mind that had never settled on what she had wanted or on what she could have been.

In thinking it just then, Norman forgave her.

The Mexicans moved eventually through a double-door of paned glass to the patio and the garden. The double garage out back had a set of prized die-cast tools his father had owned and an air-compressor unit. The son wanted the tools included as part of an offer.

The mother, when she had otherwise been speaking Spanish, announced in perfect English that she wanted the furniture, too, the beds, the linens, the curtains, *everything*.

The realtor had done Norman no favors. No wonder there had been so little interest. He was by his parents' bedroom along a hallway. Helen's medicines were beside her bed, along with a glass of water dried to a hoary calcified coating.

It was Norman's failure, not doing what a son should have done, gone out there at least once. It was easier to blame the realtor.

Norman felt a grave and sudden loss. It felt like home again, and all that it meant.

A wind-up clock in the hallway, a Woodland songbirds clock bought at Lake Geneva so long ago, had stopped at 4.15, either a.m. or p.m. Time had ended in their absence.

Norman remembered the trip gained for the correct answer in a write-in answer contest for a talk show where the result was read from the flick of card, in the index of answers read over the air, the sound of each answer, each card, the anticipation.

The win had included a romantic cruise around the lake and dinner for two. There was a picture somewhere of Norman in a nautical cap. The man who had invented the foil that went on the tops of old milk bottles had a mansion on the lake. It was his one invention. There was no envy, just a providence of luck. A house like that was always just one good idea away.

They stalked Norman suddenly, his parents. He took the songbird clock key, felt the key in the heart of the gears, turned it, felt the tremor of movement.

What was time, in a home without the quiet tick tock of Eternity, a feeling lost to a digital age of clocks with their buzzers, time, a bully of responsibility, and not something felt and experienced?

Joanne came out of Norman's bedroom with Grace. She pointed to a poster on the bedroom wall. She said, 'I would never have pegged you as a *Star Wars* fan.'

Norman said, 'I was in love with Harrison Ford.'

Then he smiled and Joanne smiled.

The realtor ascended from the basement and seemed concerned about the billow of steam gathering in the bathroom. She said tentatively, 'The windows are painted shut.'

It was a strike against the house, then she added, 'But the shower pressure is strong.'

Norman confided, 'There's a vent above the window.' He caught the realtor off-guard, and then she suddenly understood. He went into the bathroom and opened the vent.

A fan whirled in a funneling suck of air like the house needed to exhale.

25.

IMMENSITY WAS THE mistress of all. This Nate understood in his aloneness against the advance of his own passing, and yet there was hope in the remotest of places, something more readily apparent when facing the anonymity of a world outside a hotel window. Nate had the run of it in his head, what he would do after Norman Price stopped banging on his hotel room door at The Drake.

He would put his trust in the socialism of the Canadian healthcare system and not in the Philippines. He knew it better, Canada, the Wild, where, for years, industries had always flourished, then petered, where life was never a certainty.

He could better navigate this unknown. This is what he knew, the assumed history, first the natives, then the trappers, then men come up from the south in search of quick fortunes in the mines and forestry, and nearly all finding, eventually, the summer too clotted with black flies, the winter too cold and long, and the wages not profitable in the way they had anticipated. He felt the flux of hardship in the mere conjuring of it, this history.

There were the most desperate always, the newly arrived on the continent. Of the immigrants, though, in the latter part of the twentieth century, few did not know the hazards of the North, so the Canadian North became the province of men like Nate Feldman, men escaping civilization for any number of reasons – the law mostly – men who settled with the understanding wages were paid through a system of credit at a company store, so there was little real saving, and those who came were consigned that this was the best it would get, this allotted freedom, when it might not have been secured elsewhere, so they were safe from the reach of the law and bureaucracy of provincial and federal governments.

You could not take a picture when Nate Feldman arrived in Grandshire, because of the native superstition that, in doing so, you captured a soul. Ostensibly, it was the reason given, when it was more about eluding the law, so there was no definitive identification of who existed up there. It predated, of course, the proliferation of cell phones, this willful and respected détente between authorities, that this life up there was perhaps banishment harder than prison, but, on one's own terms.

Of course, it had changed, the largesse of a natural bounty, the great wealth of resources, with the emergence of fracking, the advent of chipboard and plywood, the resurgence of new growth cutting, the rise of impermanence and the lightness of life, in the way a house might now be furnished in faux-wood-finish panels, a kit assembled with an Allen wrench, in a world where there were no longer heirlooms, where nothing lasted, and everything needed to be made, or made again, recycled and rebought, and this constituted the illusion of progress.

The great and ancient woods were again protected in an emergent eco-politics that was essentially anti-human, or, at best, it vilified what humans had done, and were still doing, to the planet, a movement that ran counter to the collectivism of Marxism, to that old-world view that all human activity was about class and economics, so it was obvious, how the serviceability and truth of ideas changed with the times.

And yet, Canada distinguished itself. It kept a hold on certain values. Economically, the provincial governments abided by a socialist policy, without overtly referencing the rhetoric of compassion, because there were still few enough to share, and there were boom towns, like Edmonton, and the Pacific influx of the Hong Kong expatriates to Vancouver.

The reach of the Empire was not the curse it was in the heart of London, but something else. In Canada the land was too vastly big, its isolation, its disconnectedness, its greatest virtue, so all that came before was put in the context that nothing survived. It staved a certain fanaticism. It set human existence against a greater presence.

In the intervening years, he had seen the change. He was under no illusion, going back across the border. There was more attention to school board meetings and PTA meetings, so you might think there was progress and enlightenment, when it was all bureaucracy, and education was more a holding pen for the great majority, an institution that sapped what youth represented once, a revolutionary force.

Nate Feldman felt the maudlin sense that he was of another age. He put his hands to his face. He had lost the love of his life. He missed her so very much. It was a white man's curse to want to seize and take hold and possess.

Ursula told him this many times, but he could not let it go.

The Canadian Border Authorities were almost as insistent and inquiring in letting him back into Canada as the Americans had been in letting him into the United States, this, part of the great interconnectedness of the terror threat.

He thought he might be done then, caught for taxes he had not paid the American government. Perhaps there was a warrant now out for him. The three lawyers had seen to it. His papers were checked. His Pakistani son-in-law was, no doubt, a great liability, or so Nate felt. If there was an indictment on suspicion of tax evasion, he would be connected with his radicalized daughter, even though they had not spoken in a long time. It was suspicious in and of itself. He could, in fact, if pushed, imagine her as a suicide bomber and imagine further the RCMP advising him of what had happened.

How could *mounted* and *police* be used in the same breath concerning law enforcement, and in the twenty-first century, for God's sake? There were moments, expressions and realities that would always seem strange. *Oh, Canada!* Despite appearances, he was the outsider.

Nate drove along the 401 toward Brampton, waited at a Tim Horton's for the early light, entered the rush of traffic descending on Toronto, then turned onto the 400, going north, when everybody else was heading south.

It was premeditated, timed in the cycle of urban life. Nate wanted to more readily understand it. If there were a great disaster ever, most would die in their car. It was a terrible thought, though, if an enterprise could be pitched just right, a survival camp specializing in how to survive, it might attract a strain of people committed to the prophetic destiny of End Times.

He had the specs on a wooden lodge with a field stone chimney, a central cabin, along with more rustic cabins, all with rights to fishing.

He had priced at one point the added expense of a hydroplane to deposit avid fishermen at any of a number of lakes, remote and inaccessible, where wrangling of the heart and contradictions were best contemplated and settled once and for all.

It was an old idea, come upon first as Ursula lay dying. She had the restlessness of a spirit wanting to go further north. There was a history book opened at the time related to the discovery of the Gaspé Peninsula on the St Lawrence. Nate had read it to Ursula.

They had a name for those who ventured inland, *Coureurs de Bois*, meaning *Runners of the Woods*; white men who took their wives from the native tribes in what was described as *à la façon du pays – after the custom of the country.*

In reading it, to explain it, he fell on how it took a multitude of languages: the native language, French and English, and sometimes the non-translation of French when a term or word was not fully translatable, and how certain ways of knowing were the exclusive province of a time and a people, and all that could be ever known was the hint at what was then lost.

There was much of a practical nature in what he read to Ursula. She wanted to hear it. Nate read from the journal of a man called Daniel Harmon, who, in describing an ancient wedding contract, recalled how,

> the groom shows his Bride where his Bed is, and they rest together, and continue to do as long as they can agree among themselves, but when either is displeased with their choice, he or she will seek another partner... which is law here...

Ursula liked the idea very much, these proud, independent women, though she confessed she would not share Nate. She said it, reaching for him.

Nate was beyond tears. A great reconciliation was close at hand. He felt the faint creak of his joints as he moved to pull apart the curtain to let the light in.

It was cold here still and would remain so for a month yet, the snow faintly falling. Cold frosted the window.

His breath warmed the glass. He made a circle with his sleeve.

He was barefoot, in pajamas with the buttons in the rear. He was no longer the man who had felled trees, the young man who had ventured so long ago into the North. The greater part of his life had been spent here, the sum of all acts great and small amounting to a life. They had slept like bears, he and Ursula, contained and provisioned, their own world organized and managed along a time of plenty and scarcity.

It came as a revelation. The name of the enterprise would be *Coureurs de Bois – Runners of the Woods*. Those who came would learn, among other things, how to make fire, to erect shelter, to survive those first days of chaos and distress. He could see fear as an approaching reality. He had plans for safe routes, meeting places, points of connectedness for a family to reconvene in Toronto, and stores of dried food. It would call for an outlay and investment, but he had the Organics windfall.

He would preach that it mattered how one accounted for the days and years, for, though a tree might outlive a man, live 100 or 500 years, it did so reliant on wildfires to break open and spread its resin-coated seeds, or the wind, or the pollination of bees. Fate, a thing decided for a tree, whereas a man could just up and leave if he so chose, and this was why God ordained the years were so much shorter for humans, the decisions so much more immediate.

He would begin with the stabbing hurt of mortality, knowing, at all times, not a minute should be luxuriated and wasted. He would rely on the benevolence of a car crash victim. He would ask Ursula to watch the roads, like an eagle soaring above, for what might be scavenged – the fate of one, a donor.

It was gruesome, no doubt, but less so than what was offered in the Philippines.

26.

Y OU COULD FORSAKE sexuality, or sublimate it to a point where it mattered less and less. It happened eventually, the great suburban rut and the associated purchase of so damn much – washers and dryers and home appliances – the essential lure and eventual containment, so you turned to your side of the bed, seeking the escape of sleep, wondering what had become of your youth, your passions and great expectations?

Norman didn't believe in the Kinsey Report and the decided swapping out of a politics of economics for a politics of sex. This was part of the great distraction of late modernity. As for his sexuality, well, he would watch out that he didn't end up strangling kittens, or whatever was said that went on in the minds of the sexually repressed or the sexually confused.

He told Joanne about the kittens, just to be on her guard. She shook his hand, like a deal had been struck. He could trek across the border anytime he felt the need. She had been through enough. She understood that warranties and marriages weren't worth a damn, not in the way they used to be, and honesty was as rare a commodity as gold.

They took a long, meandering journey south to Florida and Disney World, planned by Joanne, for what she called a greater inspiration and view of the world, and, of course, for Grace. They did it on a strict budget. Norman agreed to it and gave Joanne control of the purse strings. In so doing, he bestowed on her a sense of permanence in this new existence.

In the latter stages of the house negotiations, Norman had given Joanne Power of Attorney, after she had insisted she could do better, which she did eventually. She came out almost $6,000 ahead of the initial offer, bargaining hard and holding fast when Norman would have caved in. The great secret to negotiating was not to analyze your own worries, but to assess what the other side gained or lost in walking away from the table.

Joanne, it turned out, had deep insight into how certain aspects of life worked. Norman discharged the debt he had paid off on her credit card. He called it her commission.

Joanne was asleep, her mouth half-open in the sunshine. They were across the Kentucky border. Norman tuned the radio to an a.m. station. He came upon the last of the spring baseball games played out in the Arizona Cactus

League. He had his hands on the wheel in the earnest way of someone who had mastered a new skill.

It stalked him, that old life, the absence of it made greater suddenly. He recalled a lazy afternoon long ago, Walter drinking cold beer after mowing the lawn, catching the tail end of a game on a small transistor radio. What Walter had loved about the game were the stats and the cluster of the teams with their old-fashioned stripes, knickers and stockings, the antiquated side of it, when, even into the seventies, heroes like Babe Ruth were still revered, despite how in vintage footage Babe looked like a big-diapered baby and was no athlete, or not in the way they were now, but Babe had delivered on what was asked back then. He had swung at dreams, led the way toward manhood with a trot around the bases, his cap tipped, reverent and appreciative of the applause, and the other greats of the game, known ultimately for the gravitas of their courage. Lou Gehrig's farewell speech at Yankee stadium, declaring that he was the luckiest man alive, and dead two years later, an account his father could not tell without crying.

It was there again. Walter calling the Cubs 'bums', the pennant race lost early, his relationship with them contentious, and yet he stuck with them out of loyalty. Walter attentive to the line drives, the walks, the loaded bases and the sacrifice fly – a play that had always smacked of an invention dreamt up by shakedown mobsters, or tied to political gerrymandering, when there was a deep humanity underpinning it. The assumption, that, under certain circumstances, you might be asked to make sacrifices for the team, and that a quirk in the scorecard, in the very game itself, might protect you and allow you to keep the sheet clean. This national pastime, at its essence, it tended toward the appointed time when each man in the wind-up and strike stood alone at-bat.

That was it, when it came down to it. A game that could be communicated in words alone, in the voice of commentary, so it was no great loss if you weren't there. In fact, it was a game better heard than seen, and decidedly set up that way in the ungodly number of games that constituted a season – the double-headers and clusters of mid-week games – so, in the end, it was TV that diminished the game, exposing the paucity of attendances and the slowness of any real action, an accommodation cameras could never quite invest with an essence of mystery, and even less so with the advent of color, when the texture of reality took from what was and would always be a game of nostalgia and ghosts.

Hours passed.

Norman drove deep into the Kentucky Mountains, before descending into an overgrown valley where a shadowy town stood by a carving, meandering river.

Joanne roused, her finger on a map like a field marshal. She denied that she had slept. There were quirks between them, but Norman could see the look on her face, the miraculous sense that you just close your eyes and wake into another world.

They stayed at a schoolhouse turned historic hotel in the

heart of coal mining country. The brick façade glowed in a brown dinge of light behind laced curtains.

It rained in sheets in the Blue Ridge Mountains. Through a series of tall picture windows in a classroom turned spacious bedroom, they played cards and Scrabble made of real wooden blocks, aged and played with by schoolchildren over a matter of decades.

Joanne made a meal in a small alcove, Norman standing alongside her, helping, aware of the solid wood chairs, the rounded tables and bone china, the bite of a breadknife with a worn handle and the teeth of a saw, all of it of a vintage of great permanence.

Joanne had on a wedding ring. Norman noticed it, this unannounced union decided upon by her alone. It somehow did not involve Norman, or it involved him, but in a way that acknowledged how love was always one-sided and kept alive more so by one partner than the other. He felt the advantage and disadvantage of what she quietly offered.

He looked askance at her, her hair flat against her head in an unadorned plainness of domestic life. She was in a shirt with the sleeves rolled above her elbows. It was something that would be decided, her faithfulness, over days, weeks, months and years, this decision of hers, and better configured in looking back on what had been decided and not voiced.

They were in a valley cut from a river, encased in an earthen mass of dead foliage, the layers of past life dating back millennia, predating the rise of humans, the V of the valley blocking sunlight so the day was more shadows, greyness and fog.

It took the reach of the sun across the cosmos to find them, the void of distance, a faint light eventually finding them on occasional days of blue skies, so it was not such a great burden to go into the mines against the characteristic slate grey of a webbed fog. You limited the possibilities, cut yourself off from alternatives.

Beneath the earth it was simply all darkness. You came up to the possibility of rain or sleet or maybe sun. It was a veneer, this world of light, when the greater reality of the universe was darkness. He heard a church bell toll that might have been for him alone, if he believed in miracles.

It was the two of them, and Grace, the compact of a life and the reach of Florida in the offing, but for now they were arrested here in the quiet of a schoolhouse, this weigh station between the past and the present. He liked this about Joanne, how she had found the schoolhouse in some informational flyer and sought it out, because places like this argued for simple choices or no choices at all.

Choice, or how it was now envisioned and experienced, was a new phenomenon, and what people decried when it was denied them was, in fact, the opposite of the truer essence of life and how it had been lived for the greater part of human awakening.

He was mindful of this against the scroll of fog and the diaphanous leech of true color, so Joanne was a shadow beside him. He watched her out of the corner of his eye.

She cracked a series of eggs in a deft one-handed way, so it was a magic trick, the sudden glob of yellow like a contained sun run into a ceramic bowl. This was a late afternoon lunch materializing before his eyes – scrambled eggs and bacon, a pot of coffee on the stove over the blue whisper of a crowned gas ring.

There were memories laid down, a series of acts that defined her presence, back at the apartment, her panties stained with a rusty blood, the discoloration of the water in the bathroom sink, the intimacies of the body's workings. There were nylons, too, wrung and hung casually over the shower railing.

He liked all this. He would not have anticipated it, but, when it was presented, he thought, here was a life, and he was a part of it. He sensed her creating it for him in the simple act of making lunch, and that a life was not any one thing, but a series of concatenated actions that created a greater context when viewed in their totality.

Norman poured a cheap, screw-top wine into a tumbler. They were in for the afternoon, locked in shadows. In a small library on the second floor, Norman held the weight of books stamped and worn, a hardback cloth threadbare and shiny with the oil of thumbprints – a library containing Joseph Conrad's *Heart of Darkness*, Hemingway's *The Old Man and the Sea*, and Jules Verne's *Twenty Thousand Leagues Under the Sea*.

He looked through a porthole window, saw a small church and, beyond, a hole in the ground where men had descended daily. In observing it, he understood better what an education must have offered in the past for those who could make a living above ground, what a powerful inducement it must have been to study here, and to witness Hell, to see a hole consume and disgorge human life and to know there was an alternative in books, to study and hear the concussive explosive blasts deep underground, the horror and ever-present danger always there and that took so many.

In the associated history of the area, there had been worker unrest and strikes. Norman paged through a book with accompanying black-and-white photographs of miners in an age when people made a living here on coal.

He went out eventually into the pouring rain in search of a statue and found it by an abandoned spine of rail track – a bronze statue of a miner wearing a hard hat with a miner's lamp, a pick in his hand. Veins showed in a defining grip and strength that was little needed anymore, though, in standing alongside it, it put into perspective the life Norman's father had inhabited, the reach of Mayor Daley and the Machine, and how protective a class of men had to be to ensure dignity and a living wage.

He checked the toll of death in the mine and the surrounding mines at a small museum dedicated to miners above a post office. The deaths were all accounted for in handwritten ledgers. The museum had been underwritten by Loretta Lynn, the famed Coal Miner's Daughter, a woman of great beauty and voice, who, for a time had brought the plight of the miners into the American consciousness – what they had offered the nation, and, in return, how they had been treated, the insidious slow death of black lung and the sudden cave-ins – solidarity, the only foothold the working class had against management.

Norman felt it, a gathering sense of what was then needed, and needed again, the rallying defiance of a generation, of a class consciousness that had been eclipsed somewhere during the Reagan Presidency.

He found a computer with an Internet connection back at the small schoolhouse library, and, searching archives, he found footage of the old Mayor Daley of his father's vintage, Daley, glad-handing, tipping his hat along a St Pat's Day parade route, in a coronation of the ordinary, a river run green with Irish pride and the color of money.

A voiceover echoed Daley's 1968 post-Democratic Convention statement, 'Gentleman, get the thing straight once and for all – the policeman isn't there to create disorder, the policeman is there to preserve disorder,' a gaff glossed over by a reporter who, in the spirit of the times, declared, 'We reported what he meant, not what he said.'

There was accommodation of interests and sympathies then, words not parsed and put under scrutiny, when it was so damn hard to get said right, what needed to be said, when, for most of your life, you spoke around a feeling and never fully understood it.

For Norman Price, it accounted for honesty, when contradictions, missteps, were an essential divining rod of how life was lived, and that there was nothing inconsistent in holding any number of contrary opinions on any number of subjects. It was the human condition.

Norman looked up into the glare of light. He had witnessed it even in the new politics of a supposedly unfettered history that came after the corruption of Daley, how Obama, a would-be presidential hopeful a year earlier, had mysteriously not recollected his former church pastor's alleged statements against white injustice and American Imperialism, suggesting either that Obama was a liar, or that there were Truths one told among one's own kind, or to oneself, that fed only a part of the font of who one was, and that a person could hold two histories simultaneously, two contradictory histories, and still somehow be true to oneself.

At times, survival necessitated looking beyond apparent incongruities.

For a moment, Norman thought again of Mr Ahmet, a great friend to his father – Mr Ahmet who, as a lawyer, had spent the greater part of his career defending the indefensible because it needed defending, so careers in such circumstances often ended with inevitable regrets, in willful compromises where a different set of laws and underlying truths superseded what might be arbitrated and made sense of in a court. What Mr Ahmet had hated – he, of all people, a lawyer – was factuality, too much evidence and not enough understanding.

It was deeply appreciated. Mr Ahmet's humanity evidenced in the comportment of how he carried out his duties. It was a way of negotiating life that Norman had never fully understood in his aloneness. This was how cities had once survived. Chicago, to be sure, this city that had sanctioned only so many histories, so there could be only one St Patrick's Day, so that Mr Ahmet and Joanne's Armenian boyfriend's father, with his little known nation's genocide, were left bereft, their histories held sacred in small Orthodox communities and yet somehow, their histories had survived among their kind.

They were gone the following morning, time collapsing in the run of mile markers and state borders crossed, the subtle and almost unnoticeable change until it was upon them. The retreat out of the Blue Ridge Mountains, the sharp flint brilliance of an azure tropical light replacing the dappled interlace of a forest canopy with its slow dialed movement of bluebells and ephemerals, small faced flowers tracking the sun like a congregation of faithful in the slats of a radiant, life-giving light.

There was so much to be observed and praised.

Captain Cody's outside Daytona had an All-U-Can-Eat seafood salad bar buffet done as a sandbar on an isthmus of castaway islands set against a wallpaper background of the bluest sky imaginable. A low level hush of breaking sea surf underscored the tranquility of this island paradise made real, the floor sprinkled with sand, the buffet done up like a shanty beach shack draped in fish netting and garlands of seaweed and fake starfish.

Norman was in the process of sprinkling a benediction of crumbling crackers over a bowl of hot chowder. They were in a clam-shaped booth.

Grace sat wearing a pirate's patch over one eye, just like Captain Cody. The waitress called her 'a pearl', not once or twice, but every time she refilled Grace's Pepsi. Grace was so taken with the name that she called herself Pearl.

The name Grace belonged to an affectation bestowed by Kenneth. She materialized in this new name, with an orientalism and beauty that eclipsed the Christian idea of Grace. The name, bestowed on her so casually, augured a cosmological order. This child would become his daughter in the best way he could accommodate and be her father. He would try his very best.

Norman felt the flutter of providence. All round him, half-alighted painted seagulls hung, suspended on filaments of invisible fishing line, turning in a breath of air conditioning. The restaurant's namesake, Captain Cody, was a grizzled plaster cast with disconcerting blue doll eyes. Every so often, the cheap mechanical pulley apparatus mouth opened like a trap door, and he said, in a cragged English accent, 'Ahoy, Matey', and brandished a cut-throat sabre in a jolting contraption of wires. This all miraculously conjured daily, during the early bird lunch for $7.95!

Norman looked across as Joanne said, in a quieting conspiracy, 'I'd stake a wager there's not a woman of childbearing age in a vicinity of ten miles. I'm Queen Bee.'

She made a buzzing sound that immediately annoyed Norman, but he just smiled.

Norman was writing on a napkin with the logo of Captain Cody. A hot, radiant sun fell across the table. He was aware of other convergences. Helen's sickness had been uncovered at a buffet like this, the single greatest debt paid out of her will, the six-minute Medevac airlift that cost $11,000.

Maybe Captain Cody's was tied to a medical conglomerate. It seemed feasible. These cheap eateries, the hook, given there was a great trawl in the catchment of monies associated with end-of-life care. Everything else here was the lure – the sun, the palm trees, the beach and the sunsets.

There was no great hurry. The tickets to Disney were for the following day. They whiled away almost two hours. The sun grew in intensity until the asphalt wavered.

Norman regretted having declined valet parking with the reflexive opinion it was a great trap when tipping was at one's discretion, and the service that much better for there being no set charge, no social frontloading of fees or hidden taxes. It's how they liked it down here. You were underwriting nobody else. Individual rights remained intact. In tipping, you helped the economy while equally inflating your own benevolence for a dollar bill stuffed into the brown hand of a valet.

There were refills on the refills on refills, or that's how Joanne described it in rising and coming back with another Pepsi in a beaded goblet in keeping with pirate booty. She held the Pepsi up like a chalice. This *bad choice* would end back home, but this was the grail of an earned vacation, a souvenir goblet to cherish and bring home for ninety-nine cents.

Toward the end, a garish fluorescence eventually killed the tropical mood. The waitresses were off smoking in a booth. Grace walked the aisles and eyed Captain Cody, circling him, prying. He was a great source of curiosity.

The waitresses got a kick out of it, while another waitress in her sixties, some castaway beauty of pageants, a one-time mermaid who had not fared so well on land, came out in waders and hosed down the remaining ice with steaming water, and the magic that had been the shanty beach shack was laid bare.

Norman took his time, observing and writing everything on napkins, to the amusement of Joanne, who wanted to see what he was writing.

He said shielding it, 'You'll read about it eventually.'

Joanne had aspirations of appearing in print. It ennobled her life to be in the discerning eye of someone reckoning with life's great mysteries. She said this, while eying up a dessert, a key lime pie still beached on a sandbar not yet cleared.

Norman watched her rise, feeling in her absence what aloneness might feel like.

He had followed up on Nate and the enigma of his sudden return to Canada. It played in the deeper reaches of his mind yet. A month and then two had passed, before he uncovered Nate Feldman's online obituary.

Nate had died of kidney failure related to medical complications arising from water contamination by legacy mining operations close to his property, the case in the courts, in a protracted battle of legal motions. Nate's wife

Ursula was referenced. She was a named plaintiff in an ongoing suit against a number of mining operators.

A week after he had uncovered the obituary, the law offices of Weatherly, Sutherland, and Saunders contacted him. Nate Feldman had bequeathed a set of reels and a projector to him. It was not formally disclosed how Nate had come into their possession, though, in procuring the reels, he learned that they had been bequeathed by Helen. Nate had traveled to Chicago to procure them.

What the reels revealed, well, it explained Nate's abrupt disappearance.

Norman watched the tapes while Joanne was out. He kept them from her. He came across Mr Feldman holding him for the first time. Mr Feldman might have been King Solomon tasked with the great accounting of whose child this was. It changed little. Norman determined it shouldn't change anything. Walter Price was his father. What he thought of his mother, well, his feelings were less generous, but then who was he to judge?

There was a sum of money bequeathed to Norman, and, upon receiving it, he sent a sum to Kenneth and wished him the very best. He was open and candid in what he had the Latino secretary transcribe, as he dictated a letter and authorized the legal transfer of funds to Kenneth. As for Thomas Strait, there was money sent to him as well, in the great discharge of what had been earned, not by him, but simply bequeathed him. There was the offer of bringing Sherwood up to Chicago in the summer for a ball game.

He was aware of the secretary's beauty as she wrote this

all down, and aware, too, of her subtle alignment with Nate Feldman's wife, Ursula, a shared beauty. It could not have gone unnoticed by Nate. There was, on the Internet, a blog of Ursula's writings connected to the circular spirituality behind existence. Norman had read it and gained a view into how Nate Feldman had been saved, or reoriented, in the sphere of his wife's influence.

He had a great and abiding sympathy for what it must have felt like, being Nate Feldman, and arriving at that point where your wife appeared incarnate, here and there, though, in the end, it was not enough, and Nate had sought a reunion with his wife on the other side of life.

He might have said something to the Latino secretary, but it would have been inappropriate. She laid claim only to the professional front of Weatherly, Sutherland, and Saunders, and he better understood her presence, her divested interest in how she might have otherwise lived, in finding a man, whereas now she existed as something beyond reach, and, if you could withstand her influence and not spend your time trying to fuck her, if you could go about your business, then you were a man of great restraint and moral conviction.

Obviously, Weatherly, Sutherland, and Saunders were all that, all three of them. They had set Eve among them. They had their war pictures from Vietnam proudly displayed on a wall, alongside their law degrees.

Norman looked out on the wavering heat. It seemed like the continuation of one long life really. Florida had been an abiding dream of his father's, a retirement here discussed when Norman was young, so he had a scenario in his head that his parents were, in fact, down here. It wasn't hard to imagine. There had been no closure, no ceremony. He had just not seen his parents in a long time, in the way relationships continued over time and distances, and in the divide of a past life from a present life.

In thinking it, he was not unlike Nate Feldman and his wife. He had read Nate's blog, his appeal for a reunion with his wife, whose native name meant 'Something Good Cooking by a Fire'. The name held within it such an invocation of what a man might want in the closing dark of a hunt, the succor of food and companionship.

Norman set his hand on Joanne's hand when she came back with her key lime pie.

He was a man with a singular interest, with no other apparent qualities, and Joanne, for her part, was satisfied that, between them, they would see this through in the apportioning of civility and good manners. This was not discounting love. It was just arriving at it in a way that was out of fashion, when time and understanding were most often needed.

They might go down along the coast for a cruise to catch the sunset later. Joanne had brochures guaranteeing sightings of manta rays and prices circled in a comparison with other brochures. She had a book of coupons and their AAA card that guaranteed 10 per cent off all listed prices.

Norman let her manage it. He would get on whatever boat he was told to get on.

Joanne eventually got the check, peeling her legs from the sweat of the vinyl seating. She suggested that they all use the bathroom before leaving, in a testament to all-things practical.

In the offing, Norman stared at Grace still preoccupied with Captain Cody in the quiet investigation of life and its mysteries. There was a box inside him, hidden, containing every word he ever said or would say.

For a moment, Norman was again left alone in a drifting euphoria, entering a liminal emptiness that was not emptiness at all, but the process of life. He imagined his parents caught up in a generational entanglement of new worries. Walter wading though the new economy of geriatrics teeming with predatory financial advisors trawling the pension funds of former union zealots turned conservative, all united against a welfare state intent on supporting so-called bums and welfare mothers; retirees submitting to the sway of latter-day Tea Party conservatives, with their mega-church ministers calling for moral accountability, tough love and lower taxes.

It was in his head: a trailer park with a low-maintenance pea gravel lawn, their life aligned with the so-called last of the greatest generation, patriots turned scrupulous coupon cutters, who had seen their influence extended in the hanging chad debacle that would determine the course of a new imperialism, emboldening further the would-be 9/11 hijackers logging their flight class hours along the Florida panhandle, box-cutters in hand – the box-cutter the great Excalibur of the disenfranchised.

It was not come to terms with fully yet, the great wound of 9/11. He had seen it in the cast of flags and bumper stickers down through so many states. At play in the collective consciousness, still, the terrifying truth that, in a country where God was asked to confer his blessing, bags had been packed, wives and children kissed, cabs hailed, and all dying before the in-flight service began. Though the stories told were not those stories now, but invariably, the outlier stories of those who woke up too late, the late connection, the hangover, those without upgrade points. In these isolated stories of survival, Jesus's mercy was made known, and not so the improbable sequence of actual events that got the rest to their appointed death with the assuring sense in their hearts that, on that day, there was a God watching over them and determining their destiny all along.

They made a dash across the furnace of the shimmering asphalt to their rental, to the delight of two parking attendants witnessing it. The car roiled in a wave of heat. Joanne had on big-framed black Jackie Onassis sunglasses. Norman saw just her smile and not her eyes. Yes, they should have paid the dollar for parking. All life was not a scam.

Out back of Captain Cody's, a screech of birds hung over two Hispanics emptying plastic containers of an icy slush of leftovers. A pelican, its wingspan immense in arresting flight, landed, its low-hung belly like a transport carrier.

The busboys fed it amidst the clamor of seagulls, the pelican's bill filling with a turgid bulge in a tidal wash, as one busboy hosed and the other threw it a flotsam of shrimp, crab leg, oyster, pot roast, and all manner of salads, beets, and slaws.

Then the pelican, in a waddling gait, crossed the scorch of asphalt, seeking flight.

Buoyed on an uplift of unseen thermals, an indiscernible aerodynamics was suddenly made apparent, the tuck of the head and spread of wings, so this majestic creature might go for a very long time out over the ocean caps, Norman Price, made mindful of so many things in life, what might be achieved on the right thermal, with the right attitude, and aware he was riding such a thermal, and in the midst of great flight.